The Nocker

The Nocker

Nachash Keeper

STONE Pulp Press Presents

A Mystic Island Story

The Nocker

Copyright © 2025 by Nachash Keeper

Printed in the United States of America

Stone Pulp Press
Imprint Mailing Address: PO Box 23
Zip: 02339 US States: MA
Country: US

Paperback ISBN: 979-8-9898749-8-9
E-book ISBN: 979-8-9898749-9-6
Library of Congress Control Number: 2025945453

They can lie to others. They can lie to themselves. But they can't lie to me.

The Keeper

PART 1

1

The guy's good looking enough. But good-looking with muted charisma. Think a Clive Owen paint-by numbers who has yet to be filled in with any vitality. Or just think Clive Owen. And the guy's rich. Very rich. According to him anyway. But he's one of those rich guys who thinks he's self-made. Telling me over and over how he graduated from Yale—on a "scholarship," which I know means trust fund—and how he'd been forced to start out in the "slummy" world of mutual funds—questionable mutual funds, mind you—fleecing some so-and-so with a short sale, or scamming whomever with some put option. But he's beyond all that now. Now he's a reputable banker (whatever that means). He says, "We all have to do what we have to do to survive." At one point, with a forced look of contrition and shake of his head, he even says: "The suckers never saw it coming."

I like to think someday that will be his epitaph: *Sucker never saw it coming.*

This guy, John Thompson is his name, is an asshole. Narcissist is the clinical term, but I prefer asshole. It's simple. Uncomplicated.

We leave the bar in the guy's Jag. *A fucking Jag.* Not a Porsche. Not a Beemer or a Benz or something with actual high-performance capability. A Jag. The ultimate in poser, look-at-me status symbols. Might as well be a Maserati.

After pulling up to some big post-modern house in Westchester, we climb from the Jag and stumble up the walkway. It had clearly been John's intention to get me drunk back at the bar. The guy challenging me to shot after shot of Patron. He'd even suggested body-shots for the last one. Which I had accepted, being sure to blow a stream of extra-warm air on his neck before licking the salt off. But what the asshole didn't realize is I can hold my liquor far better than he ever could. Hell, I could drink Jose-fucking-Cuervo under the table, if need be.

We make it to the front door of John's Pad. That's what he actually calls it, his *Pad.* John is the type of guy that likes to invent hip, insider lingo—John-speak, if you will—and this lingo breaks most things down to three letter identifiers. *The Pad. The Jag.* He'd even called the Patron, *Ron.* "Wanna do a shot of *Ron*?" "Another shot of *Ron*?" I wanted to say to him, *Who the fuck is Ron?* But instead, I just smiled, saying, "Another shot of Ron it is."

At the front door of his Pad, he drops his keys and, with me hanging limply in his arms, retrieves them with limited dexterity. As we stand, I slump a little in his grasp. This slump is by design, of course.

"Whoa," he says to me, "you okay?"

"I'm great," I say with a big, goofy smile. "Just drunk."

Just drunk: the fucking asshole's call to action.

Most men might find this situation blurring ethical lines, and at this point they should be overwhelmed by a prevailing blanket of morality. Many men—I'd like to say all men, or even most men, but let's face it, it's only many men—will be struck with disappointment at this point, knowing that, despite what their libido is screaming, they would never actually take advantage of a drunken young lady. The really decent guys will immediately turn back for the car, saying they'll take me home right away. But not John. John closes deals. And at that moment, John gets a look in his eyes like he's just hit the fucking jackpot. Or hit the "Pot" as he'd probably put it.

When we regain our balance—I have to be honest, I thought we were both going to topple for a moment—he fumbles the house key into its lock, unlocking the door and kicking it open. As soon as we enter, a Shih Tzu bolts up to us, its plumed tail wagging, the thing jumping around as if its excitement is electrocuting it.

A Shih Tzu. The final confirmation that there is a *Mrs.* John Thompson. It isn't enough that he lives in Westchester rather than Manhattan, or that he lives in a house twice the size that's needed for a bachelor, but he owns a Shih Tzu. There are only two types of men that own Shih Tzu: gay men and married men.

Although none of this is necessary to deduce John's marital status. The fact that he'd answered my Craigslist ad was proof enough. The good-looking ones are always married.

I bend down to greet the dog. Shih Tzu are basically neuroses-personified (like their owners), and I half expect the thing to bite me. "Hey. Cute dog," I say, and the dog backs away, growling, and then approaches again to be petted.

John says, "Yeah, that's Wee."

"Wee?"

"Well, Stewie. But I like to call him Wee."

"Of course you do."

I regard the house. Meticulously decorated. Lots of floral designs—another sign of a wife.

"I like the *Pad*," I say, staggering drunkenly into the living room.

Again, this staggering is by design.

"Yeah? You really like it?"

I turn toward him, pretending to stumble, and then I lunge into his arms, saying, "It goes with your car."

He grins. "Yeah? Well, the Jag's for fun. The Pad is a necessity."

I plaster another smile on my face. "We can have fun in the Pad, too."

He smirks and pulls me up to his lips for a kiss. The kiss is tender at first, but then he opens his mouth trying to acquire my tongue.

I pull away, leaning a little off balance, and say, "I could use a drink."

He smiles, that jackpot-winning look back in his eyes, and says, "I can provide that." He kisses me on the forehead. "Stay here," he says. As he walks away, I wipe my forehead with the back of my hand. The stench of his cologne lingers; it's like some company bottled his smile and put it in spray-on form—a sweet and musky smell like the anal gland of some weasel.

When he disappears into the kitchen, I turn my attention to the living room, making a slow, circling sweep of the space, inventorying the furnishings, the gizmos and the trinkets, the different knick-knacks on the shelves.

I call toward the kitchen, "This really is a nice place."

He calls back from the kitchen. "Thanks." He then says, "Is wine okay?"

"Wine's perfect," I call, spotting a bookcase in a side nook of the room. As I head toward it, I notice Stewie at my feet. I quickly scruff the top of the dog's head before returning my attention to the bookcase's contents. I'm not surprised to spot a locket-sized wedding picture of John and a high-strung-looking woman. He most likely hid the pictures of the wife, or children if there are any, but he must've missed this one.

I look down at Stewie and smirk.

The dog doesn't seem to give a shit about his master's infidelity.

John calls from the kitchen, "I'll open a ninety-four Stags Leap. Got three bottles. Hard to find. They're about four-hundred bucks a bottle." He pauses a moment and says, "Hey, four hundred bucks for a bottle of Stags Leap. Get it?"

"Yeah, that's funny," I call. I look down at the dog and raise my eyebrows. "Is he for real?" I say to the dog.

The dog cocks its head, looking as if he doesn't give a shit about his master's lameness either.

I call toward the kitchen, "Four hundred bucks, you say?"

He returns from the kitchen with two glasses of red wine, handing one of the glasses to me. "Yeah, I got them at auction, along with an eighty-five Cristal worth a cool G." He clinks my wine glass and we take a sip. "Smooth, no?" he says.

"Quite."

We take another sip.

"So what's with your balls?" I say.

"Excuse me?"

I motion to the three baseballs on the bookcase. "You've got these baseballs here." I pick one of the balls up, saying, "Doesn't really go with the rest of the Pad."

He grimaces, as if I'd grabbed one of his actual testicles, and takes the baseball from my hand, saying, "Those *balls* are worth a fortune. Signed by Ruth, Maris, and McGwire, all from the years they broke the homerun record."

It was no accident that I'd picked up the Ruth ball, knowing it would elicit the most anxious response from him.

"Oh, so sorry," I say in my best I'm-just-a-girl voice.

He returns the Babe Ruth ball to the bookcase as if it's fucking plutonium, saying, "I'll have to get a Bonds eventually."

"Oh, yeah? Whoever that is," I say, again with my just-a-girl voice.

"You don't know who Bonds is?"

I want to smack the motherfucker and say, *Of course I know who Bonds is, dipshit*, but instead I say, "James Bond?"

"Um, no, Barry Bonds."

"Oh. Right," I say, rolling my eyes.

We sip our wine again, and then I say, "Hard to believe that such a successful guy like you would need to answer an ad on Craigslist for a date."

He shrugs. "What can I say? The price of success can be loneliness."

I kind of almost throw up in my mouth, and to be honest, part of me wants to douse him in the Stags Leap, but instead, I allow my gaze to drift toward the wedding picture on the bookcase.

He quickly takes the glass from me and sets it on the coffee table, saying, "Why don't we sit on the couch?"

I let that goofy smile slip onto my face again and say, "I was thinking more like, how about we hit the sack."

It doesn't take long before we're rolling around on Mr. and Mrs. Thompson's bed. I'm wearing nothing but a pair of boyshort panties and a spaghetti strap top, John wearing his silk boxers and black, knee-high dress socks. I always make them keep on their socks. Something about a guy stripped down to nothing but his dress socks cracks me up.

While we're making out, John stops suddenly and, pulling his head back to look earnestly into my eyes, he says, "Hard to believe that a smoking hot girl like you needs to post an ad on Craigslist for a date."

I say, "Well, sometimes the price of adventure is taking a chance."

"Just how much adventure are you looking for?"

"Why? Are you feeling adventurous?" I say.

"Definitely."

Could he make this any easier?

I smile and flick the hair of my blond wig from my face. Glancing around the room, I spot something and dart from the bed to the room's curtains. I'd actually spotted the ties on the curtains when we'd first entered the room, and I'd known exactly what I was going to do with them, but still, I act as if the notion has just spontaneously popped into my head. I pull the ties free and turn back toward him, holding the ties in my fingers as if about to make a cat's cradle. I say with the most child-like smile I can muster, "Ever been tied up?"

It is my experience that if a girl flashes a child-like smile and uses a baby-doll voice, she can ask a man to do just about anything. Especially if that anything has an element of kink to it.

John, lying there half-mast, looking as if he's about to pop right out of his boxers, hesitates. "From what I've seen so far, maybe I should do the tying."

Yeah, you'd like that, Johnny-boy, I think.

Guy can't subdue me with alcohol, so he figures he'll subdue me with bondage.

I dart back to the bed. "Nope. You're first," I say, and then add for good measure, "because you're such a bad, bad boy." I say this in another baby-doll voice, and of course John's hands obediently come up to be tied.

And there it is, the moment John Thompson, master of the universe, taker of fortunes, is bested by a baby-doll voice.

I tie one wrist, all the time teasing him with blown kisses.

He growls like a tiger, feigning scratches with his free hand.

I tie his other hand and then step back to inspect my work. Scrunching up my face in a displeased look, I glance around the room as if something more is missing.

Again, I've known what that something is the whole time.

"Here we go," I say, snatching up John's discarded shirt. I blindfold Mr. Put-option, wondering how much he'd have made if he'd shorted this date.

"Don't move, tiger," I say.

He purrs.

I step back again, inspecting my work, taking a moment to enjoy it all: millionaire adulterer bound to his king-size bed with curtain ties, blindfolded with his own shirt, erection trying to free itself from his silk shorts, and, of course, the black knee-high socks.

Beautiful.

I gather up my clothes and begin to dress.

John, still blindfolded, cocks his head and says, "What are you doing?"

"Getting ready. Now, don't you move, tiger."

"Where are you going?" he says, raising his voice an octave, sounding as if the first pangs of blue balls are about to bloom.

Slipping on the last of my clothing, I start toward the door, saying, "I'm going to get the wine." Out of the bedroom, I bound down the stairs.

Stewie is eagerly waiting at the foot of the steps, the dog's tail a blur. I dart into the living room with the dog at my feet, almost tripping over the thing.

After grabbing my pocketbook—an over-sized leather bag I'd left on the couch—I go to the kitchen. There I find two wine refrigerators—the pretentious Sharper Image, yuppie-specials. I open them up, plucking out the remaining bottles of Stags Leap and the bottle of Cristal. I also find a couple of bottles of Dom Perignon, and wonder why he hadn't offered the beverage with three letters to its name. *Want some Dom? I have plenty of Dom. We can take my Jag to the Pad for some Dom.*

As I stand from the wine refrigerators, the bottles clinking in my bag, I almost step on Stewie again. The thing looks up at me accusingly, as if wondering why I'm taking his buddy's wine. I say to the dog, "Don't look at me like that. You know he's an asshole."

On cue, John calls from upstairs, the blue balls probably taking full effect, "Hey, baby, where are you?"

I call toward the ceiling, "Just getting some goodies, tiger."

He calls down, "There's whipped cream in the fridge, how about I be your dessert tonight?"

I look down at Stewie, asking the dog, "Seriously?"

Stewie cocks his head, his tail going nuts again.

John calls, "C'mon, baby, I got a sweet treat for you right here. It needs a little whipped cream, and you can be the cherry on top."

I scrunch up my face, saying, "Ew." Looking down at the dog, I say, "See? Asshole." I then call up the stairs, "Be right there, tiger."

I return to the kitchen, walking to the fridge, which is one of those industrial, silver, Sub-Zero monstrosities that belong in a restaurant. I rifle through trendy condiments and cooking sherries to find the whipped cream. Heading back up the stairs and shaking the canister, I call to the dog, "C'mon, Stewie."

In the master bedroom, John is writhing on the bed in anticipation.

I say to him, "I got a surprise for you, tiger."

"Oh yeah, baby?" he says, offering his tiger growl again.

"Oh yeah," I say, spraying the whipped cream on his now fully erect member, which is sticking out of the fly of his boxers. The guy groans with delight. I say, "Ready, tiger?"

"Oh yeah, baby."

I pick up Stewie, putting the dog on the bed, the dog immediately going to town on the whipped cream. John groans in ecstasy, saying, "Oh yeah, there you go, baby."

I tilt my head, holding my hand below my chin as if admiring a fine work of art. Which it kind of is. The scene belonging in a fucking museum. A true masterpiece. I could relish this sight all night, but it's time to get going. I head down the stairs, and as I reach the bottom step, I hear John yell, "Hey, wait a minute, hey."

I run into the kitchen, retrieving the bag with the wine, and then head to the bookcase in the living room, all the time listening to John yelling from upstairs, "Stewie, no. Stewie, stop." I place John's baseballs in my bag along with their certificates of authenticity, and a few other expensive looking knick-knacks to boot.

John is yelling, "Hey, Shauna, where did you go? This isn't funny."

I head to the door, laughing. For one thing, my name isn't Shauna. And what's more, it *is* funny.

2

My name is Carl White. I'm the type of guy who sweats a lot—it's a genetic thing or something that's always been—and sitting in this lawyer's office isn't helping. I sweat and I bite at the inside of my lip while the woman to my right keeps yipping. Like one of those little dogs that never shuts up. The *dog* in this case (dare I say bitch?) is my ex-wife Mandy. Correction: my soon-to-be ex-wife. But that is our future. In this moment, we are still legally married. Still some kind of unit. Which gives her the prerogative to rub my face in the stink of our shared past.

I've not said a thing during this meeting, mind you; after all, she's already saying everything. As usual, each of us is adding our own unique value to a conversation, which is nothing. It dawns on me that moments like this have become old hat. Nothing of value ever shared. I remember the first time Mandy was this close to me, and now I wish I'd shut my eyes, plugged my ears, and walked the other way. It would have spared me from having to endure this spectacle.

I catch the disapproving frown of her slimy lawyer Vincent Stone, and I decide to occupy myself by glancing at my surroundings. The office is a world of polished dark wood. Even the walls are wood. My attention falls on a slightly ajar door behind Stone's desk, and the human skeleton peeking from behind it. I dart my eyes from it, the thing creeping me out, but like a car wreck, or like my failed marriage—hell, my failed life—I just can't get away from it. Why the hell is it even there?

Personal injury cases, dipshit, a voice, which sounds just like Mandy, says in my head. The imagined voice lays over her actual speaking voice at that moment in a bizarre, hellish harmonization. Still trying to block out the woman's yipping, and now trying to block out the gazes of the lawyer *and* his skeleton, I focus on the artwork scattered throughout the room. Klimt's *The Kiss* hangs on the wall. I remember studying the painting during an art history course I took in junior college—back when I still had a chance at a decent future. As I stare at the painting now, it occurs to me that such a vision of romance is an odd choice to have on the wall during divorce proceedings. The painting seems to suck me into it, as if I now stand over the figures with their looks of passion and bliss on their faces. I try to imagine that look on Mandy's face, but I can't. Before I met her, I had been starved for sex, so one can imagine my exponential disappointment when sex with her became a chore I hurried through so I could dislodge myself from that cold sack of boredom.

"—See what I mean? He never listens."

I fall out of Klimt's painting and find Mandy glaring at me. I offer a limp, "Huh?"

"I was saying, *Carl,* that I will decide what is best for *my* son. Visiting rights are non-negotiable, I'm staying firm on this."

At some point, our son Rudy became some sort of weapon in all of this. Something for her to wield. Something with which she'd parry my accusations and thrust her digs. It isn't like it matters to Rudy one way or the other where he spends his time, my place or Mandy's place, it's all the same to him.

I gaze back at the Klimt painting in order to avoid her

eyes, and say, "I want more say in what goes on in my son's life, that's all."

Mandy says, "You're lucky I'm not cutting you out completely."

Against my better judgment, I take the bait. "And what makes you feel a judge would give you that right? It's 2004, plenty of fathers get custodial rights now."

"Not fathers with anger management problems."

"Or wives with fidelity problems," I snap, unable to avoid the hint of self-righteousness in my voice. But in reality, I wish I *was* the one with the fidelity problem, or with the means to acquire one. It no longer matters to me that some other guy is sticking his dick in my wife; I just care that it happened on my watch: that I'd stuck to my vows, while she'd disregarded hers.

"I don't have a fidelity problem," she says.

"I don't have an anger problem," I say.

"The cops needed to be called to the house over you kicking the coffee table into splinters."

With my elbows digging into the armrests, my fingers locked, I carefully reply, "That is a matter of semantics. The police didn't *need* to be called. The police *were* called. And I think I had a right to kick *my* coffee table after finding out my wife was *banging* someone else."

I use the term *banging* for the harshness of it, even though I can't picture Mandy banging anyone.

Mandy rolls her eyes and looks out the window, murmuring, "At least I didn't *bang* a piece of plastic."

"I did not bang—"

"It's true," Mandy says to Stone. "He got fired once for having sex with—"

"All right, look," Stone says, shifting in his seat. "We've been over this. Do you think we can agree on the terms we've already spelled out about visitation?"

Mandy says, "Look, *I've* already agreed. He's the one that, *as usual,* questions everything. As soon as he commits to something, he can't follow through." She turns toward me, saying, "Make a damn decision for once, Carl, and stick with it. You are consistently…"

Here we go again; it is now time for a succession of grievances, illustrating how everything in her life is all *my* fault. She is the master at ripping me apart and leaving the pieces strewn about like petals pulled from a flower—*I hate him, I hate him more, I hate him, I hate him more.* Her rant is liable to take a while, and it is futile to tune her out. I might as well go out and grab a coffee at the café down the street and watch the pretty girls walk past.

"…you are lazy and boring…"

My attention shifts to the skeleton as it leers from the closet. Only now, it isn't staring at *me.* It is staring at something on Stone's desk. I look at the desk and see a shiny, gold Cross pen. I stare at the pen and then at the skeleton. The skeleton seems to nod, and then the pen is in my hand. I drive it into Mandy's forehead, right between her eyes.

Her eyes widen and cross, looking at the pen sticking from her forehead before she slumps in her seat like a balloon draining of air.

Stone stares at me for a moment, silent with shock. Then the lawyer says, "Thank Christ, I didn't think she was ever going to shut up."

"Think that was decisive enough for her?" I say, and the two of us laugh. Even the skeleton seems to be laughing.

I snap from the fantasy. Mandy is still ranting beside me, saying, "He's weak and he's…" Stone is still sitting, pretending to be interested. The skeleton is leering at me again.

"All right," I say, standing from the seat and lifting my hands like a conductor calling a symphony to attention. "Look, just do whatever you want. I don't even give a shit anymore." I deliver this message to the skeleton—I can't stand to look at Mandy or the lawyer anymore. I then say to the skeleton, "Just send the papers for me to sign." I storm to the door, turn and say, "And you're not getting any of my collection."

When I storm out of the room, I hear Mandy saying, "Like I want any of that shit in his *collection*." With that word, *collection*, her voice takes on a warble I know all too well, and I picture her waving her hands in the air to emphasize the point.

I walk from the office building and down the street. The sidewalk is pocked with mid-afternoon pedestrians, each with a unique agenda. I wonder if any of them feel the way I do at that moment.

Which is what, exactly? I'm not even sure what I am feeling.

Klimt's lovers linger in my mind, and I wish I could experience just one moment of that brand of passion. I am actually envious of the painted figures forever entwined in that embrace.

As I walk, I feel the fluorescent NKOTB keychain swinging lamely beneath the umbrella of my palm. Mandy had given the keychain to me one Christmas long ago. She'd always been good at passing off her judgmental bullying as *all in fun*. I wonder if convincing me to get a vasectomy—a botched vasectomy, mind you—days before announcing she wanted a divorce, was also just for fun.

I hate The New Kids on the Block.

Hate vasectomies, too, botched or otherwise.

When I'd point out that I was not a NKOTB fan,

Mandy would say, "What's the difference?" *NSYNC, New Kids, same fucking difference. Balls, no balls, same fucking difference.*

Couldn't she just let me have my joys? Calling me a "pedo" for liking boys. "Dickless" for not having a working dick. And I'd correct her by saying: I don't like boys, I like boy bands. And my dick works just fine, and then I'd try explaining the workings of the male reproductive system. Then I'd given up trying. Given up arguing. Given up the parrying and thrusting and deflecting. And so I kept the keychain out of spite. To prove to her that she couldn't break me.

As for my dick, I still haven't figured out what to do with that.

I stop and lean against a tree to shake her face from my mind. I take a few deep breaths and cultivate my standard fantasy. There I am, standing on the *American Idol* stage, belting out a song as the crowd and the television audience drop their jaws in adoration. Ryan standing off to the side, his perfect white teeth chiseled into a smile. Randy bobbing his head. Paula gazing approvingly. And even Simon shrugging and conceding that he can't argue with what I'm selling. I call out to the adoring crowd—

"Oh, shit, wait. I got it."

A parking enforcement officer is placing a ticket under the windshield wiper of my Crown Victoria.

I trot the rest of the way to the car, saying, "Wait, I got it. I got it. I'm leaving right now."

The woman, squat with blotchy skin, says, "Sorry. Already recorded it in the book." She smiles as she pushes her pen back into its holster like a gunslinger having felled the town thug.

"Don't you know who I am?" I say to her. My voice is rising in speed and cadence. It sounds whiny, and I imagine Mandy shaking a disapproving scowl at me.

The woman says, "I don't care who you *think* you are. It's in the book." She snaps shut her ticket book and walks away.

3

I stare at Klimt's *The Kiss* on my computer screen. I've been a prisoner to the image since I huffed out of Stone's office. The man in the painting seems to smother the woman against her will, but the look of bliss on her face betrays this notion. Instead, she willingly submits to the protective cocoon they share. I play these diametric possibilities in my mind, wishing to climb into the painting, to know their passion atop the apron of blooming flowers. The painting has the addictive pull of porn. I've always been one to resist the simplistic ease of porn—just one more way to take a stoic stand against my apparent lack of sexuality—but this picture is something different. It has the guilty voyeuristic pull of pornography, that feeding of my inner lust. Fine-art-porn. Is there such a thing?

My fingers drum beside the mouse along to a Clay Aiken CD on the stereo, and I imagine myself in bed with a beautiful girl nestled in my arms like the girl in the painting, my lips nuzzled into her cheek. As if my hand is independent of myself, I open a new window on the computer screen and search: SINGLE WOMEN DATING.

The instant results of dating sites on the screen are overwhelming. I could choose anything my fantasies require, from race to fetish to religion to political orientation.

Comparability to works of fine art? I suppose this is not an option. And I begin to wonder if I really want to put forth the effort of trying to build my perfect girl with a template of interests and desires on a dating site. What I really want is to find a diamond in the ruff, so to speak. Stumble across that perfect woman and fall into her arms as if accidently. I want to find Klimt's passion, not try to manufacture it.

I click on a link for Craigslist.

A menu of anything pops up on the screen: from cars to furniture to activities, forums, jobs, computers, haiku, diets, crafts, events, personals.

I click on personals.

More choices pop up.

WOMEN SEEKING MEN.

I click.

Several descriptive taglines stretch along a sea of white. Some of them are straightforward and filthy, such as the amateur poet who proclaimed: *On top or from behind, they're both all right, as long as you can give it morning noon and night.* Others are timid and simple. *I'm just searching for a decent man.*

I wonder if Mandy would ever advertise on one of these sites. That would be a hoot if I respond and it turns out to be her, "*If You Like Piña Coladas*"-style.

Yeah, a real hoot. That would probably be the day I shoot myself, or jump off a bridge, or self-immolate: the day fate confirms that Mandy is my one true match.

I spend a few minutes reading dozens of these posts before one hook catches my eye.

WILL BE IN TOWN FOR A COUPLE OF DAYS. LOOKING FOR SOMEONE TO HAVE DRINKS WITH.

Not the best grammar, but I was drawn to it nonetheless. As I read the message out loud, a new Clay Aiken song scores the statement. It is the *looking for someone* that caught my eye. The three words tug at some deep-rooted part of me with breathtaking torque. I click on the link.

I scroll down to the attached photo.

Another high-torque pull on me. The girl in the picture is stunning. Not the type of woman I expect to be searching for companionship on Craigslist.

Black hair, tanned skin, gray eyes. I stare at those eyes, almost convinced that we are gazing at each other, that we are sharing a moment in the digital universe. I envision our faces superimposed onto *The Kiss*, imagine her falling limply into my embrace as I pull her from the computer screen. I absorb her image until the den becomes silent, the Clay Aiken CD having ended. I break my gaze from the computer screen and my eyes shift to the shelves of war memorabilia scattered about the room. What Mandy called my *bullshit clutter*. A silver door knocker in the shape of an eagle and swastika hangs on the wall above my computer screen. A relic from my great uncle's service as a Nazi-hunter in World War II. A hideous symbol with an amusing backstory.

I am suddenly filled with giddiness, and I find myself saying out loud, in a high, womanly voice, "Knock-knock. Avon Fräulein calling."

4

I nestle in among the magazine display, a place where I can remain semi-hidden while keeping an eye on the bustling sidewalk outside the bookstore's window. The magazine area tends to cater to the lurking, loitering customers—some with a few minutes to kill while waiting for a companion to finish browsing, others just wanting to be alone, others with intentions I don't care to know.

Beside me, a twenty-something scratches at his beard with one hand and pulls an issue of *High Times* with the other. An older man swivels his head this way and that before snatching the last copy of *Maxim*—the guy then retreating to the edge of the magazine rack. Two teenage girls stand a few feet away, the two of them regarding a teen pop magazine. They jockey for position to view pictures of NSYNC.

I grab a car magazine from the rack and start flipping through it, scanning the pages of jacked-up muscle cars and new-age Italian sports cars as I edge toward the girls. They are gushing at the pictures in the magazine, one girl saying, "His hair…." The other saying, "I would do anything for that to happen…." One of the girls spots me drifting toward them. She nudges her friend. The other girl looks up at me, now standing beside them. The girls set the magazine down and rush away into other parts of the store.

I grab the magazine the girls had been looking at. The aroma of their perfume lingers around me—fruity, floral, cheap. I unfurl a poster of Clay Aiken stapled into the centerfold. I imagine it is an action shot of myself, the microphone stand riding between my legs, one hand gripping the mic, the other hand extending out to the adoring crowd, index finger curling backward to invite them all to love me. I feel the crowd's eyes on me…but I suddenly realize it is not the eyes of an adoring crowd on me. I look up to find a man staring at me, an issue of *Field and Stream* having gone limp in the guy's hands.

I say, "What?"

The man shakes his head and goes back to his magazine.

Before I have a chance to return to the poster and my fantasy, something from outside the store's window catches my attention. Out on the sidewalk, a girl with black hair and flawless tan skin passes the store. I watch her absentmindedly, wondering why the girl looks familiar, wondering for a moment if she is a celebrity. But then I remember the Craigslist ad, the whole reason I am here in the first place.

You're such a fucking dope, Mandy's voice rings in my head, and I say it out loud, "Fucking dope," as I return the magazine to the rack.

The *Field and Stream* guy looks up abruptly.

I can feel the expression on my face at that moment, a fish suddenly out of water, "No, not you," I say to him breathlessly. "I'm the dope."

"You got that right," the man says.

I dart out of the bookstore, looking down the sidewalk. It is littered with casual daytime pedestrian traffic. An elderly woman is pushing an old-timey stroller, which looks like something out of *Rosemary's Baby*, a smartly dressed young man in a suit waits patiently with a plastic bag while his Pekingese squats on an island of grass. Beyond them, I spot the young woman striding into a restaurant. I follow her. I didn't want to be the first to arrive for the date. Didn't want to have her walk in, take one look at me, and walk back out. Better to have a captive audience for at least enough time to try and charm her.

You charm her? Mandy says in my head.

"Yes, *me* charm her," I say to myself in a huff and enter the restaurant.

I hesitate in the darkened foyer. The place reeks of stale garlic, as if the smell is manufactured, like some kind of air freshener to fake ambiance. Red, velvety curtains shroud a small podium where a hostess is having a conversation with one of the waitresses. I stand there and finger a cup of toothpicks, taking inventory of the other items on the podium's lip—matchbooks, business cards, a bowl of Starlite Mints. Finally, mid-conversation, the hostess turns to me and says, "Just one?"

"What?" I say, realizing that my voice sounds more edgy and more confused than intended.

Without a break in her smile, the hostess says, "Just you today, sir?" The waitress standing beside the hostess stares at me blankly.

"No," I say, again sounding annoyed, as if she suggested some asinine premise. I tip the toothpicks a little too far, and they spill from the pedestal. I look down at the pile of toothpicks and then step into the bar area of the restaurant.

I scan the room, a seed of panic germinating in my mid-section. I'm not going to charm anyone. Jesus, what the hell am I doing here? Meeting a girl *that* beautiful on a blind date? *I* am going to be the one to run from the restaurant, but then my eyes fall on the girl with the black hair, and I am frozen in place.

She is sitting alone at a table. I start toward her, but then stop, again gripped with an overwhelming urge to run away. It is similar to the feeling I had before bolting from Vincent Stone's office. But when I took off from the lawyer's office, I was nudged forward by anger. Here, in the restaurant, it is something closer to fear. Fear of what, I'm not entirely sure. Failure? Humiliation? The dull cycle of hope and disappointment when, like everything else in my life, this fizzles out too? I'm not the type of guy who approaches strange women like this.

Or maybe I am; I'm here aren't I?

I contemplate my next move and regard the people seated at the bar. They all seem to know what they are doing there, chatting in easygoing, confident manners. An older woman is drumming her fingers on the bar beside the stem of her martini glass while a portly gentleman, wearing self-importance on his sleeve, drivels on with some story; I can hear snippets of his voice, which sounds like a kazoo. A pair of robust young women cackle and holler comments across the shiny bar top at the bartender. I watch the bartender flash an obligatory smile toward them, and as I do so, I spot something that some might call serendipitous, ironic, maybe even an omen. The bartender is in the midst of pouring a glass of wine from a bottle with Klimt's *The Kiss* on its label. The bartender hands the glass of wine to the same waitress who was talking to the hostess when I'd arrived. The waitress brings the glass over to the raven-haired girl.

I take a deep breath, still waffling on my decision to stay or flee. The girl smiles and thanks the waitress, and then she looks over toward me. She cocks her head in a questioning manner.

By instinct, I walk toward her, but as I near the table, I am suddenly unable to summon any words. I become lost for a moment in the girl's beautiful, light eyes.

She cocks her head again and says, "Carl?"

"Stacey?" I say to her.

"Yes," she says.

Silence hangs between us for a moment. I want something witty to say, but I have nothing, just dumb silence.

The girl says, "Hey, what's up?" She says it nonchalantly, like we've known each other for years. I like that, and I feel a little more at ease. She stands, and I see she is wearing a pleated black and white polka dotted miniskirt and a tight gray, V-neck T-shirt reading: I *was Paul Revere's Ride*. My jaw drops slightly reading the words. She leans toward me as if going to give me a hug, and there I am with my hand held out to be shaken. She stops and adjusts to the handshake as I lean in for the hug. We both laugh as we meet in an awkward embrace.

She then motions to the chair across from her and says, "Have a seat."

I stand beside the table, still unable to respond as the waitress reappears at the table, the waitress saying to the girl, "He want something?"

Still standing beside the table, I glare at the waitress and say, "*He* wants a scotch and water." I don't usually drink, and certainly don't drink scotch, but this order sounds as if it has the authority I'm going for. Something someone of importance would order.

The waitress purses her lips and walks toward the bar.

I sit down across from the girl, still unable to think of anything worthwhile to say.

Thankfully, she breaks the ice, saying, "Right on time, Carl. I respect a punctual man."

I shrug, saying, "Yeah, well…." Nothing more comes to mind. My hands are sweating and I spin them in the white napkin of the table's setting. My mind is spinning with questions. How has it come to this? A blind date? How can I have wasted so many years with Mandy and let myself wind up an out of shape, socially-deprived nitwit chasing girls from internet ads? And how did I end up with a beautiful, charismatic girl like this from an internet ad? And how long until I send her running?

I realize I've been staring at the phrase on her T-shirt. On her *chest*. Emblazoned across her *bosom*. My eyes snap to her eyes, which are watching me.

I say, "Um, sorry…I wasn't looking at…I was reading your shirt. It's…funny."

She looks down at it and chuckles. "Yeah, well, that's why I bought it."

"He didn't make it, you know?"

"Huh?"

"Paul Revere. He was captured. He barely made it to Cambridge."

"Yeah? Hmm. I guess I did know that. Poem was wrong, right?"

"Yeah. Poem was intended as propaganda for the Civil War."

"Interesting."

"Your shirt should actually say Israel Bissell?"

"Pardon?"

"That's the guy that actually made it to Philadelphia."

"Really? Huh. Doesn't have the same ring though, does it?"

"What's that?"

"The Midnight Ride of Israel Bissell. Not quite the same."

I shrug. "I suppose not."

The girl smiles quickly and then takes a sip of her wine.

"Still a good poem, though." I say. I shift in my seat. "And it was good propaganda. I mean, it got the North pumped up and all."

"That it did," she says. After another awkward silence, the girl nods and makes an attempt at small talk, saying, "So, what is it exactly a guy like Carl White does?"

I begin to say, "Well, I—" But I am cut short as the waitress places the scotch in front of me.

Without a word, the waitress walks off toward the bar, and the girl across from me focuses her attention on me again. Her eyes seem to acknowledge my struggle for communication, and she invites me to continue. The expression reminds me of Jane Goodall speaking to a chimp. I take a sip of my scotch to buy some time while I think of something to say. The sudden onslaught of liquor on my taste buds puckers my lips, and I cough, feeling the liquid backup into my nose with a burn. I pray it doesn't shoot out my nostrils.

"You okay?" the girl says.

"Yeah," I cough. "I don't drink often. Snuck up on me a little."

"Gotta drink it till you love it," she says.

I nod, attempting another sip, if for no other reason than to prove I can handle it. It goes down rough again, but I'm able to camouflage my struggle with it for the most part.

The girl says, "So where were we?"

I try to build the conversation again from the ground up, aching to gain some confidence. I say, "We were at the usual get to know you chit-chat, I guess."

"Okay, so, let's see, you said on the phone that you're from an island?"

"Yeah. Mystic Island. It isn't far from here. Small community. Nice. Where are you from again?"

"Pittsburgh, born and raised."

"Are you sure?"

"Um, yeah?"

"I'm sorry, I thought—never mind. And what is it you do there?"

"Bartender."

"How's that working out for you?"

"All right, I guess. At least, when they can keep me from dancing on the bar top it's all right."

"Really? You dance on the bar?"

"No. I was just making a joke. Or trying to."

"Oh." There is more awkward silence. I finally say, "So what brings you to this area?"

"Just visiting. I wanted to check out the historical sites and all."

I perk in my seat. "Really?"

"Oh, yeah. I love history. Especially Revolutionary War era stuff. I mean, to think, birth of a nation, Sam Adams"—she gestures to her chest—"Paul Revere's surprisingly short ride and all that."

"That's amazing," I say. "I'm a huge history buff. Especially military history."

"Yeah. I know. You mentioned something about that when we spoke on the phone the other night. You collect historical memorabilia and such, right?"

"Yeah. I have some great pieces."

"I'd love to see them."

"Why didn't you mention anything about being into history when we spoke on the phone?" I say.

"I did. Remember?"

I shake my head, feeling a flush of heat in my face, a fusion of embarrassment and scotch.

The girl laughs. "First you don't remember where I'm from, now you don't remember that I love history. Real observant, Carl."

"I'm not that good at talking on the phone," I say. There is another beat of awkward silence, before I say, "For some reason I thought you were from Ohio. And I don't know why I don't remember the history bit. I remember mentioning something about my interest in it, but…like I said, I'm not so good on the phone. I must've been nervous. I don't really respond to those Craigslist ads."

"I guess that's understandable. So, do you have any recommendations for what historical sites to see? I'm not even sure where to begin. I feel like I need a personal tour guide just to navigate it all."

I perk more in my seat, my voice's cadence winding up. "Well, this is certainly the place for history, especially Revolutionary War era history...."

As I speak, I envision myself with this girl, entwined like the figures from *The Kiss*, only instead of the bed of flowers, we are making love on a pile of war memorabilia. Could that be the direction this is going? And then a sudden dread comes over me. How do I get this girl to my house? I never actually picked up a girl like this before. Is there some code to get her to come home with me? And should I take her home on the first date? It seems a long time since I read the book on dating etiquette. And even back when I had, I seemed to miss several chapters.

"Hey, have you ever heard of Mystic Island?" I say.

"Um, yeah, Carl, you just said it's where you're from."

I flush again, but my voice keeps speaking, seemingly independent of my brain, "Well there is a ton of history there, right back to when the Indians populated it. It's a hodgepodge of different eras. There's Puritan era stuff, Colonial era stuff, Civil War.... It's also been voted by several paranormal societies as one of the most haunted places in America—if you believe in that kind of stuff— but the structures on the island are very cool. A huge hospital and prison from Victorian times, both of which are still used today. There are old churches, one with a stained glass window from a medieval basilica, the other supposedly built on the gateway to Hell." I chuckle a moment. "There's more legends surrounding the island than can be counted. There's Captain Price and Captain Damon, and the wreck of the Dutch Horse...." I stop.

The girl is staring at me. She chuckles and says, "Wow, that sure was a lot of information, Carl."

I look down at the table. "Sorry. I can get a little carried away at times."

"So what's some of the historical memorabilia you have?"

"Mostly World War II pieces. I have some Nazi pieces that are pretty valuable with the skinhead crowd."

The girl twists her expression. "Skinheads?"

"Not that I like skinheads," I say. The words sound forced and ridiculous. After all, who *does* like skinheads? Or, at least, who would proclaim that they do on a first date? "But they can really drive up the value of some of the pieces," I say. "I also have Infamy Cards." I say this with an air of self-importance.

"I'd love to see them."

"Really?" my voice cracks slightly.

"Of course I would," the girl says.

For a moment, I am a fifteen-year-old again, and the hot cheerleader is thrusting her cleavage my way, asking if she can copy my homework. And, even though I know that she'll never look at me until the next time she needs to copy my work, I oblige.

But this is different. This girl seems to have sincere interest in what I am saying.

"You sound surprised by that," the girl says.

"Not many girls are interested in that kind of stuff."

"Well, I'm not like many girls."

I say as if to myself, "I guess not."

"So how about it?" the girl says. "You want to show me what you got, Carl?"

5

You've probably figured out that my name isn't Stacey (or Shauna, or Vivian, or Alana, or Veronica, or Rochelle). It's Sophie. Sophie Monroe. I don't know why I went with Stacey this time to be honest. I hate the name Stacey—it's something for trailer trash royalty. I can't stand the name Carl either—a name with an almost built-in snarl or whine when said, making it sound like an insult in itself—but there's nothing this schmuck can do about it at this point; it's the name this poor motherfucker was stuck with. We're in his car, an old Crown Vic (early-nineties era), approaching the bridge to cross onto Mystic Island—why the fuck I'm going onto an island for this, I'll never know. Laughter fills the car—mostly thanks to me. The two of us laughing at something about *American Idol*, which he seems to know an amazing amount about.

We bump onto a bridge and are immediately engulfed in wispy fog. No discernible beginning or end to it, and I have a sudden, anxious stomach-drop, my laughter fading. This is uncharacteristic, my nerves generally never falter, but suddenly I feel like a swimmer who'd just passed the point of no return. There is only forward now, and I'm not quite sure what the far shore looks like. Carl says the bridge is often covered in fog—something about the island's currents—and when we make it off the bridge and onto the island, the fog clears, and so does the anxiety.

Carl is accurate with his description of the place; the island is a hodgepodge of different eras, as if we are driving along a school textbook's timeline. I say to him, in my giggling, ain't-we-so-fun voice, "So this is the famous Mystic Island."

"I don't know about famous. Infamous is probably more like it."

"It's in the middle of nowhere."

"Well, it is an island," he says with a shrug.

"True," I say, and again question what the hell I am doing.

He pulls his car into a driveway at the end of a sparse street. As we walk from the car, I notice a slight weave in Carl's gait from the two drinks he's had at the bar. This is good. Drunk means clueless. Although, so far this guy doesn't need any assistance with being clueless.

His house is a basic ranch, low and squat. I note a seeming wall of black behind it, as if the night sky above has spilled into some kind of void around his house, like some kind of black hole.

Filled with that unexpected anxiety again, but still with that giggling, ain't-we-so-fun voice, I say, "Your house is apparently in the middle of nowhere, in the middle of nowhere. Are those, like, trees or something?"

"My property butts up against Parson's Woods, so there's a lot of trees around. It only appears that we are in the middle of nowhere," he says. "The woods are pretty thick though…and supposedly haunted. A lot of missing kids over the years." He then adds almost defensively, "They went missing before my time living here." He chuckles awkwardly. "Like over a span of hundreds of years. Just more of the place's legends." He looks off into the dark a moment and then adds, "Don't worry, we aren't that far from the bridge."

I've met up with enough of these dweebs to know what he's really getting at here. He is already preparing for my departure. He's fantasized seducing me for a night of crazy sex, but deep down, he's already accepted that I won't be staying the night. Although part of his ego can't believe this smoking hot girl is here with him in the first place, he knows the score; Carl is a lot of things—boring, the most obvious—but he is also a realist. He knows guys like him don't convince girls like me to spend the night. I can use this lack of assuredness to my advantage. Easier to string him along.

He says, "So, you know, it's not a long cab ride back to where you are staying, or I can give you a ride, although"—he teeters a little where he stands, as if butchering a field sobriety test—"I'm a little drunk at the moment."

"Well," I say, "We'll just have to see where this night takes us." I give him a seductive look, but not too come-fuck-me-like—I need Carl to believe he still needs to work for something, rather than believing he'd already hit the jackpot. Even if that *something* doesn't exist. I prefer not to get physical if at all possible. Sometimes, like with the aggressive, good-looking banker types, it's necessary (I wonder how long it took for John to get Stewie off his dick), but I try to avoid it. Especially with the dweebs like this guy. When dweebs get a little taste of the physical, they often become possessive, even obsessive, which can make my egress more difficult.

Carl opens his front door and leads me into the living room. As he flips on the lights, I quickly size up the space. It is scarcely decorated, but very neat. There is a beige carpet on a wood floor. Secondhand, mismatched furniture. Obviously no wife in this picture.

Carl and I are laughing again at some inane thing, and I try to keep the laughter going, launching into one of those drunken giggle fits young, silly girls are prone to have. I'm not drunk of course, nor am I silly. Just loosening him up, making everything seem much more fun than it is. Which isn't hard to do, seeing as he doesn't seem the type that has fun too often anyway. I'm just happy he isn't ultra-obnoxious. Or ugly. It is more that he is charismatically challenged. His hair thinning a little. Standard haircut. He isn't fat, but not in shape either. He has a collapsible chin—from the front it looks more clenched than strong, but from the side, it seems to disappear altogether. Every so often, he'll absentmindedly sweep his hand across his forehead like a windshield wiper snuffing out a gathering of misty sweat. There is a strange lost puppy way to him. It brings about a sense of pity for his apparent loneliness. But I need to be wary of that loneliness, too.

He motions to the couch. "Have a seat."

I sit.

There is a chess set on the coffee table. The board is the kind that folds into a box to hold the pieces, but right now it is open and its carved, wooden pieces set. I pick up the bishop and begin caressing the piece in my fingers. "I like this," I say.

Obviously, my caressing of the phallic piece is supposed to turn him on a little, but instead, he says, "The chess set? You play?"

Something tells me I could have outright blown the piece and he still wouldn't have caught the inuendo. "I play," I say.

"You any good?"

"I can hold my own in just about any game, Carl."

"Is that a challenge?"

"Maybe," I say coyly.

"You really want to play chess?" he says.

I pause a moment, biting back sarcasm, thinking this guy couldn't catch a double entendre if it were lubricated with every sexual innuendo and rammed up his rectum. I offer an easy-going grin and say, "No, Carl, not now."

He looks disappointed for a moment. "Too bad," he says. "It's hard to find anyone that's a challenge."

"Well, I'm certainly a challenge."

"Sure you don't want to play?"

Is this really his idea of foreplay?

"No, I'm quite sure," I say sweetly. "What I want, Carl, is a drink. Got anything?"

"I have whiskey."

"Whiskey's good."

He says, "I don't drink often. Don't even think the bottle's been opened."

"Well, there's a first time for everything."

"It was a gift. I generally don't go out and buy booze."

"Carl, get the drinks," I say playfully, not wanting him to feel as if being scolded, or that I'm expressing how incredibly annoyingly boring he is.

He grins, as if realizing, all on his own, how incredibly annoyingly boring he is.

I like this. It shows that my tone is working. I want to make everything he thinks and does seem like it is his idea, or that it is the product of his own will, when, of course, I'll be the one controlling his every move.

After he walks off into the kitchen, I immediately begin a cursory sweep of the living room. Aside from the chess set, there is no sign of expensive trinkets or knick-knacks—and even the chess set is questionable. Whatever is worth taking is somewhere else in the house. Or, at least I hope it is. I pray I've nocked the right arrow. He seems too sincerely clueless to have been bullshitting me.

There is an old stereo system with big speakers and a turntable CD changer. A bookcase with history books and framed photographs. My attention shifts to photos of Carl with a boy of about eleven. In all of them, Carl has a big, goofball smile on his face. The boy has an absolute, deadpan expression. I've seen this scenario often enough:

dad trying to play comedian to the perpetual straight man of adolescence.

"You have a son?" I call toward the kitchen.

"Yeah," he calls back.

"Where is he?"

"He lives with his mother."

I flip through a few history books from the bookshelf, searching for publication dates or signatures. Nothing.

I walk toward what looks like a diploma on the wall, calling toward the kitchen, "I can't wait to see your—" My voice drops off when Carl returns with the drinks.

"My son?" he says, as if taken aback a little.

"Your collection," I say with a smile. "The memorabilia. The Infamy Cards. I can't wait to see them."

I have no idea what the hell Infamy Cards are, but if they are as valuable as the Internet search says they are, then, yes, I can't wait to see them.

"Oh, yeah, right," he says, as if forgetting the whole reason we are here in the first place. He hands me a drink, saying, "I had ginger ale, so I made—is whiskey and ginger ale even called anything?"

"Highball," I say.

"I made highballs, then," he says, sounding impressed with himself.

"Perfect." I clink my glass with his.

"Cheers," he says with an awkward smile that makes the word seem like a foreign language. He sips the drink and makes a sour face, stifling a cough.

"Remember, drink it till you love it," I say and drain my glass.

His sour face drops into a gaping expression.

I say, "You're gonna need to keep up if you're going to hang with me, Carl."

He looks at his drink as if it's hemlock. He drains it with some difficulty, coughing when he's finished. "Jesus," he says. "Like I said, I don't drink often."

I say, "Why don't you grab the whiskey bottle and the memorabilia, and we can get this party started."

6

We put a good dent in the whiskey. He is sitting on the couch; I am on the carpet—to give him an opportunity to catch glimpses of my cleavage—with all sorts of World War II memorabilia spread out on the coffee table between us. Clay Aiken is playing on the CD turntable, one track ending and another beginning like a chain-smoker's succession of butts. I say, "I can't believe you listen to Clay Aiken." I giggle this statement, not wanting him to think I'm questioning his manhood—even though I am.

"I can't believe you don't," he says.

"Believe it."

"Didn't you see him on *Idol?*"

"Um, no."

"It was incredible. And he seems like such a nice guy. Visiting cancer patients and all...."

I've come to the realization that it might be harder to seduce this guy than I'd originally thought. I decide to shift the subject in a random direction to catch him off guard, take back control of the conversation. Interrupting him in a playfully sarcastic tone, I say, "So why do you have a bubblegum card of Hitler?"

"Huh?"

I pick up what is in essence a bubblegum card of a cartoonish ranting Hitler. Beneath the Hitler card is another card with what looks like a Japanese man's face on a balloon with a dart flying at it while floating over Pearl Harbor. Beneath that card is a card adorned with a snowman beginning to melt in blazing sunlight; the snowman's baldheaded face looking a lot like Benito Mussolini's. I read what is written on the back of the Hitler card, "'Führer Hosenscheisser?'" I giggle. "What are these things?"

Carl looks stunned. He gently takes the card from me. "A bubblegum card of Hitler?" he says incredulously. "These are Infamy Cards."

"Oh, right. Of course," I say.

"I thought you said you knew about them."

"I know *of* them," I say. "Meaning, I've heard they existed. I just never really understood what they are. I'd love to hear about them."

Something tells me he'll love to tell me about them.

He holds the card delicately, as if inspecting it for blemishes or scratches. "They are very rare and worth quite a lot of money. Infamy Cards were created during the Second World War, designed by two men: Louis Ting and Samuel Carey. I guess describing them as 'men' isn't even right here. They were just a couple of kids, really. Showing aptitude for art and design, they were assigned to create propaganda. It was these Infamy Cards that they created. They were pretty successful, the cards being dropped all over Europe, but when the Allies were storming Normandy, one regiment was short and they grabbed Ting and Carey, and sent them up the beach. They were dragged along with their foster regiment all the way to The Battle of the Bulge, where Carey was killed. Ting became so disheartened, he went AWOL and began making rogue Infamy cards, attacking everything from American politicians to popular culture. He disappeared and is in hiding, still wanted by the government, and continuing to create Infamy Cards to this day. He works with different artists from around the world. There are supposedly cards out there designed by Andy Warhol, Keith Haring, even Banksy. My great uncle actually fought with Ting in The Battle of the Bulge—" Carl stops abruptly, reading my expressionless face. He flushes.

"Wow," I say. "Once again, that was *a lot* of information, Carl."

"Sorry."

"No, it's interesting," I say.

There is a brief awkward pause.

I then say, "So where did you get all this memorabilia?"

"Most of it is from my family," he says, his demeanor perking considerably. "A lot of the stuff's just been passed down and all."

"Nice that they gave it to you."

"Yeah. They knew I collect the stuff," he says. "Most of them are gone now." He pauses a moment, regarding his collection, then says, "So, how about you? You have a large family?"

"I come from a long line of only-children," I say. "I'm an only-child. My mom, dad, grandparents, all only-children. I guess it's what gives me my independent spirit."

"You certainly seem independent. And spirited," he says, glancing at me, his eyes lingering on my cleavage a moment.

The conversation is hovering dangerously close to personal territory, which means that it is heading to a comfortable silence, and subsequently, a potential make out session. I'm hoping I can get Carl so hammered he'll pass out and I can merely walk out the front door without any physical entanglement at all, but the guy is holding his liquor surprisingly well for a supposed light-weight. Maybe I can get him rambling again about *Idol,* or World War II, or haunted churches and forests, or whatever. Maybe he will literally talk himself into a stupor. Or, maybe I can speed up his stupefaction by getting him drinking and rambling at the same time.

"Okay, time for a drinking game," I say.

"Drinking game?"

He has this way of processing information, asking rhetorical self-clarifying questions in a manner that is not unlike a village idiot. But this guy is far from idiotic. It is more the way he comes to grips with the things going on around him. A slow building of understanding in his mind. As if he needs to take apart and analyze every word said to him and rearrange it into a recognizable narrative, translating it all into his own understanding of the world around him.

"I'm going to make up a game right now," I say, inspecting the memorabilia spread out on the coffee table. "Let's see…." I'm searching for the object that will have the longest anecdotal potential. I pick up a bayonet—the thing about fourteen inches long, an apparent perpetual polishing having accentuated the battle scars upon it—but something about it brings up the hairs on my neck. Holding it feels like holding dread. Its story will surely be a buzz-kill, and I return it to the table, brushing my fingers across my skirt, as if wiping the negative juju from my fingertips. I search the table again. There are medals and documents, the stupid bubblegum cards, and then— bingo. There is a door knocker in the shape of an eagle and swastika.

I say to Carl, "Okay, You need to tell the story behind this object without using the word *and.* If you do say *and,* then you finish your drink. Got it? It's a lot harder than it sounds, so concentrate. Ready? Go."

Carl says, "I can't say *and*?"

"Shit, Carl, you already lost."

He sits there for a moment as his intoxicated, over-processing brain works out the joke. Then it dawns on him, and he smiles a sloppy grin, saying, "Whoops. Sorry."

"Okay, try again," I say. "And no *ands*, got it?"

"Got it," he says, picking up the door knocker. "All righty-then. This lovely item my uncle Herbert Palmer—actually, my mom's uncle, my great uncle—he got it off of an SS captain's house…." He pauses, obviously about to say *and*. He sits a moment gathering his thoughts again.

I smile. It is my first legitimate smile of the night.

Carl continues his story, saying, "They knocked on the door with this knocker. Generally, they'd have just busted down the door and raided the house, but something about a swastika door knocker cracked them up…." He pauses, reeling in another *and*. "They couldn't resist cordially using it. After knocking, my uncle calls up in this high-pitched voice, 'Hallo, Avon Fräulein calling.'" Carl begins laughing uncontrollably, but he stops when he notices I am not laughing.

It would have been a good time to laugh with the guy, a good bonding moment, gaining his trust and all. But if we both start laughing uncontrollably, there is nowhere to go but make out city, so instead, I arch an eyebrow to get him back on track.

Carl continues, saying, "My uncle used to laugh his ass off telling that story, but you probably had to be there. He had one of those infectious laughs. Know what I mean by an infectious laugh?"

I nod and smile another genuine smile.

Carl says, "I once had a skinhead offer me a grand for this knocker. I would never sell it though. Because it had such sentimental value to my uncle, and—"

"Wait," I say, "You said *and*. You owe a drink."

"Really? I said *and*?"

"Two drinks," I say.

"Oh, man," Carl says, "I don't even know if I can."

"A rule's a rule, Carl. No reneging. It's drinking-game etiquette. You don't really have a say in the matter."

"All right. All right. Give it here," he says. His extended arm sways a bit, like a branch in a strong breeze.

I am both sincerely impressed and sincerely disappointed when he downs the drink like a champ. But after a moment, I can see he's feeling very un-champ-like.

He stands, wobbly, from the couch and says, "I think I need that one to hit to my head."

I'm not quite sure what he's trying to say, but I figure it is his saying two different things at once—trying to say he needs the bathroom and that the alcohol has gone straight to his head.

"Jesus, you are drunk," I say, laughing, as he stumbles off in the direction of the bathroom, almost tripping over the threshold into the kitchen.

When I hear the bathroom door click shut, I grab my bag and begin stuffing the war memorabilia into it. I figure I have plenty of time—he'll most likely be in the bathroom for a while, if not for the rest of the night—but still, my precision is as flawlessly automated as an assembly line, and I clear the table in seconds, even dumping the chess set, pieces and all, into my bag. I do leave the bayonet, however, not wanting to touch the thing. Then I turn and head for a swift exit.

For some reason—one I can't quite explain—I stop.

I return to the coffee table—again, I have no idea why I am doing this—and I dig through my bag to find the swastika door knocker. I place it beside the bayonet before heading back for an exit, grabbing his car keys hanging on the wall beside the front door.

I stop again.

I notice something I hadn't paid enough attention to when first inventorying the room. I can't believe I'd missed it. It is what I'd earlier assumed to be a framed diploma on the wall. I paid it no mind then, but now I realize it is a framed certificate. It reads: *For ten years of loyal duty with the Salem Police Department.*

"Uh-oh."

He's a cop? How did I not pick up on this?

Well, I guess in retrospect, it was easy not to have picked up on it; he is way too boring and timid to be a cop. Cops are generally too stupid to be boring and too arrogant to be timid. But still, there it is, despite being in no way cop-like, he is a fucking cop.

His voice comes suddenly from behind me. At first I don't realize what he says, the sound of his voice jolting me, his car keys jangling in my hand. For a moment I hear only my heart pounding, giving me time to realize what he'd said: "What are you doing?"

I've only been caught in the act once before. It was in Chicago, and I was able to get down three flights of stairs and out of the building, disappearing into the crowded streets before the fat-fuck I'd robbed even made it out of his apartment. But now I'm in the middle of nowhere, and if I have to run, I have no idea in which direction to even go. Can I make it out to his car before he grabs me? It's not like I can go running off down the street with this guy chasing me, it would attract far too much attention. And I certainly don't want to end up lost in those woods out back. Haunted or not. And what's more, I've already made three cardinal mistakes.

My first mistake had been to take the time to return the knocker.

The second mistake was freezing when I'd seen the certificate.

But my third mistake is the game-changer. I can't remember if Carl locked the door when we'd first arrived. I always note that. It is an amateur move to not know if I'm locked in here or not—I should have noted if he'd locked it, and if he had, unlock it before snatching his things. But I neglected to do that. I must be slipping. Or I've become over-confident. Or this is just one of those days, full of surprises.

I turn around to find Carl standing in the middle of the living room. Standing beside the now-empty coffee table. My only option at this point is to talk my way out of this, but if he is a cop, that probably won't work. There is no way a cop can let this go.

A cop turning his head on a crime? Yes.

Turn his cheek on a personal affront? Never.

How did I not see this coming?

In my defense, generally cops will happily tell you they're a cop at least twenty times a night. In fact, it is like they can't *not* tell someone, which is why I've always had the chance to bail before ending up at one's house. Had he mentioned he was a cop during our phone call? Definitely not. Had I even asked him what he did for a living? It is something I always do. Man, I am really slipping on all accounts with this one. And now, I'll most likely have to sleep with him. I've never had to sleep with a mark. Never so much as a hand job. But sex is generally the only language cops understand when it comes to a girl talking her way out of trouble.

I say in a light, airy, don't-mind-me tone, "Um, well, Carl, I'm not feeling so great. I think I'll just get going."

He looks down at the coffee table, empty now, save for the bayonet and the door knocker, and his brain begins to do that slow crawl to comprehension. The confusion slips into his eyes and voice. "You're robbing me?"

"It was nice meeting you, Carl, but I've got to get going," I say, stepping to the door and yanking on the doorknob.

Of course it's locked.

I reach up and fumble with the deadbolt.

He is now right behind me. I can smell him. The reek of alcohol and some other underlining metallic smell.

I say, "It's been real, Carl."

Finally there comes the beautiful music of the deadbolt clicking out of the jamb, and I'm able to open the door.

He slams it shut again, saying, in that village idiot way of his, "You're really robbing me?"

I turn to face him and smile, trying to lay on the charm.

But he looks different. His eyes are intense, nostrils flared, teeth bared. I never would have guessed him capable of it, but he actually looks menacing.

Menacing was not the right word. More like unsettling. And it is not the anger in his expression that is so unsettling; it is that confusion.

I say, "Look, Carl, why don't you just take your stuff back, and I'll be going. No harm, no foul, right?"

He still seems to be working it all out in his mind, the anger and the confusion seeping across his face like a stain, and he says, "But...I thought we...you're really robbing me?"

At any other time, this bewildered look on his face would be funny. It would be funny if I wasn't so utterly and completely fucked at the moment.

"Carl, I need to get going now. Here's your stuff." I walk back to his coffee table and begin returning the stolen items to it.

I know this is my fourth mistake as soon as I do it. Now Carl is between me and the door.

I continue pulling items from my bag, but my fingers keep falling onto individual chess pieces, and I find myself returning his stolen items one pawn at a time.

"You bitch," he says. He says it almost conversationally, but there is a growl to that tone that I don't like at all.

This is all wrong. The mistakes I've made. The look in his eyes. The black hole seemingly swallowing this house from outside. The dreamlike fog I'd crossed through to get onto this island. It all feels dreamlike and surreal. I've crossed into some dicey situations in the past—more than I can count—but I'd always known I would get out of them. However, there is something about this one…what it is, I can't quite put my finger on. The bayonet is still on the coffee table. Will I need to use it? Am I willing to use it?

"Look, Carl, calm down. I can explain." My tone is steady, subdued.

"*Me* calm down? *You* can *explain*?" His voice is anything but subdued; it is screechy and out of control.

I lunge for the bayonet, but he grabs me, hard, before I can get to it. I drop my bag at his feet, and he flings me back toward the kitchen. I have nowhere to go now. The front door may as well be in Istanbul. There could be a back door, but it is probably locked, too. If I run at this point, he'll be on me, most likely with the bayonet. Like the old adage goes, never run from an animal, and the wild frenzy in his eyes makes him look like exactly that.

I need to stay calm. I can still talk—or fuck—my way out of this. "Let's talk about this, Carl. This could still have a happy ending."

"A happy ending?" he says in his confused way. Again, he doesn't seem to get the sexual overtones of my words.

He picks up my bag and checks the heft of it in his hand. "How much did you take?"

All of it, asshole, I want to say, but instead I muster my sweetest smile and say, "C'mon, Carl, let's not ruin the night."

"*Ruin the night?*" he screams. He looks like a Ralph Steadman drawing (I'd snagged an original in Vegas a couple of years ago; still haven't sold it), his eyes protruding from their sockets, his lips peeling away from his teeth. I can count every cavity in his teeth and see the vein bulging in his forehead.

I am now witnessing a man who has come completely unhinged. I've seen unhinged before—unhinged is often the default of most men—but this is a different unhinged. And I'm not quite sure what to do with *this* unhinged. Like a lion-tamer trapped in a cage, I now have no control of the situation. My only option is to see where he is going with this, and to stay ahead of him. But I may be too far behind already.

With an unsettling quickness, he swings my bag—a good fifteen pounds of war memorabilia in it—and catches me right in the chops. I lose my balance and hit my head on the coffee ta—

PART 2

1

The bed's sheets cling to me. Feverishly, I think this is what it must be like to be Saran Wrapped. And for a moment I envision I am encased in giant strips of the clear plastic. But I can feel the softness of the linens pressed against my skin. My chest and back are sweaty. The back of my neck, too. My ankles itch beneath my bunched socks. I wonder how I could've climbed into bed with them on. I hate wearing socks to bed. Hate wearing anything other than my pajamas. But I'm not wearing my pajamas. Instead, I feel the binding constriction of my clothing—the jeans' denim wrapping around my legs, the collared shirt around my neck. I am floating in some murky state, my fragmented dreams drifting away from nauseated reality. It seems like a small fissure is wedged into my brain, and I massage my temples with clammy fingers as I debate whether or not to open my clinging, sleep-crusted eyes.

The gentle ticking of my watch—still on my wrist—sounds uncomfortably loud, and my mind drifts to the stories of torture I'd read in my military history books.

Sensory disorientation. POWs and terrorists alike driven to the edge of madness. I count off the *tick-tick-tick-tick* rhythm, my semi-conscious mind drifting back toward sleep, painting a cartoonish dog walking on hind legs, its steps keeping pace with the ticks. Thin ropes of saliva fall from the dog's jowls, then a dim, almost muted sunny summer sky and the silhouette of a bloodhound from some far away memory is above me. I feel a tongue lapping across my chapped lips. When was that? The dog? Was it the neighbors' or some stray I'd picked up? Why were my lips chapped? Were they? Why the hell am I thinking about this shit now?

Jesus, I wish I had a bottle of cold Gatorade at my bedside to wash out my dry, filmy mouth. My eyes jolt open and the lurking dog dissolves back into my childhood.

The phone is ringing.

More, it is suddenly reverberating through my head.

I roll over and adjust my eyes against the light peeking through the blinds, hoping the insistent ringing, and subsequent pounding inside my head, will cease.

It doesn't.

I sit upright, the world taking a sudden, rogue-wave lurch. I recognize the high probability I will puke onto the floor beside my bed; it makes it up around my larynx before I can choke it down. I smack my lips, to rid my mouth of its rancid state, and then pick up the receiver. If for no other reason than to stop that dreadful head-pounding ringing.

Still smacking my lips, I manage to whisper, "Hello?"

"White. Where the hell are you?" It is Ben Walters, my supervisor.

"I…I'm sick. I'm real sick. I can't make it in today."

"Were you planning to call and let us know?"

"Sorry. I…" I look around my sun-drenched bedroom. "I was out dead to the world. Must be the flu or something."

"All right. Get your rest, because you *will* be here tomorrow." He has that scolding tone he always takes with me. "You are out of sick time."

"Yeah. All right."

I hang up the phone and roll onto my back, groaning, "What the hell…?"

I try to piece together what had put me in this state of nauseated, head-pounding torture, trying to cognitively trace back to the last thing I remember from last night, the last thing I—

I hear the far-off voice of a woman calling.

I put my head in my hands and say, "Oh, shit."

2

Let's back up a few minutes. I'd been dreaming. In the dream, I'm in the room of a house. The place is gargantuan, as if the walls are that of a canyon. I look up and see there is no ceiling. It is a black, starless night above. The floor is under an indeterminable depth of water, and I make my way through the giant room on oversized, partially-submerged pieces of furniture. I'm not quite sure where I'm going, but I feel there is some task I need to perform. Maybe it's to answer the ringing phone—the sound of it is muffled and far off.

There's a crag in the room's wall, a doorway to another room, and I leap from a chair, which is the size of a platform, to an ottoman with the dimensions of a king-sized mattress. But I slip from the ottoman and go right into the water. It's too deep to stand, so I swim toward the distant ringing phone. I'm a pretty strong swimmer, no problem getting to where I need to go, but I have a sudden feeling I'm not alone, and as the thought seeds itself in my mind, something grabs me. It is all tentacles, caressing and binding me. I try to swim harder, but the tentacles have my wrists—I can feel the actual suction cups puckering at my skin—and it is dragging me under the water. I feel the room's floor beneath me and I flatten my feet on it and struggle to launch myself toward the surface, but I am fettered to some beast, and I know I am about to drown.

Under the water, the ringing phone seems to get louder and clearer, and somehow I'm able to break the water's surface and gasp for breath, and that's when I realize it's a dream. I'm not even in water. Or drowning.

But my wrists are bound.

I reach through that very hazy, deep sleep—you know that kind you can't quite climb all the way out of—and as consciousness takes hold of me, I notice the headache. Not a usual headache, but a trumpet-blasting, jackhammer of a headache. My eyes spring open with a crashing wave of nausea. I often have that feeling of not being quite sure where I'm waking—given the number of different hotel rooms in the number of different cities—however they all tend to blend into a recognizable sense of place. I can always confidently say, I am going to open my eyes and I will be in a hotel room, even if I'm not at first exactly sure which hotel, or even which city. But this…this I am not prepared to see.

I'm in a dim space. My wrists jerk against binds that dig into my skin. Dizzying with the confusion and panic, and desperate for an answer, my eyes adjust to the dimness. With sinking dread, another wave of nausea hits me as the situation takes hold fully in my recall. Coming back to me in blurred and streaked memories of the prior night.

"No fucking way," I say, regarding the dim space around me.

I'm in the center of a basement. The only light is from a low-wattage light bulb hanging above me and sunlight streaming through the streaked panes of a narrow, horizontal window. To my left is a workbench with varied tools—everything from construction to gardening. To the right is a furnace and water heater. In the corners are boxes and flats of bulk supplies. Bottled water and canned food. Beside those are neatly stacked bottles and cans for the redemption center and a few pieces of forgotten equipment and mementos. Straight ahead of me are stairs leading to a closed door.

I'm seated in a wooden chair, the type one might find as part of a dining room set. My wrists are bound to the chair's armrests with duct tape. Which I foolishly try to get free of by sliding my wrists under, only bunching it into stronger binds.

I bang my back against the chair, trying to break it.

No good.

Only my wrists are bound, my legs remaining free, and I flatten my feet on the concrete floor, just like I had in the dream, trying to get the best leverage to bust the chair apart. I push back with all my strength against the thing's back, but no luck. The chair is pretty fucking sturdy.

"This isn't good," I say. "I can't believe he tied me up in his basement." I look around the basement again, saying, "I can't believe I got myself into this." I then say, while staring up at the ceiling and blowing a strand of hair out of my eyes, "I can't believe I'm talking to myself." After taking a deep breath and blowing it slowly through pursed lips—a technique acquired from several failed yogi careers—I begin calling out to nowhere in particular,

"Um, Carl? Carl? This isn't funny. Yo, Carl, I'm not really into this kind of bondage shit."

No answer.

I blow the hair from my face and call up toward the basement's ceiling, "Hey, Carl, this really isn't fucking funny."

Still no answer.

"Fucker," I mutter before taking another deep breath and flexing my legs. They're stiff—having fallen asleep during the night—the remnants of weak pins and needles still pulsing through them. With the chair still bound to my wrists, I stand, bent over, looking like some demented turtle.

I call, "Yo, Carl. Carl."

Nothing.

"Fucker," I mutter again and take my demented turtle show on the road, waddling toward the stairs. Then I waddle up the steps, feeling as if I'm in one of those old Harold Lloyd movies, or Buster Keaton, or any of those old black and white movies my grandmother used to have on Sunday mornings. There I am, climbing riser by riser, bent over in the chair, finally making it to the door. And there, balanced precariously atop the steps, I call through the door, "Carl. Hello, Carl."

No response.

"Hey, this isn't funny."

Nothing.

Still bent over, and with no other way to knock, I use my head to pound on the door—the action sending bright flashes of pain through my skull—and I scream, "Hey, asshole, you hear me?"

The door bursts open.

And of course the shock of the opening door causes me to lose my balance and tumble down the steps—still bound to the chair, mind you—and I strike the basement floor. Luckily the chair breaks, freeing my arms—and probably saving me from taking a bad angle and breaking my neck—but when I try to stand, the room is spinning and fading in a topsy-turvy, seasickness sort of way. I hear footsteps rushing down the stairs toward me as I float away into the fading, spinning of nausea and aching pain.

3

"They'd have you believe in fear."

"Fear?" Mandy asks.

"Fear. Yes. Such a simple device, which, skillfully used, can transform continents, dictate the way people live. And die. It's quite comical, actually. How we just lie in wait."

"Weight? Like pounds?"

I'm regretting I said anything at all. Atop the fishing dock on Half Moon Pond, we stand in silence, eyes cast westward. A quarrel of sparrows shiver in the skeleton of a tree, and I watch, awaiting their flight.

"It will feel so good for it to be spring again," she says.

I think of the prospect for a moment and then consider that she has changed the subject quite unsubtly. I gather that she hasn't been comfortable with her own interrogative responses to my thoughts, but I don't really care to speak of spring. The bark on the surrounding trees remains chapped and the earth appears solid as concrete. It is hardly spring.

"The winter isn't finished with us yet," I say and am disappointed to see her look downward in a pout. Her aura begs for agreement, and her tactic is to remain casually silent during discordant conversations. "What's your favorite thing about spring?" I say, attempting to compensate. As the silence continues for a moment, I feel guilty for surrendering my position. I don't want to discuss something as finite as the seasons of the year.

"Well…" she begins, and then stops abruptly. A few of the birds take to the air and then return to their perch in the tree's crook. Testing the air. "Just the return of sunshine. Of life. The flowers and the green grass and no more of the brutal cold and snow," she says.

"Are you afraid of the snow?" I ask.

"Afraid?"

"Yes. Afraid," I say. "Forget it."

I look toward the water beneath the dock. The ice has been reduced to a thinly crusted sheet. I imagine dropping a pebble and watching it heroically push a tiny hole through the perfectly smooth layer, only to be hidden from the world in the murk. I fiddle with my wedding ring, loose on my finger, then look at my windburned hand. If my finger follows the example set by the ice's expanding molecules, my ring will suffocate the blood supply. Intrigued by the notion, I raise a finger before my face and imagine it engorged. Slowly evolving to blue, like the sky, then to the purple of a bruising sunset, until a thin line bleeds through the cuticle, fingernail flecking away, skin stretching and pulsing and ripping and—

"I like to watch the birds fly, too," she says. "That's another thing I like. You know, about spring and all."

I remain silent and watch the sparrows. Beyond them, the dissolving sun rouges the sky and I stare toward the hidden horizon. With one raised arm, I point toward the sunset and inhale deeply, about to say something. But I don't say anything. I lower my arm. The ring slides from my finger with ease, and as it descends, I close my eyes and listen. It passes delicately through the skin of ice below. I look up at the woman standing beside me, but it is no longer Mandy. It is the girl in my basement.

"You really are a useless prick, Carl," she says.

I break from my thoughts, unsure for a moment where I am, or what I'm doing, as if I'd fallen asleep standing up.

What you're doing, Mandy's voice says in my head, *is waiting for the girl to wake up…again.*

After my abrupt waking and phone call with Walters, and then hearing the girl's shouting, and remembering what exactly had happened the night before, I'd checked on her, shocked upon finding her at the top of the basement stairs. And then she goes and falls, knocking herself out…again.

Mandy's voice in my head saying: *Again? She didn't knock herself out the first time.*

I am standing in my living room. The scene of the crime, so to speak.

Mandy again: *So to speak? It is literally the scene of the crime. Two crimes, if you want to get real technical.*

I begin to assess the aftermath while waiting for the girl to wake up…for the second time.

Is waking up the correct terminology? More like coming to.

I glance at the woman's bag on the floor. *My* belongings spilling from its open mouth.

"What the fuck?"

I look at the coffee table that was heaped with my memorabilia the night before, but now it only holds my door knocker and my bayonet.

"What am I supposed to do now?" I say.

Besides wait for her to come to…? Again.

If she comes to, I suppose. The *if* is a major part of the equation now. The girl having been knocked out for the second time in less than twelve hours, there is a chance she won't wake up at all. Maybe she *won't* wake up at all, I think hopefully. That will solve everything.

Will it?

Actually it won't solve anything. But what other options do I have? Let her go? She will obviously turn me in.

Or would she? *She* tried to rob *me.*

I can always bring her to the station.

And then what? The publicity tour about how I'd actually gotten a beautiful girl home with me, only to have her choose my Infamy Cards over me?

So let me get this straight, I can hear the guys saying, *you were so charming that she found old bubblegum cards more desirable than you?*

Is that so hard to believe? They're *Infamy Cards.* Any collector would find them irresistible. She must not have been able to control herself. After all, we'd been having fun.

Right?

Sounds like she was having a blast, I hear the guys saying.

Think of the scandal of it. They can put me on display in the break room. Like the Elephant Man or something. They will laugh and point.

Why will they laugh? *I* am the victim. She *robbed* me.

But with a sinking feeling, I realize she never actually left my property with the merchandise, so she never actually robbed me.

Holy shit. I am screwed.

She will say she was kidding around with me and I attacked her.

Could that be what actually happened? Was she just kidding around with me?

No. She'd spotted something she wanted for herself and took it. And I...overreacted.

Doesn't this make her nothing more than a common thief?

I hate common thieves. Or any thief, for that matter. People taking what other people work hard to obtain. Taking what other people love. Things with sentiment. If one were to think about it, aren't thieves really a kind of murderer? Killing trust? Killing sentiment? Killing memories and hopes?

Thief or not, she is currently tied up in your basement.

What was I *supposed* to do with her?

Maybe scare her? Put the fear of heaven and hell into her and get her begging, and *then* let her go? Make her believe I am going to kill her, and then she'll be so grateful that I actually let her live that she won't say anything? Maybe she'll even want to sleep with me, or at least a blowjob—

Jesus, stop it.

It is up to me, and me alone, to right karma's wheel. I need to punish this girl. Give her a good scare. Scare her straight. I'll be doing her a favor in the long run.

Is it really to help her?

Well, no. It's more that I can't live a life knowing she got one over on me like this. That she thinks so little about me—about humanity—that she can just take someone's things and get away with it.

I could kill her. Bury her. Who even knows that she went out with me?

She must have friends.

A boyfriend?

A really big boyfriend?

Will he come looking for her?

Would she tell a boyfriend she was going on a date with another man?

Why am I so worried? I've done nothing wrong. This is all *her* fault. She *made* me hit her. She *made* me tie her up. This is *not* my fault. I need to teach her a lesson. It's my duty to do it. For Karma's sake. I'll scare her. Make her think I'm going to kill her. Give her one of those life-altering, scared-straight, come-to-Jesus moments.

But that might be harder than you think. A lot harder. Will she even scare? I'm not so sure about that. How exactly does one scare someone like her? Mandy's voice still in my head.

I grimace; the sentiment is unfortunately accurate. It isn't like I was able to intimidate Mandy and her lawyer into conceding anything the other day.

You're weak, I hear Mandy saying.

But I'm not weak. I *acted* weak the other day. That's how it has always been for me, acting weak when there is resolve in my heart. Why is that? Was I just raised to be meek in the face of opposition? No, not weak or meek…passive is the better word. Was it my mother that instilled this in me? This trait of not rocking the boat? I need to not act weak. And what better time to start than now? In the face of conceit herself.

I once took a public speaking class in college. Something I was terrible at. Standing up there and trying to compel others to listen to what I had to say. My professor told me, *Pretend you're the guy that is good at public speaking.* And it worked. I gave a great speech.

I need to construct a persona. I need to *act* like someone threatening. I am good at pretending after all. Pretending to be a father. Pretending to be a husband. Even pretending to be a cop. But I have no idea where to begin with this kind of pretend. No idea where to find this kind of persona.

Movies, maybe? Or television? Think about people acting that way on screen. Who is an in-control, take-no-shit badass?

Horatio Caine. *CSI: Miami.* I'll Caine the bitch. Okay, I can do this. I'll threaten her Caruso-style. *Then* I'll let her go. Or, as they say on the show, *cut her loose*. I'll open the cage, and like a frightened bird, she will be gone so fast she will never think to come back. I'll never hear that bird's demented caw again.

I hit the nail on the head there, comparing her to a bird. Her calling my name sounded precisely like a crow's cawing.

Carl. Carl.

Like *Cawl. Cawl.*

"Carl? Carl?"

And there it is again. I hear it coming from the basement.

She is awake.

Not in a coma.

Damn.

"Hey, fuckhead," she shouts.

Fuckhead? Did she just call *me* a fuckhead?

Rage fills me, my breaths coming in deep waves. A girl who forced me to tie her in my basement, is calling *me* a fuckhead?

Forget scaring her. Forget teaching lessons or balancing Karma. I am going to kill her. Plain and simple, I am going to kill this bitch.

No. Stay calm. Get in character.

Closing my eyes and shaking my arms like a stage actor warming up, I envision Horatio Caine about to enter the interrogation room to intimidate a witness. Scare her straight. And then I'll let her go.

No, I will cut her loose.

I stride into the kitchen, grab one of the two remaining chairs at the dining table, and I storm down the basement steps.

4

I'd been dreaming again. Before coming to…for the second time. In the dream, I'm holding a personal check in my hand. *One thousand dollars* written in a rushed scrawl on the amount line, with a familiar signature scribbled in the corner. Above the memo line, in the same rushed handwriting, is the statement: *This is the last one.* Below the memo line are the words: *You are such a cunt.* The check suddenly bursts into flames, the fire rushing up my arms and engulfing me in blazing agony.

I wake from the dream, snapping to attention, my eyes blinking to adjust to the dim light. In a jerky panic, I inspect my arms, which are no longer ablaze. But they are again bound to the chair. A new chair, apparently. And this time he'd bound my ankles, too.

I take another yoga gulp of air and let it out in a loud, slow stream, but it sounds more like a sigh than someone trying to gain calmness and enlightenment. I've had enough enlightenment for the day already.

"You've got to be kidding me," I say. "Again? He tied me up again? You've got to be *kidding* me. And to think for a moment I thought it was just a bad dream. But fuck if it's not real." I gulp another breath. "Why the fuck do I keep talking to myself?" I then call up toward the ceiling again, "Carl? Carl?" Without leaving him time to answer, I scream, "Hey, fuckhead."

I'm about to scream again, but the basement door snaps open and Carl comes storming down the stairs, awkwardly carrying another chair.

Fall, I think. I'm literally willing the piece of shit to fall. *C'mon, motherfucker, fall and break your neck.* But he doesn't.

He places the chair a few feet away, facing me.

"You gonna let me go now, Carl?" I say.

Clearly ignoring me with some effort, he sits calmly in the chair, even folding his hands on his lap. His eyes become heavy-lidded and distant, and he stares at me with an expression I can only imagine is him trying to be intimidating. He doesn't say a word.

"Okay, fucknut," I say to him, "time to let me go. This shit ain't funny."

Still in this over-calm way, Carl says, "That was quite a fall."

I take another deep breath and let it out in another breathy sigh, saying, "You knock me out, *twice*, and then tie me up in a basement? No offense, Carl, but this date really sucks."

"Date was going fine until you took my stuff."

"If you say so."

His dispassionate expression drops a moment. Clearly taken aback by how smooth and sarcastic my own tone is. This is good; I need to keep it up. Show this dickweed I'm not scared about being tied up in a stranger's basement. Even though I am. Fucking terrified. But I'm not going to let this asshole know it. As far as he's concerned, this type of shit happens to me all the time. I continue with my smooth, in-control tone, saying, "Did you tie me up so I'd listen to more of your boring history shit?"

His expression falls further. Weak-ass punk. I've seen this before, with men. He'd had this speech all planned out for me, and I just ruined it. Men love their fucking speeches. They love their lectures and convoluted explanations for how something happened or how something is a woman's fault. Probably been rehearsing it all in his head for however long I'd been out. And I'm sure in all those rehearsals, I'd been crying and looking frightened and penitent. However, now, instead of penitence, I'm regarding him with a blank, fuck-you-expression.

Carl says, "No. I've been thinking about this—"

I can't help but roll my eyes. He's going ahead with the speech anyway.

He says, "At first, I was going to turn you in. But then I was figuring you'd just get off, and probably have a good laugh about it, too. And that just can't be. I'm tired of people like you."

"People like me? What does that even mean? Are you talking about women?"

"Doesn't matter man or woman. You are everywhere now. On the highway, in lines at supermarkets, walking down the street, in bars and restaurants, on the fucking highway—"

"You already said the highway," I say.

Carl sizes me up, his eyes narrowing. "Takers. You think everything is yours. Like you're entitled to anything you want. All the things others worked to obtain. You're a sickness. Nothing more than a virus."

"You didn't seem to think I was a virus when you wanted to stick your dick in me last night."

"You are disgusting, and you know, I might just have to eliminate you."

Eliminate me? Did he say eliminate me, like…? Wait a minute. Something's amiss here. Is he…? I say, "What's wrong with your voice?"

"What do you mean?" he says.

"Your voice. It sounds weird. Are you like trying to do a Clint Eastwood or David Caruso impression or something?"

"What?"

"I think you are." I really think he is. "You're trying to sound like someone tough."

"No."

"Then why the voice?"

"I have a cold," he says.

"Uh-huh."

He sits silent a moment, obviously trying to regain his bearings in the conversation.

I prompt, "Eliminate me."

"Huh?"

"You were saying you were going to eliminate me."

He takes a deep breath, rolls his neck, and lets the breath out. His eyes becoming heavy-lidded again, and the coolness returning to his voice. "That's right. I'm going to kill you."

I stare into his heavy eyes for a moment. And then I burst out laughing—partly to fuck with him, but mostly because, despite the situation, he looks so fucking stupid trying to act tough like that. Actually, maybe not despite the situation, more like *because* of the situation; what kind of absurdist shit is this? "Drinks and elimination?" I say. "That is a hell of a date, Carl. What is this *The Bachelor*, psychos edition?"

He doesn't respond right away, and we regard each other for what seems goddamn weeks, and I realize he's going to keep going with this shit. So I try shifting gears some, flashing my tone from sarcastic to seductive. "C'mon, Carlsy, wouldn't you rather pick this date up in the bedroom? Let the Avon Fräulein take good care of you?"

He stares at me for what seems two more weeks, several expressions threatening to steal his face. He finally regains his composure and says, "You disgust me."

Still in my seductive way, "Wouldn't you rather be a lover than a fighter?"

His soft, growly, Eastwood voice breaks a moment as he says, "You're a piece of work."

With the seduction obviously not working, I return to my default sarcasm, saying, "So people tell me."

Eastwood, or Caruso, or whatever he's going for, returns. "I really will be doing the world a favor by eliminating you."

"C'mon, Carl, you're no more capable of murder than a Disney character."

Carl's tone breaks again, becoming defensive, "There's been murderous Disney characters, there's—"

"Look, literal-boy, what I'm saying is, you don't strike me as the killing type."

Whispery, and growly again, he says, "Well, that's where you're wrong. You fell into the wrong web, said the spider to the fly."

I can't help but laugh again. "Said the spider to the fly?"

"Laugh all you want. But you see, you've caught me at the shittiest of times." He nods, like a pensive man coming to a hard-fought decision—or like a television cop coming to the case's solution, and I am stuck wondering, is he really doing a David Caruso impersonation? He says, "You see, I'm in a transformational period here, and I think you need to be dead for me to move forward with it. For society to move forward, really. Sorry. Nothing personal."

"Sounds pretty personal, Carl."

"It's time for you to beg."

"How?"

"How, what? How should you beg?"

"No. How do you plan on killing me?"

He looks deep into my eyes, trying to pull off the heavy-lidded, man-with-the-answers, look. But I see nothing but confusion. And panic.

I don't flinch. After all, I know he has no idea how he'll kill me because he has no intention of killing me. He's trying to scare me. And doing a piss-poor job of it, frankly, so I'm calling his bluff. He won't kill me…I think. Pretty sure he won't. No, he won't kill me.

He stares at me for a moment, those cogs turning in his brain. Then he stands and strides up the basement steps.

Alone again in the basement, I say, "You've got to be shitting me."

Carl then trudges down the stairs and plops into the chair in front of me again. He has the long bayonet that had been on the coffee table the night before. Holding the bayonet up between us, he says, "This bayonet was used by my great-uncle at The Battle of the Bulge."

Despite the drop of my stomach upon seeing the implement of death, and the hairs of my neck standing on end, I groan sarcastically, saying, "Yeah, Carl, I had to sit through a story about your uncle last night."

"No. Not my *Avon Fräulein* uncle. My other great uncle. My father's uncle."

"Yeah, you told me about him, too. How you have his diary from the war. It starts out light and carefree at the beginning of the war, but gets ultra-twisted in the end because he'd lost his marbles. Wasn't that it?"

He says, in a tone not unlike a camp counselor telling a ghost story around a campfire, "Yes, that's right. I do have his diary. And it does get more and more twisted as it goes on. But do you know why?"

"Because psychos run in your family?"

"No, that's not why. You see, when he first got to Europe, he didn't see much action. In fact, he came up onto Normandy after it was already secured."

"There's the men of the White family for you, never getting any action."

He ignored me, continuing his tale, "His unit followed

the allied forces as they pushed toward Berlin. And it's here you can really witness the change in his writing. You understand, a soldier in the thick of it, like the ones storming Normandy, learned to justify all they did as survival. But my great uncle, viewing the aftermath, had time to process all he saw, to take it all in. Like Kurtz said: 'The horror.'"

"Thought Brando said that."

"My uncle came to realize just how shitty the world is, how shitty the human spirit can be."

"Yeah, there's assholes that tie women up in basements."

"He wrote about bloated bodies blackened with decomposition, and puddles of blood. Here, one can actually trace the breaking down of his mind. In retrospect, we know what he didn't; he was heading into the worst of it. The Battle of the Bulge. And his diary goes into great detail about what he did with this bayonet while there." He brandishes the bayonet before my eyes.

Again, my stomach drops, and I feel my heart twitch, like it's a jigger on a fishing line, but I keep my eyes steady—a poker face on par with Phil Ivey.

Carl says, "At one point, he came across an injured Kraut, and he slipped this bayonet from its sheath. Clasping his hand over the man's mouth, he stared deep into his eyes and slit his throat. The man's blood sprayed across his face like driven rain."

"Lovely visual, Carl," I say. My voice almost cracks, but it doesn't. I keep it fucking steady and cool.

"As my great-uncle watched the light leave the man's eyes, he felt righteous. A kind of cleansing of humanity, you might say. Because, to him, that man embodied the worst horrors of the human spirit."

He stares into my eyes, letting the story hang in the air

a moment.

I blow out another sigh, and say, "You know what, Carl, if I have to listen to another of these fucking history lessons, I'll be begging you to kill me." Saying this, my heart is picking up pace, beating with hummingbird wings. This is unlike me; I haven't had these hummingbird wings since…well, it's been a while.

Carl leans forward suddenly, finally achieving some true menace—not an orchestrated soft growl to his voice, but a real one—saying, "Oh, you will beg. Because, you see, Stacey, to me, you represent the worst of humanity's spirit. You're a leach, a parasite that takes from people."

It wasn't enough menace, however, to strip me of my cool gaze or wiseass tone. And I pause for a beat, letting my stare linger, not by design, mind you, I was just thrown off a moment remembering that I was still Stacey. I let out a stream of breath, as if blowing cigarette smoke in the fucker's face, and say, "At least I'm not a boring loser that listens to teenybopper music and could put a meth addict to sleep with his pointless stories."

Carl stands, knocking over his chair with the backs of his legs, and he flashes the bayonet in my face, turning the weapon back and forth so its scarred surface can catch the dim light of the basement's light bulb.

I still don't flinch, despite the fact that the hummingbird wings are now that of an albatross. I am still quite certain he is bluffing…pussy.

I say, "Carl, you're not your great uncle. You're not even your mother's uncle. You're not a Disney Villain. And you ain't Clint Eastwood, or whatever you're trying to pull here. You're nothing. And you're not gonna kill anyone."

"Shut up," Carl growls—again, a real growl.

I say, still as if blowing cigarette smoke into his face,

"It's tougher than you thought."

He growls, "I want you to beg for your life."

"I can see it in your eyes, you ain't got the balls for this."

I realize the blade is at my throat. There in a flash, but it stays there for what seems hours, his frenzied eyes staring into my unflinching eyes.

"Beg," he says.

It's a bluff, it's a bluff, it's a bluff, I tell myself, and don't flinch. "Nope."

"Fuck," he howls, turning and kicking the chair he'd been sitting on.

I watch coolly, as if dragging on that invisible cigarette. He storms up the stairs. When the door slams shut behind him, I can't fucking control my sobs.

5

I stand in my office, which is actually the house's dining room. It's not like I use the room for dining. When's the last time I was even a participant of an actual sit-down dinner? Even with my family intact, dinners were really just everyone staring at their plates. I use the room as my office mostly because of the inlaid hutch I assume the old owners had filled with plates and such, but which is now used for my memorabilia. I have the girl's worn leather bag, feeling like a little boy fumbling through his mommy's purse as I snake my hand inside the thing. It feels wrong somehow, as if I'm violating her privacy, and I have to remind myself that it is *my* stuff in there. I retrieve the pieces one by one and return them to their rightful places on the shelves, using the opportunity to finger away the tiny aprons of dust I'd missed during my last cleaning.

Jesus there's a lot of dust, Carl, I imagine the girl saying. *Where did it all come from? Didn't you just clean this place?*

"Shut up, bitch," I snap at the empty room.

Bitch? Damn, Carl, that's rude. So you're going to blame me for everything, now, huh? Even blaming me for the dust you were too lazy to clean?

"I said shut up, bitch."

Stop calling me bitch, bitch.

"Bitch. Bitch. Bitch."

I stop myself and take a breath. But the breath doesn't do what it's supposed to. My hands are trembling as I lift my great uncle's purple heart—the last of my items in her bag—and place it on the shelf. I peek into the bag to make sure I've gotten everything, and then shake the bag upside down. A wallet tumbles to the floor. A woman's wallet. It sits on the carpet and I feel a surge of adrenaline similar to what I might feel if I'd found it on the sidewalk. I have to consciously fight back the urge to crane my head, as if checking if anyone else is looking. I pluck it from the floor.

Its cheap clasp is sharp against my thumb and forefinger and it flips open easily. The plastic sleeves that are supposed to house credit cards, licenses, library cards, are all empty. Nothing in the change compartment. There are a few dollars twisted together in the bill holder—not even enough for her to pay for a drink had we actually decided to go Dutch on the date.

"Bitch."

I need to put an end to this right now. I could still scare the shit out of her. Send her running. That didn't work before. Why would it work now? Maybe I should up my game? Maybe cut her a little with the blade?

I remember her cool gray eyes staring into my own.

The berating taunting. What would cutting her do? She'd bleed, maybe say ouch at the most, and then call me a dickless bitch.

Okay, then drag her scamming ass to the station and lay it all out in the open—the whole embarrassing tale.

And *I'd* be charged with assault.

Goddamn it.

Oh god, I might really have to kill her.

I suddenly realize I've been pacing circles in the room. I stop. Stand still. My heart stutters, but then it lurches forward into a beat steady and heavy. Like my whole torso is a Chinese War Drum.

Am I really capable of killing someone?

I look at the bayonet in its case on the shelf, and a vision strikes me: the girl is shoveling my things into her bag and heading for the door, grabbing my car keys and out into the night, taking off in *my car*—the bitch did have my car keys, right? Why'd she take my car keys? I would have given her a ride.

With all your stuff?

Well, no. But why was she taking my stuff? All on a whim? What kind of person is this? Who, out of the blue, decides to steal the belongings of a nice guy who'd taken her out for drinks?

In my vision, I see her standing on the field near Malmedy, donned in a Nazi uniform, covered in the mud and the blood and the stench of smoke and death. She trains her machine gun on the line of American POWs, their hands on their heads, and she opens fire.

That girl embodies the degradation of society. She is the personification of a coming crisis, society's lack of empathy for others. For others' things. For others' lives. She is the living representation of all of it. Should that living representation *be* living? Or is it my *responsibility* to snuff it out?

Can I kill her?

"Damn right I can," I say, and the words feel like a call to arms, ringing out over the war drum.

I storm out of the office to the basement door, then down the basement stairs. She looks up at me in that cool, fuck you, way of hers, and I feel something surging through me like a sickening orgasm. I smash my fists into her face, and then rain blows down on her. It is as if I am watching it on TV, the blood droplets springing from her mouth and nose in slow motion, staining the cement floor in constellations around her. I retrieve the chair I'd been sitting on earlier and hoist it above my head. I then beat her with it until her own chair tips over and she is a hump on the floor, twitching, then still, twitching, then still again.

I shake from the homicidal fantasy.

Still standing in my office, I listen.

The room is quiet.

The house is quiet.

The girl is quiet.

There is only my own heavy ragged breath.

No sound comes from the basement. She's probably been listening to me pacing the floor above her. Or she fell back to blissful slumber. What's the saying: only the guilty sleep well?

Seriously, Carl, she says in my head. *You're not gonna kill me. No sack. No follow through.*

"You're wrong."

You're weak, Carl. We can't all be wrong. Everyone knows it.

"You fucking bitch," I scream and I storm from the house, slamming the door shut behind me.

6

A door slams shut somewhere upstairs. I'm guessing it's most likely the house's front door. Then I hear a car speed away. This all after hearing him scream, *You fucking bitch*, at the top of his lungs. I'm assuming that I am the bitch in question, but who knows with this guy?

I want to cry again. But what would that accomplish?

My head is splitting.

And I need to pee.

Badly.

How I didn't piss myself when he lunged at me with the bayonet, I will never know. Sheer will, I guess.

For a moment, I really thought he was going to kill me. It was in his eyes. The bloodlust. I've seen that look before. Back when I was fifteen and dating some nineteen-year-old douchebag. I was into them back then: douchebags. Sleeves of tats on wiry arms, straight brim baseball hat cocked crooked over one eye. I'd ask him why he only seemed concerned with protecting one eye from the sunlight, but he didn't get it. The only thing lower than his I.Q. were the jeans on his hips. But I was in love.

The guy—Dan Kelly was his name—he had a pit bull. A sweet dog he'd named Hellfire. The thing would look up at me with that eager-to-please look that dogs have, and it loved to get scratched behind its ears. What I didn't know, however, was that Hellfire's dipshit owner had been convinced to enter the thing into a dogfight. The fucking douche actually brought me to one of the fights as a date. When Hellfire got into the ring, this new look came over that sweet dog's face. A look like he'd fully intended to rip that other dog apart, and didn't care what happened to himself in the process.

That was the look that flashed in Carl's eyes as he

brandished that bayonet. The look wasn't present when he'd been making his dumb spider and fly speech, but for that split second, as he'd brandished the bayonet, it was there.

It was the same look he'd had the moment he'd knocked me out with my own goddamn bag.

As for Hellfire, he'd regained that sweet, eager-to-please look in his eyes after he'd gotten his ass kicked in the fighting ring and died in the douchebag's arms. I never saw Dan after that. I did, however, smear dog shit all over the interior of his Impala, leaving a note on his dash, reading: "Payback from Hellfire, motherfucker." Signed with a paw print.

Throughout the years, I've had enough experience with human nature and basic psychology to know Carl's deal. His rage stems from being an omega dog all his life, and his desire to finally be alpha. He recognizes the alpha in me, and he can't let me go until he breaks me. Thinking that will somehow make *him* alpha. Which it won't. That guy could never be alpha. But if he *is* finally able to break me—and it is a big *if*—then he will most likely kill me. And then himself. Because let's face it, that's how these sackless fucks do it. He'll come to the realization that a broken girl is a weak girl, a girl that will go straight to the authorities, a girl whose damaged spirit will weigh forever on his conscience. And if I don't break, then he certainly can't let me go…and, well, he'll have to kill me then, too. Not a lot of options for either of us. I'm not the only one trapped here.

My only chance might be to break *him* first and convince him to let me walk out the front door. Or I might need to, like that *One Thousand and One Nights* chick, survive long enough to formulate a plan of escape.

I look around the basement again and then down at the

duct tape binding my wrists to the armrests of the chair.

Why wait the thousand and one nights? Let's formulate a plan now.

My wrists are close enough for me to lean over and use my teeth on the tape, but the seams of the duct tape are facing away from me. I'm not entirely sure if this is by Carl's design or just his dumb luck.

Can I tear them? Maybe.

I'd tried this before, but I try again, inching my forearms back and forth, but, again, the bindings only tighten and bunch and become stronger. I try to rip free of the ankle-bindings, but it's the same deal: the tape only bunches into stronger bands. And what would I do if I freed my legs anyway? It's not like I can free my wrists with my toes. There's plenty of talents I can perform with my feet—opening and lighting a Zippo being one of them—but somehow reaching across my body to my opposite wrist to pick at duct tape? I'm certainly out of yoga shape for that maneuver. Although, I suppose if I free my legs I could walk again—not walk up the stairs, but rather to something in the room that can help me get the fuck out of it? That probably would have been a better plan than trying to walk up the stairs earlier like a dumbass, but live and learn.

I inventory the space again. The bottles and cans. Boxes of who knows what. And the workbench…the workbench with a pair of pruning shears hanging from a nail on the bench's edge.

Decision time. Do I try to get the shears, or do I try to bite through the tape? Can I bite through the tape?

I really need to pee.

Jesus. Don't think about it. Focus.

I dip my head toward my right wrist, and I begin to gnaw at the tape.

7

The struts of my car squeal in protest as the balding tires crawl down the dirt road. Low brush pocks the embankment at the road's margins, and my imagination paints frantic images of my car slipping into the shallow ditch, a snapped tie rod leaving the wheel uselessly angled in defeat. I envision some stilted conversation with a half-witted tow truck driver as the guy scratches his scruffy chin and wonders what brought me out to this desolate area. Possibly even a police cruiser sent out to the scene to verify there are no injuries. And then the cop gives me a ride home and…and what? And nothing. Why would the cop go down into my basement? Why would I run my car into a ditch? And who even comes out here to the island's isthmus? The effort to get here isn't worth the sightseeing aspect of the trip. Only thing out here is Mystic Light, and I'm sure the lighthouse is automated at this point.

I take a deep haul of the air rushing in through the car's open window, but instead of getting a breath of the fresh sea breeze, I get a lungful of dust kicked up by my car's tires.

I cough and hack and swap my Backstreet Boys tape for NSYNC, pushing the cassette into the car's radio. My nerves settle a bit as "Giddy Up" segues into "Here We Go," and I sing—more like shout—along with the guys. The lyrics seem to mirror my situation, and while I know this is impossible, I am convinced for one fleeting moment that they are singing just for me. Rooting me on. Offering encouragement to get out of this dilemma. By the time "Bye, Bye, Bye" comes on, this feeling is reinforced, and I sing along with the chorus, accenting its sentiment with a sharp "bitch," at its end, pounding on the steering wheel while doing so.

I'm going to have to kill her. I've come to this conclusion right here, while driving in my car. Away from the house. Away from her. I now know I can't intimidate her into changing her ways or not ratting me out. And what's more, she deserves to die. I've been toying with this thought since waking and recalling the dreadful situation. Like a little kid playing with clay, I'll push the thought back into an amorphous ball every time any hint of definition surfaces—kill her, scare her, let her go...but out here, in the open marshes leading out to the lighthouse, it is clear to me: I can not allow someone like her to survive. That bitch is a representation of a greater plague in the world. One willing to take the things I've spent a lifetime to acquire and cherish. I will dispose of her, and no one will probably miss her. It is more likely that society will celebrate the loss. Karma will right itself. All will balance in the universe.

I sift through the events from the prior night: the date, the drinks, the game and conversations, and her treachery. Tears suddenly threaten my eyes, and I fight them back, unable to decide if they are tears for the loss of what could have been or what will now have to be.

Or perhaps it is something else entirely.

Up ahead, an occasional ball of dried scrub shrub flutters across the road, cradled by the breeze. I watch one dance into the ditch and consider how, although it will lie with many similar to it, none will be identical, like scrubby snowflakes. Like deceptive women. All different. All the same. While I am locked into this half-attentive assessment of brush and women, I notice suddenly that I am bearing down on a chipmunk sitting in the middle of the road.

Fuck it. I grit my teeth and tighten my eyes into a determined stare as I accelerate the car, yelling, "Bye, bye, bye, *bitch*."

But before I flatten the rodent, I slam on the brakes. Everything in the back seat—pickaxe, shovel, work gloves—tumbles onto the car's rear floorboard.

I yell what sounds like a squeal to my own ears, like some kind of little girl, and I stare at the chipmunk as if the sound that had emanated from me is its fault. The chipmunk stares back with that same cool, blank stare that the girl in the basement offers. Then it leaps over the ditch and runs off into the brush. I drive a little further before pulling the car off to the side of the road, singing one more, "Bye, bye, bye…" but my voice falters on the "bitch."

I climb out of the car, glancing up and down the deserted road, and open the back door. Regarding the wares assembled there on the floor, I feel the same confused indecision that used to grip me when Rudy was a baby, and I would look into the back seat before scooping him out of his car seat. As if asking, what am I supposed to do with this?

I take out the pickaxe, shovel and gloves, and head off into the brush.

8

I smack my lips. The taste is awful. The duct tape's glue seeming to coat my tongue and the sides of my mouth. I run my tongue over my teeth. Jesus, it's even on my teeth. "What is this shit made of?"

"Glue," I answer myself.

My neck and lower back are already stiffening from

bending at such an unnatural angle. It's going to take a chiropractor years to undo this shit, including the sciatica I can already feel creeping into my ass. Asshole couldn't have at least tied me to a more comfortable chair?

I inspect the tape. I'm no closer to splitting it. And I need to pee. Badly. Like really badly. Should I just piss myself?

And then be sticky and itchy and wet for who knows how long?

Would Carl even let me clean myself?

No. Probably not.

And how would that change the dynamic, me begging him to let me clean up because I peed my pants like a little fucking child? Once I pee myself, it will become the only solution to the bathroom problem; he'll expect me to pee myself all the time, instead of forcing him to figure out a solution, or taking me to the bathroom. And if I can convince him to untie me and take me to the bathroom, then there is a chance I can get away. Fuck it. I will show this motherfucker what real fucking will is.

I can hold it. Be a fucking camel. Is that the right term? Someone who can hold their pee for a long time is known as a camel, right?

But why? Do camels not pee? No, of course not, they live in a fucking desert; there's no water to pee out. If they could drink enough water, I'm sure they pee just fine. They probably find some oasis, drink up, and have the longest most glorious pee one could—

My bladder gives a groan. Why do I keep thinking about pee? Fucking stop it.

I try to gauge the time of day by the dim sunlight streaming in through the window, but I can't tell. Why can't I tell? I should have some indication of—What am I, a fucking boy scout? I can only decipher that it is in fact day. I don't have my bearings as to which direction that window even faces. I'll have to come to that determination in the coming days, watch the light in the early morning as opposed to the evening when…wait, coming days? Am I really going to be stuck here for days?

If I don't get my ass out of here, then yes.

I look around the basement. My eyes falling onto the hanging shears again. I stare at them like I'm Carrie, trying to will them to me through some kind of mental power. Or maybe I can will them into Carl's fucking face when he gets back. That's what I'll do: put those sheers right through his—

"What the fuck is wrong with you?" Stop with this fantasy bullshit. This is a real situation, requiring real solutions.

Can I angle the chair and tiptoe over to them?

And shift too far forward and fall on my face, most likely losing most of my teeth in the process? If I were lucky enough not to break my neck, that is.

I don't need the fucking shears. I have teeth.

I smack my lips again, looking down at the tape around my wrists. Little teeth indentions and frays pock its surface. But no real headway. I bend over and start gnawing again.

9

The crunch of dried branches beneath my feet is white noise as I trace a path deeper into the marshlands, toward the scattered islands of tangled trees that would provide me cover. The fingers of pricker bushes claw at my pant legs like tiny creatures pleading for me to stop.

Nope. Sorry. Nothing is going to stop me now…right?

Why the qualifying *right*? I'm determined; I'm digging a fucking grave aren't I?

You do a lot of things, Mandy's voice says. *Doesn't mean shit.*

Shut up, I'm doing it. I'm digging a grave…in case I need it.

In case you need it? See what you did there?

Shut up.

I push on at a decent pace, leading with the pickaxe and spade like a blind man pushing into some mysterious void.

Through a tight strangle of dogwood trees, I spot an open clearing and take my eyes off the path long enough to step into a patch of moss-skimmed mud. My foot sinks into the mud and then makes a dull sucking sound as I pull it free. Is it the same sound a bayonet would make when pulled from the chest of a beautiful thief.

I backtrack toward higher ground, reach a clearing in the woods' center.

This is the spot.

The tools tumble from my grip and clang together on the ground. Beyond the woods, an embankment dips down toward streams and I listen for a moment to the gentle gurgling of water as it slips over rocks and meanders through the marshlands, in and out of a series of pools toward the sea. I wonder if there are any fish in the streams and if they treat one another with more respect than the people I know?

I brush the thought aside, and contemplate a plan.

Plan? Dig a hole and put the bitch in it…

And then get caught because I don't have some kind of plan.

It would be wise to stay away from the streams and the marshier areas, as to avoid digging down and hitting water—although the thought of giving her a watery grave is also appealing.

I pull on my gloves, grab the shovel and begin digging.

I'd been hoping the work would keep my mind from racing, but the thoughts keep tumbling into my head. And even if I could block them, they seem to scurry into my stomach, residing as a low, heavy nausea.

I'm screwed.

So screwed.

I try to focus on the delicate crumbling of damp soil beneath my force. Chunks of it breaking apart exposing an intricate series of thread-like roots that course through the soil like veins. The blade of the shovel severs them and pushes the dirt into small piles. There is a therapeutic aspect to it. After all, I am in control. Way out here, there is no danger of anyone bitching about how I am doing it wrong or not fast enough, or whatever. I imagine this must be what it feels like to work as a farmer or a gravedigger, or a miner in the deep, echoing darkness, far from anything. My breathing escalates with the work. And I like that feeling of hard-fought accomplishment.

I pause when I hear a rustling. My body going rigid, hands tightening on the shovel. I glance around, fighting off an immediate blast of fear. How would I explain my actions to a birdwatcher, or hiker, or maybe the ghost of the mysterious lighthouse keeper?

But there is no hiker, or cop, or ghost, just a chipmunk who'd scurried from the brush and now stares at me with that blank, cool stare.

I stare back at it, wondering if it is the same chipmunk I'd almost squashed in the road. I say, "I'm gonna kill that bitch."

The chipmunk doesn't move.

Then I say, "I'm gonna kill you, too."

It still doesn't move.

I toss a shovelful of dirt at the thing.

It scurries away.

Before returning to my digging, I announce, "That's right, motherfucker. I'm not one to be trifled with."

10

I look at the window again, still unable to assess any passage of time. I then examine the binding around my wrist. I certainly don't want to assess time's passing from how far I've gotten on the tape.

I've added only a few more teeth marks.

A few more frays.

Using the tape as reference, maybe ten minutes have passed. Using my bladder as reference, ten days have passed. I'll split the difference and put it at about two hours.

Is that splitting the difference? Wouldn't splitting the difference be five days?

Stop with this shit. Focus.

Focus on what? I have all the time in the world to do pointless math problems. And maybe it would take my mind off my bladder. Okay, problem number one: how long have I been here, minus how long can I hold my fucking pee? Is it true someone's bladder can explode from holding in piss? People have to be able to go a long time, right? I mean, look at all the movies, when do you ever see characters stop what they're doing to take a piss? Okay, sure, that's movies, but some of them are based on real things, like what was that one with Jimmy Stewart, where he has to talk for like days (I never saw it, but I did have a signed photo from that movie)? *Mr. Smith Goes to*

Washington. I mean, the filibuster is a real thing; did all those congressmen just piss themselves in front of their opponents and constituents? When did I last take a piss? Must have been like 1:00, 2:00 am? And I haven't had any liquid since, and even before that, I stopped—the real problem is more likely dehydration, which I guess is good for my bladder situation, but…so much for taking my mind off my bladder.

You know what would take my mind off my bladder? Going to the bathroom. Getting free and going to the fucking bathroom.

I begin gnawing at the tape again.

11

I stand beside the shallow hole in the ground, small pyramids of moist earth rimming its perimeter. I lean on the shovel and regard my work. The calluses on my hands are burning and swollen. It is the first time in a long time that I actually admire the fruits of my own labor. Peering down onto the grave's concave floor, I watch an earthworm move along its length, and I consider all of the things that could possibly fit in that hole: two good-sized suitcases, a couple weeks' worth of groceries, one dead bitch.

Perfect.

Now I can kill her and bury her out here in the middle of nowhere. Nothing but gulls, and rodents, and the ghost of the lighthouse keeper to keep her company.

Or, I could maybe bring her out here still alive. Show her the grave. Scare her. Make her stand on its edge. Maybe I should fill it back in and have her dig it herself. I could make her stand in it and say, *Don't you ever do anything like this again, or so help me, I will put you in this grave.*

But you're not going to put me in it now? She'd say.

I will if you try me again, you bitch.

You'll do no such thing, you dickless pussy.

Damn it.

I flinch, breaking free from my thoughts, a rustling sound nearby. The chipmunk is back, staring at me from the base of a tree.

"I really am going to kill her," I say to the chipmunk.

The chipmunk continues to stare at me, it's tiny mouth pulsing gently, as if at any moment it might formulate a response. Or burst out laughing.

I don't wait to hear if it does; I gather my tools and return to my car.

After sliding each tool through my gloved hands to remove some of the dirt, I drop each instrument into the back seat where they clang against one another. Lowering into the driver's seat, the springs of the door groaning as I pull it shut, I think about trading in this old Crown Vic. It would be nice to have something roomier. A van, perhaps. Something to pile that thieving bitch's lifeless body into for the ride back out here.

I turn the key, restarting both the car and the NSYNC song, and after a multi-point U-turn, raising fresh plumes of dust, I point the car toward home. With a deep breath and a flex of my sore fingers against the steering wheel, the jumble of fatigue and stress embrace me. I squeeze my eyes shut for a moment, praying for a second wind. The empty road calms my nerves and I actually feel a bit of optimism. There is an end in sight. A solution. Until I open my eyes and look in the rearview mirror.

The girl, Stacey, is sitting in the back seat. And she starts her yapping: "Do we really need to listen to this shit, Carl? Stuff will turn you queer, you know. Not to mention, how much longer can I put up with listening to it? Jesus, Chinese water-torture me, bamboo shoots under the fingernails, anything, but please, for the love of all things rational, lose this music."

I watch her for a moment, my hands gripping the wheel with force despite the calluses. "Won't have to put up with it much longer," I say. "When I get home, you'll be begging me to kill you."

"I'm begging you now. Just to end this shrill screeching. Leave it to me: killed by a guy obsessed with boy bands. Can't you think about my reputation for a moment?"

"Do you ever shut up?"

"Hey, I got it. They can call you the New Killer on the Block."

"I never listened to New Kids."

"Sounds like I hit a nerve, Carl. You got something against the New Kids? Too hardcore for you?"

"No. I just never—look, will you please just shut up? I mean it, not another word."

"Or what? You'll kill me?"

"No, I—"

"You'll what?"

"What you say doesn't matter."

"Oh, that's right. For my opinion to matter, I need to be some asexual teenage boy, singing like a whiny neutered dog."

"I can't wait until you're in the ground, you miserable bitch. This world will be such a better place with your existence erased from it."

"*So much better with your existence erased from it,*" she says mocking my voice. "You sound like a comic book villain, Carl. It's kind of hot. A Backstreet-lovin, New Kids-hatin, super-villain. Instead of The Joker, they can just call you

The Joke."

I turn and swipe at her, the car swerving on the road. The gravel spraying beneath the tires. I imagine that the chipmunk is watching from the edge of the embankment.

Straightening the car, and my nerves, I look over my shoulder to the back seat.

The girl is gone.

"Okay. Get a grip," I say. I take a deep breath, feeling calmer. And I contemplate how to kill her. And when to kill her.

Later, I think.

I glance at the clock. How the fuck is it already 3:30?

I will kill her later. After *Idol.* Maybe I'll kill her after *American Idol* tonight.

There's that word, *maybe*, again.

I take another deep breath. "I am so screwed," I say.

12

Not bad. I actually got pretty far with the tape. I smack my lips, trying to eradicate the glue taste. Looks like I've chewed about halfway through its length. Soon I'll be able to tear through the rest.

Maybe.

And I'm at the point now where I need to pee so badly that I don't feel like I need to pee at all. It is as if it has become part of my being. I am now Sophie plus urine, my bladder seemingly accepting its new state, perhaps somehow redistributing all the fluid back throughout my body.

Above me, the house's front door opens and closes, and there are footsteps striding across the floor.

"Uh-oh."

I work the tape, trying to tear it, feeling the glue pulling at my skin. The tape's fabric tearing a little more, sounding like the stretching tear of a shirt's collar or the slow split of a seam. Fuck I'm close, but I stop when the basement door opens and Carl comes striding down the steps. He's doused in dirt.

Do I *want* to know what the fuck he's been doing?

He stops and stands there before me, the two of us staring at one another, fucker with the expression of a husband coming home to his wife, as if saying, *You wouldn't believe the day I've had, honey.*

I say, "Jesus, Carl, you look like Al Jolson. What the hell have you been doing?"

He doesn't answer. He just shakes his head in a *not now* manner.

"You should probably get cleaned up for dinner, dear, it's getting late."

He looks around at the basement.

"How about cooking us up some eats?" I add.

He stares at me, his eyes narrowing. "Something's up."

My right shoulder twitches back, instinctively, subconsciously trying to hide my right wrist. I say, "Something's up, Carl? Yes, something's up, you have a girl tied up in your basement. I'd call that being something's up. And that girl is hungry, so why don't you cook us up some grub?"

His eyes narrow again. He steps toward me.

I say, "You were raving about your cooking skills last night, Carl, now—"

"I never raved about my cooking. I'm a terrible cook." He's now inspecting my face.

"You were drunk, Carl. Talking up about how Emeril got nothing on you," I say, but mentally I'm screaming, *Don't look at my wrist,* like some kind of Jedi mind-trick.

He inspects me more closely, then turns and walks back up the basement steps.

When he's completely gone from sight, I frantically work at the tape again.

"C'mon, you bitch," I mutter, the fabric's threads tearing slowly, the glue pulling.

Carl comes back down the steps, carrying a bundle of items.

"Fucker," I say, yanking my arm up, the final inch of the tape tearing.

The bayonet is against my throat.

"You keep that hand right there," he says.

"Fuck you, dickless."

"You should have said that a minute ago. I knew there was something up when you didn't insult me."

"You're as manly as a cunt-flap, Carl."

"There you go. See? You should have used that one before. Stay still, or I'll open your throat."

"Whatever butt-lint."

He puts the bayonet in his back pocket and produces the duct tape. He rewraps my wrist with a thicker layer of tape. Then produces several large, industrial plastic ties, binding two ties on each wrist.

"Chew through those," Carl says, turning and walking away.

"Carl, I need to go to the bathroom."

"Fuck off," he says over his shoulder, walking up the steps and shutting the door.

I scream after him, "You dickless, pansy-ass, twat I need the bathroom. Carl. Caaaaarrrrrl...."

13

I assess my parking job. The car is angled slightly in the spot, the front tires six inches closer to the curb than the back. My bumper slightly over the front line.

Should I fix it?

Of course I should. I can't leave it like that. I start back toward the car.

I stop.

Leave it. It's fine.

But I can't leave it like that. I step toward the car, but then stop again.

Fuck it. The new, take-control Carl is leaving it as it is. I take one step toward the front door of the bar, but then stride back to the curb and straighten out the car.

After approving the parking adjustment, I return to the door of The Dutch Horse Pub, but I don't go in yet. Is this really where I want to be? In a local bar?

Yes. Anywhere. I *need* to get out of that house. The girl won't stop her incessant screaming, and she most likely will scream throughout the entire *American Idol* episode. And then I *will* kill her.

Gonna have to kill her anyway.

I push the thought away, thinking if I killed her now, I'd have to take care of the body before the end of the episode, giving me a very real and logical reason for not killing her. Cleaning up a dead body would be too much of a distraction for tonight's all-important results.

I chuckle out loud, but I'm not sure why.

I glance around the sidewalk. Pedestrian traffic is light. I study an approaching couple, their hands locked, the woman's head tilted casually inward as if listening for a secret. I try to remember a time when that was me. With Mandy. But did that time ever exist? Even in the early days, she never leaned against me like that, and there seemed to be a lack of authenticity in any hand-holding we did. Like most things about our relationship, it seemed an obligation rather than natural inclination. The way she raised her eyes slightly when I spoke to her, as if she were thinking about something else, as if waiting for me to shut up. Her stiffened embrace during sex, as if—

"Staring problem, pal?"

I snap from my daze and recoil half a step from the passing couple.

"See something you like?" A slight taunt resides in the man's smile, and the woman softly giggles, playfully punching the man's chest.

The door of The Dutch Horse opens and a man in a disheveled suit emerges, causing me to have to dart out of his way. The man hurries down the sidewalk, squinting at the display of his flip phone. I catch the door and step inside.

I cringe at the music spraying from all corners of the room. Classic rock shit by some dead, or soon-to-be-dead, drug addict. It doesn't make any sense why anyone is still hanging onto these inane ramblings and stale guitar riffs from so long ago when there is such great new stuff coming out.

I hoist myself onto a barstool. The bartender nods toward me and finishes pingponging a jovial conversation with a crusty fisherman at the other end of the bar. Probably reliving some booze-soaked interlude from last night, or the night before, or the night before that. I eye the narrow row of bottles lining the shelf along the bar's back then look up at the TV angled from the wall on a steel arm, a muted episode of *Wheel of Fortune* on the screen. A woman, wearing a dress that reveals an abundance of cleavage when she leans over, is giving the wheel a spin before the camera zeroes in on Pat Sajak's grin, brimming with manufactured enthusiasm as if he's never seen such an amazing spin in his whole redundant career. I wonder if the host ever secretly hopes a contestant will fall over the rail onto the spinner, just to break up the monotony.

The fisherman slaps the bar in a gale of laughter, an ice cube bouncing from his glass onto the bar top. I begin to chew my lip, willing the bartender to come down to me, but the bartender towels down the spot where the ice cube fell and then goads the fisherman into a fresh chuckle with some sort of impersonation that has him flapping his elbows like a chicken. I watch them, trying to mask my annoyance as *Wheel of Fortune* slips into a commercial break and the final verse of "Sunshine of Your Love" rains down on me from speakers above the bar.

It has been a while since I stepped foot in The Dutch Horse Pub, and at this moment, I appreciate the hiatus. The place specializes in domestic beer and booze from plastic bottles, but it was standard for date night when Mandy and I would mill about the beach around sunset and grab a few drinks afterward. I could never bring myself to tell her that I would have preferred Chilis or TGI Friday's back toward the city—a place where I could've gotten one of those fun drinks with a blue sugared rim on the glass and gummy bears bobbing among the ice cubes. She would have made fun of me and issued her standard *you would* reply.

Those two words were her trademark response to most of my joys as our marriage dissolved.

The bartender pulls away from the fisherman, picks up a remote control from beneath the bar and aims it up at the TV. Final credits for *Wheel of Fortune* are racing past—Director, Executive Producer, blah, blah, blah. Vanna

White's fucking wardrobe provided by? What a waste of airtime. And then the channels flip.

Anderson Cooper. Toothpaste commercial. College softball game. Baseball.

It stays on baseball.

Please God, no. It's the *Idol* results, you douche.

The bartender rests his gaze on the TV, satisfied with the Sox vs. Toronto game, and returns the controller to its hidden spot beneath the bar—I imagine it is probably stowed beside a sawed-off shotgun or blood-stained Louisville Slugger. The bartender walks slowly toward me, a slight swagger to his gait.

My fingers fidget and then lock together atop the polyurethane bar top.

"What can I get you?" The bartender pulls the towel slung over his shoulder and twists it between his hands. I imagine the towel continuing into its tight coil and then lashing out at me in a version of the locker room gag that regularly tormented me after middle school gym class.

"I'll just have a beer," I say and then regret it. I recently read that using the word *just* diminishes your power in a conversation and I am working up toward a big ask in a moment. "A big beer," I say, hoping to compensate. "Biggest one you've got."

"A big beer?" the bartender asks. "Big as in size?"

"Size doesn't matter. Or at least that's what the actress said to the priest." I'm certain I botched the joke as the words tumble from my mouth. "I'll just have a Bud Light," I say. "Or Sam Adams. Do you have Sam Adams?"

The bartender saves me with a smile. "Yeah, we have Sammy. About the only decent thing we carry." He fishes one from the cooler, pulls the cap and places it in front of me. "Tab?"

"Tab?" I repeat. "The soda?"

"Tab," the bartender says. "You want to run a tab or settle up as you go?"

"Oh, right," I say. "Sorry, man. I'm spacing out tonight. A lot on my mind."

Like a girl tied in my basement, I want to blurt out.

Aren't bartenders supposed to listen to your problems? Is there bartender-patron confidentiality? I shake these thoughts from my head, saying, "Sure, I'll run one in case I stay for a few." I dig my wallet from my back pocket and slide a credit card across the shiny bar top. The bartender pockets it and turns away from me.

"Excuse me," I call. I cringe at the feeble edges framing my voice as I prepare my question.

"Yeah?" the bartender says. "Ready for another one already, huh?"

"No, not yet," I say, the guy's sarcasm skittering over my head. "I was just wondering…."

There it is again. The feeble edge in my voice. And the *just*.

"Yeah?" The bartender says. His face beginning to betray his true feelings for me.

"I was wondering if we could put on a different show. And turn off *this*." I point up to the speaker as Mick Jagger's voice gyrates a line from "Paint it Black." I say, "*Idol* is on tonight. We could watch that. And it comes with music, too."

It comes with music, too? Like that was some add on—the prize lodged in the bottom of a box of Cracker Jacks.

"*Idol?* What is that?" the bartender says.

I can feel my face redden as a concoction of emotions swirl within me: a thin layer of embarrassment holding down disdain for this man who doesn't even know what *Idol* is, all stirring together by the underlying nauseating anguish of my pathetic life.

"Idol. American Idol. It's just…" I pause and draw a breath. "It's a singing competition. Each week you get to vote for a contestant. Callers do. And someone gets voted out. And the rest live to sing another day. You've seriously never heard of this?"

"Sounds dumb," the bartender says. "Besides, the Sox are on." He turns and walks back to the fisherman.

I pull from my bottle of Sam Adams as the speakers overhead begin pushing out the twisted redneck joy of "Ramblin' Man." I take a long swallow of the beer, wincing a little at its bitterness, then I look toward the baseball game. A shrimpy infielder on the TV tries unsuccessfully to turn a double play. Guy will probably still make a hundred grand tonight. And get a BJ from some baseball groupie. Little twerp.

I take another sip of beer and set the bottle on the bar top. There is still time to get home for the show. That John Stevens kid might still be singing then. That's who I am rooting for. Although, deep down, I know that Fantasia or Jennifer Hudson probably have better chops. And I'd get to watch from the comforts of home, instead of this dump. I can't believe that, on my way here, I envisioned watching the show while sitting at the bar, trying to get the other patrons to predict the vote results. I imagined they'd all be gathered around and laughing with me like some goddamn Kumbaya sing-along. A vote-along.

Wait. *Get to watch from the comforts of home?* Did I really just think that? How could I be comfortable at home with my…houseguest from hell?

Houseguest?

Try hostage, fuckhead.

I have to get out of this bar. I can feel something ugly pushing up from my gut, my perception blurring at the edges.

I push off the barstool and glare at the bartender and fisherman who are certainly not watching the baseball game. They are wrapped up in some story, chuckling and sighing like a couple of girls in study hall.

"It's not dumb," I call. "It's not dumb at all."

The two men look at me.

"Kelly Clarkson? Ruben Studdard? Clay-fucking-Aiken? Dumb? I don't think so, pal. And neither do over 20 million viewers every week. Think they are all dumb? 20 million dummies out there?"

The two men continue staring at me. The final guitar twang of "Ramblin' Man" rambles into a fade. The baseball game heads to a mid-inning commercial.

I push open the door of The Dutch Horse Pub with trembling hands. "Pluck yew both," I call over my shoulder, letting the door shut behind me.

PART 3

1

I stand outside the front door of my house, feeling like a kid again, harkening back to when I'd sneak into my house without waking my parents. I used to sneak out to play with a bunny in my neighbor's backyard, until I'd accidently left the hutch open one night and a coyote made a mess of the thing. Now, before opening the door, I cradle my head with massaging hands, as if there is a chance I can rub away any memory of my current situation.

Situation? Nice euphemism. How about a total cluster fuck? This has always been the way for me. Since I was a boy, I've been grasping for "do-overs" in the sharp face of regret. Like seeing the entrails of that bunny strewn across my neighbor's backyard. How had all the things in my life gotten so screwed up in the first place? Why couldn't I have stumbled into a normal marriage instead of the shit-show that I've endured. One that wouldn't have guided me to the tempting ads on Craigslist and, in turn, into the hands of this creature in the basement.

Like the bunny to the coyote.

Wait, who is the bunny and who is the coyote?

I am the coyote. *She* is the bunny. *She* is the one tied up.

"Nope, she's definitely the freaking coyote," I say, but shake the thought away. I *need* to be the coyote. Show that bunny what is up. Show her who is in control. But first, it is time for *Idol.*

I slip the key into the lock and turn it, easing the door open and tiptoeing into the house, not wanting to alert her to my return. Knowing it will bring about her unremitting screaming and goading. I glance at the clock hanging on the kitchen wall. Damn it, it is later than I'd thought. The results show has already been on for some time, I'll be coming in mid-point.

I creep into the living room and turn on the television, the volume seeming to blast like the first notes of a symphony. I rapidly turn down the volume on the end of a teaser for the eleven o'clock news—some spiel about the rising cost of public transportation and the effect it has on the blue-collar community. I wish my only problems were something like that. The simpler time of being an everyman schlub trying to balance my out-of-control life.

Out-of-control? Is that a joke? My former concept of out-of-control is nothing compared to where my life is now. My life is now a spinning wheel losing any semblance of centrifugal force, its contents flying off in every direction.

How long until the teaser for the eleven o'clock news is: *man ties up girl in basement for rejecting him on a date?*

That's not why she's in the basement. She's in the basement for robbing me.

If you say so.

I do say so.

The *Idol* theme breaks this inner monologue. The

electric blue graphic fills the screen.

I can't help turning up the volume as Seacrest's voice builds momentum toward announcing the next performer.

I hear a shout mingled with the cheering crowd. The shout coming from beneath my feet. The timing couldn't be worse. Like a sneeze in church, an itch at the dentist, a fart during sex, if I don't acknowledge it, maybe it will go away.

"Carl," the girl shouts.

Not now, damn it. The only time I want to hear my name called out during an *Idol* episode is the day Ryan Seacrest announces me to the stage for my performance in front of the judges.

She calls again, this time elongating my name in one resonant syllable, "Caaarrrrl."

I don't respond.

Maybe she'll think I'm not here.

But she can most certainly hear the television.

She screams then, carrying out the length of my name in a teakettle whistle, "Caaaaaarrrrrrrrl."

I storm down the basement steps, shouting over her teakettle whine, "Jesus Christ, what the hell's the matter with you?"

She stops screaming and says, "You mean, besides being tied up in some psycho's basement?"

I turn to leave.

She screams again, "Caaaaaaaaaaaaaarrrrrrrrrrrrrrl."

"Jesus. Stop screaming. What do you want?"

"I have to go to the bathroom."

I regard her a moment before glancing around the basement.

I have to admit, I hadn't thought about this.

I have the foresight to dig a goddamn grave, but I

didn't consider this girl needing to take a piss at some point? Perhaps Mandy was right all those years, and I really do need to be more considerate.

Or maybe it is more that I *had* thought of it, but forced it from my head, not wanting to face the decision of what to do about it.

After all, this girl should be dead by now.

I force this thought aside, too, as I inventory the basement. In the corner, there is a neat pile of empty cans and plastic bottles for the bottle redemption. I stride to the pile, pick up an empty two-liter bottle, and return to her, thrusting the bottle in her direction.

She says, "You've got to be kidding."

I shake the bottle, glancing at the basement door, then back at her. The sound of pop music wafts down the steps from the living room. I shake the bottle again. "C'mon, it's this or nothing."

"Look, Carl, if you were looking for a girl that can piss into a bottle, then you were on the wrong section of Craigslist."

"C'mon."

Her voice rises in a scolding manner, "How the hell am I supposed to piss into a bottle while tied up?"

I turn to leave. "Fine, then piss yourself."

The girl's tone flashes to that of the hurt little girl. "Piss myself? You don't want me to piss myself, Carl, do you? Think of the smell. Seeping up into your house. Your home smelling like piss."

I turn to look at her again. She's actually right. I don't want the place smelling like piss.

She continues in her sweet, little-girl voice, "And then I'm itchy, clothes sticking to me, I might even develop a rash. And the flies—"

I can feel the stale itchiness crawl across my skin. "All

right, enough," I snap. I look around the basement again, trying to formulate a plan.

The girl says in an even tone, "You know, Carl, I have a bathroom at home. I could go there. You'd never have to see me again."

I ignore her as I inventory the basement again. A stepladder, a shelving unit, a table with tools laid out in the orderly precision of a surgeon's tray. I'd wager that it is cleaner in this basement than it is in most people's bedrooms—besides this pest tied to the chair—and, for the first time, I envision the clean basement through her eyes—the economy trays of canned goods, the jumbo bottles of laundry detergent, the pallets of bottled water. I must look like an anal-retentive doomsday prepper.

Or a cheap loser with no life. Which, of course, you are. It's her voice in my head.

"Shut up," I tell her. "And no, I can't just let you go." I note my tone has taken on a pleading edge I definitely did not intend. I reel it back and say, "Look, just be quiet for a minute." I walk to the other side of the basement.

"You tie a girl up in your basement, and you don't even think ahead that she might need to take a piss?"

I return with a bucket, saying, "I said shut up."

"I'm not pissing in a bucket, Carl."

"Shut up."

"Just take me to the bathroom, Carl, it's as simple as that."

The *American Idol* theme drifts from the living room again, and suddenly it is like I am a kid again, hearing the theme from *Batman* before I'm done with my chores. My mom would turn the show on and crank the volume to entice me to kick it into high gear. And it usually worked. I've always responded to music—and, I suppose, guys in flashy outfits. Mandy used to tell me I was a closeted homo. After living with her for a few years, I wished I were, it would've made it easier to leave her. And I wouldn't have fallen in with this evil temptress tied up in my basement.

Nah, I'd most likely have still ended up with some evil temptress. After all, wasn't that apparently my fate? Or is it that the seeming abundance of evil temptresses is impossible to get away from?

I look to the basement door. My mother would not scold me now if I were to take a peek at the television before finishing my chores. Nobody will.

Except this girl.

Fuck it, *I* am in charge.

"Look, just wait a minute," I say, setting down the bucket and rushing up the steps.

In the living room, I watch the results from the voting. Jennifer Hudson is in the bottom three.

"What?" I shout.

At least Stevens is safe. But now I am questioning if I've backed the right horse. Is Stevens better? Or is Hudson the best one? Her rendition of Whitney Houston's "I am Nothing," gave me goose bumps the week before.

"She's getting robbed," I groan. The phrase stops me for a moment.

I glance at the chessboard on the coffee table.

The phone rings.

"Christ, what now?"

I storm to the phone, struggling to keep an eye on the *American Idol* results, barking into the receiver. "Yeah?"

"Carl, it's me." Mandy's voice is even more unwelcome than usual.

"You know it's *Idol* time."

"Oh, is it? Well, sorry about that," she says, pretending

she didn't know. She often calls during *American Idol,* and generally when I scold her for it, she either ignores me or makes fun of me. But this time she'd apologized, and an apology means she wants something. I stiffen against what I know will be more unpleasantness.

Mandy says, "I need you to pick up Rudy tomorrow and you need to keep him for a couple of nights."

"Rudy? Tomorrow? A couple of nights...?"

"I hope you are repeating what I said because you are making a checklist of what you intend to do, Carl."

"But I can't...oh tomorrow, no, I—"

Mandy's voice boomerangs from apologetic to its usual bitterness. "Oh, tomorrow, yes, Carl. You have responsibilities as a father, Carl. Unless you want to go to the court and tell them that you relinquish those responsibilities, and...."

I tune her out and keep an eye on the *American Idol* results.

Jennifer Hudson is being sent home.

"Oh, no, c'mon." I shout. I feel a pit in my stomach. Buyer's remorse on some crooner kid.

"Carl, are you yelling at me?"

"No, it's...nothing."

"You need to pick him up here tomorrow."

"Doesn't he have school tomorrow?"

"It's vacation, Carl."

I groan, watching Jennifer singing her swan song.

"Nice, Carl, groaning about seeing your son. This is just like you to...."

I tune her out. Already plotting my trip to Providence for the *Idol Live* tour. I am pretty much guaranteed a good seat since I'll only have to order one seat. There is always a good single leftover.

Single seat? Don't you need two seats? the girl in the

basement's voice says. *And it will need to be duct tape accessible. You may have to ask for the bondage section.*

This thought stops me again. Brings me back to the reality of the situation here.

"Carl, are you even listening to me?" Mandy barks over the phone.

As if on cue, the girl begins calling from downstairs. "Carl. Oh, Carl."

Damn it. I should have gagged her.

"Carl?" Mandy barks.

Should have gagged her, too.

"Carl, Carl, Carl," the girl calls. She then begins singing at the top of her lungs, "Carl's got me locked up in the basement, please send some help, the man is a like a prepubescent psycho, that likes to listen to young boys trilling…"

"Okay, fine, I'll be there," I tell Mandy.

"That's more like it, because—"

I hang up the phone.

It rings again thirty seconds later, but I ignore it.

2

I hear him shout, "Fuck," from upstairs.

With my bladder seriously about to burst, I call up through the ceiling, "Carl. C'mon, Carl, hurry up."

I hope whoever he's been talking to on the phone hears me screaming. Maybe the cavalry is already on the way. But that is doubtful. After all, how could the person tell the difference between my screaming and the talentless hacks screeching on the *Idol* stage?

I scream, "Yo, Carl, asshoooooooooole."

He storms down the steps. "Christ, will you shut up?"

"Who got shit-canned?"

"Huh?"

"On *American Idol*, who got kicked off?"

He looks unsure if I'm pulling his leg, saying, "You like *American Idol?*"

"No, Carl, I'm not a twelve-year-old. But I would like to know what's going on in the world and all. Been a little too tied up to catch *Entertainment Tonight.*"

"Very funny."

"So, Carl, how about that bathroom trip?"

"Can't you just tinkle in the bucket?" he whines.

"Tinkle, Carl? Did you just ask if I can tinkle in a bucket?" I then speak more sternly, "Carl, cut the shit. I'm not pissing into a bucket. Now hurry up, I really need to go. Chop-chop."

It's not entirely shocking to see him jump to it, looking like a soldier following orders, saying, "Shit. All right, fine." A good sign he is responding in this manner. I still have some kind of sway here. But then he stops.

I say, "Carl, c'mon, let's go. Hurry up, before I piss myself."

He stands in front of me, holding his hands out to his sides, saying as if more to himself than to me, "All right, all right, just hold on and let me think."

"No time to think, Carl. I'm gonna burst."

He hops to it again, heading to the workbench and rummaging through odd items. He returns with a length of rope. A clothesline, maybe. Thin. Long. He pulls the bayonet from his back pocket and cuts a shorter length of the line. With the longer length, he fashions a slipknot.

"Someone was a boy scout," I say.

"Shut up," he says, approaching with the noose. "I'm warning you, don't you do anything stupid."

Despite the creeping feeling I'm getting from that

noose, I say in my sweet, choir-girly voice, "Sure thing, Carl, whatever you say."

He slips the noose over my head, and a rush of panic courses through me, but I show no sign of it. Not so much as a flinch. I can't show fear. And I really do need to pee.

He says, "I mean it. If you screw around, then I swear, I'll…." He stops as he visibly struggles to think up a consequence.

"Look, Carl, honestly, I just need to go to the bathroom." I bail him out, not needing him to come up with any consequences. Not to mention if he thinks about it too hard, he's liable to give himself an aneurism, and then I'll be stuck down here for good.

Aren't I stuck down here for good anyway?

No. I still have some control over him; otherwise, I'd be peeing into a bucket.

"Fine," he says. He cuts the zip ties around my wrists and steps back a moment, as if he's cut a wire while disarming a bomb. Even with the duct tape still binding me to the chair, he's wary.

I smile sweetly at him.

He doesn't move.

"Gonna need to lose the tape, too, Carl."

He takes a deep breath and then slits the tape on both sides, stepping back again.

We regard one another.

"Could still use some help getting this tape off, Carl."

"You seemed fine working to get it off earlier."

"Are you retarded, Carl? That took hours."

"Don't call me that."

"Sorry. Didn't know you were so sensitive about these things. Allow me to rephrase. Are you mentally challenged, Carl? That took hours to get one binding off. I need to piss *now*. Right fucking now, so c'mon."

He pulls the tape from around the armrest of the chair, the tape stubborn in places, and then pulls on the section of tape flush to my arm, the tape becoming even more stubborn. I wince. "C'mon, band-aid-rules, Carl. Just give it a yank."

He yanks. I yelp.

He then inspects the armrest, which is now caked with tape residue. "Shit," he says, running his finger along the residue.

That probably would have been a good time for me to make a move, with him distracted and within striking-distance, but I'm too shocked by his reaction to the chair to react quickly enough. Besides, with that bayonet in his hand, he's still too unpredictable. I know he doesn't really want to kill me. Consciously, at least. So why do something to give his subconscious the chance to make the decision for him? I still have lingering concussion symptoms from his prior *subconscious reaction*—a reaction that landed us both in this situation in the first place.

No, it was my own dumbass decisions that landed me here in the first place. The decision to break my cardinal rules. The decision to freeze like a fucking amateur.

"I think the chair will be fine, Carl, but do you think we can save some of the hairs on my other arm with the next one?"

Carl looks up from the tape residue, his eyes narrowing. He reaches over and yanks off the other tape.

I wince.

"Better?" he asks.

"Perfect," I say, a breathy squeak edging the word.

"All right," he says, "arms over your head and hands together."

I smile at him again, even batting my eyelashes, and I raise my arms, placing my palms together as if praying.

"Like this?" I ask sweetly.

"Yeah, that's fine," he says, still eyeing me suspiciously. He wraps the end of the slipknot's line tighter around his hand, as if he's hooked a marlin he's expecting to run.

I bob my head back and forth, my palms still together above my head, saying, "Want me to walk like an Egyptian?"

"No. I want you to sit there and not do anything stupid."

"You bet, Carl."

Still eyeing me suspiciously, he steps behind me and binds my wrists together with the shorter length of rope. I don't understand why he doesn't just cuff me or threaten me with his gun, but maybe he's left that shit in his police locker or in the station or whatever. And he figures the bayonet is that much more intimidating—not to mention it has such a great and interesting story about his stupid, psycho uncle.

"All right. Place your hands in your lap."

I do as he says, now sitting as if that choirgirl were sitting in a pew.

He hunkers down on one side of me, never taking his eyes from me, and cuts loose one ankle. Then, scooting behind me to the other side, he cuts loose the other ankle. He yanks the tape free with less pain than with the wrists.

"You're getting the hang of that tape, Carl," I say in my friendly voice, wanting to encourage him enough to trust me. You know, so he'll get me up to the goddamn bathroom before I explode into piss shrapnel.

He stands behind me and waits. I can feel his narrowed eyes burn into my back, the noose tightening around my neck.

I sit perfectly still.

He says, "All right, stand up slowly."

I stand. A flare of tingles explode across my feet and legs like sunbursts, and I drop back into the seat. The noose doesn't loosen.

He remains behind me, unmoving, as if waiting for the marlin to run again.

"Legs are asleep," I tell him.

My muscles are weak and numb. I try standing again, legs wobbling, and I make it upright, feeling a rush of static run down to the balls of my heels. I raise one foot at a time, trying to pump blood into them, looking as if I'm trying to stand on hot tar.

He says, "Are you able to walk?"

"Yes, Carl, I can fucking walk," I snap. I knew it was the wrong thing to do, but I have to pee so freaking bad.

"We don't have to go up there if you're going to give me attitude."

"Carl, I need to fucking piss, let's go."

"All right, fine" he says. "Now, without doing anything stupid, walk toward the stairs."

He tightens the grip on the rope as I slowly walk toward the stairs, pins and needles flaring in my feet, balance and gravity playing a game of seesaw, my legs wanting to give in to one of them. I am immediately reminded of the first time walking in high heels.

When we're almost to the foot of the steps, he tells me, "Up the stairs. Kneel on the top step. And I swear to God, if you try anything funny, I'll yank you back down these stairs head-first."

I say over my shoulder in a cordial voice, "Sure thing, Carl, you bet." Then I place a foot on the first step and pause. For a moment, I'm unsure if my legs will support my weight as I climb, but after flexing them again, I start up the steps.

Carl's voice comes from behind me, saying,

"Remember. Nothing stupid." The slipknot tightens around my neck.

I reach the top of the stairs and follow his directions perfectly, kneeling on the top step, just as he'd instructed.

He climbs the steps behind me, and I feel the slack in the line around my neck. For a split moment, I think about grabbing hold of the line and yanking it free, or kicking out suddenly, trying to knock the fucker down the stairs. But I don't like my odds at the moment. If I don't land the shot perfectly, and don't get free, there could be some real unpleasantness. Again, why give his subconscious a reason? Not to mention, if I knock him back down the stairs and he doesn't actually let go of his end of the rope, then I'm either breaking my neck or asphyxiating; and either option sucks.

It's too late anyway; he places the blade on my shoulder, nestling the tip of it into my collarbone. He says, "All right, carefully stand up and walk to the bathroom. It's through the kitchen, on the right."

I stand and start toward the bathroom, saying, "I know where the bathroom is, Carl, I drank half a bottle of whiskey here last night."

"Just shut up and get going."

"You bet, Carl."

I reach the bathroom door and open it. Before I enter, Carl says, "And don't do anything tricky in there. I have the key to the door, and the window doesn't open. If I hear any funny business in there, I swear, I'll come in there and—"

I turn and look him in the eyes.

The fucker drops his gaze and says, "You have two minutes."

"Two minutes, Carl? What if I want to do the crossword?"

"Two minutes."

I humph, and step into the bathroom. As I begin to shut the door, he stops it and says, "Leave the door cracked for the rope."

I kick the rope under the door, saying, "Look at that, fits right under it." And I slam the door shut. I press my ear against the door to hear him groan in frustration on the other side.

I dart to the window. Peering through the glass panes, I see only darkness. I'm assuming it is the seemingly endless trees of that damn forest. I test the window, unlocking it and straining to pop it open. The asshole wasn't lying, it doesn't open. I'd have bet money he'd been bluffing. But he wasn't. I actually offer a high-pitch, "Hmm," to this revelation.

I regard the door. Can I somehow barricade the door, or even wedge myself against it so he can't get to me?

And accomplish what, exactly? Besides trapping myself in the bathroom and pushing him into a harsh and desperate reaction?

This game will be won on a mental playing field, and I need to calculate my moves carefully. I've always had a mind for calculation. Playing chess, back in the day, away for the summers at the lake house, I'd always whoop the cousins and adults alike. That was before...before the thing that put an end to all that.

I go to the toilet, lowering the seat and calling, "Could've at least left the toilet seat down, Carl."

"Hurry up in there," he calls through the door.

After reaching under my skirt, with my still-bound hands, and pulling down my panties, I squat on the toilet seat, about to revel in that glorious release of emptying an over-full bladder, but, with quite a bit of effort, I stop myself. Wincing, I stand and kick off my panties, picking them up off the floor. I then shuffle to the center of the bathroom, squat, and piss, right on his nice clean tiles, all the while whistling a friendly tune.

Carl calls through the door, "What're you doing in there?"

"Just peeing," I call casually.

I glance around the bathroom and spot a toothbrush in a coffee mug on the sink. Forcing myself to stop peeing again—an especially difficult task with my body so resolved to evacuating my bladder—I shuffle to the sink and grab the toothbrush. I pee on the thing, offering a loud and content, "Ahhhh."

"What's going on in there?" he calls.

I finish peeing, doing a strange, bird-like dance around the puddle of urine that is rapidly spreading across the floor, and I return the toothbrush to the mug. I look around the room and grab a towel from the towel rack beside the bathtub, dropping it onto the puddle. I step on it and wipe my feet before grabbing a fresh towel from a linen closet.

"Let's go," he calls.

I wipe myself with the towel and drop it on the puddle before flushing the toilet and putting on my panties.

"C'mon," he calls.

I crack the door and slip out of the bathroom, quickly shutting the door behind me, saying, "Whew. I would *not* go in there for at least an hour." I head into the kitchen, saying, "So, what's for dinner?"

He yanks on the line, the slipknot snapping my head back enough to give me minor whiplash. "Shit, Carl, what the—"

He growls, "Back downstairs, let's go."

"But I'm starving, Carl." Now that I've eliminated the overwhelming discomfort of excess urine, I realize just how fucking hungry I am.

"Downstairs," he says.

We repeat the production of me being the obedient dog on the leash—not wanting another of those whiplash jerks—as we return to the basement. I sit in the chair, and he binds me again with extra tape and three zip ties on each forearm now.

I say, "You were up for dinner and drinks last night, Carl. C'mon, I haven't eaten all day. I'm starved."

He assesses the durability of the zip ties and says, "Just sit quietly and maybe I'll bring you something."

"Gee, thanks."

He finishes securing my ankles to the chair and then looks down at me as if wanting to say something, but he doesn't. Instead, he goes up the steps.

I begin counting the ensuing seconds in my head—*one-Mississippi…two-Mississippi*—imagining him walking up the steps, through the kitchen, and into the bathroom, wanting to check for signs of attempted escape. I'll set the line at thirty-Mississippi—betting the under—but I barely hit twenty when he shouts, "Jesus Christ. What the…you peed on the floor?"

I savor the scene in my mind's eye—he is standing in the bathroom with his slack-jawed, bewildered expression, his slow processing way of trying to piece together how and why I'd pissed on his floor—and I giggle in spite of myself. I then call up through the ceiling, "How about that food, Carl?"

There is no response.

"C'mon, Carl, I'm hungry."

The basement door bursts open. A box of Ritz Crackers bounces down the steps and lands well out of my reach. Not that it matters if I can reach it or not, seeing as I'm bound to a fucking chair anyway.

I really *am* hungry, though, and seeing the food so close, makes my stomach ache. But his reaction makes it worthwhile.

"Just wait until I need to take a shit, Carl," I call.

The door slams shut.

3

I stand in front of the mirror, fastening the last button of my uniform. After plucking a stray piece of lint from one of the sleeves, I sit on the bed and take a few deep breaths, dreading having to face Walters. The bastard will probably put the screws to me today. Being even more of a prick than usual.

I bend over and ease my feet into police-issue shoes, then, standing with shoulders pushed back, I assess the whole package in the mirror. "*I'd fuck me,*" I say in my best Buffalo Bill impersonation. Then my own voice says, "but apparently no woman will."

I freeze, looking into the mirror, the Buffalo Bill reference popping back into my head—it is a voice and phrase I've always found creepily hilarious in the past, but now…I *am* Buffalo Bill. I really have a girl held captive in *my* basement.

How long before you start tucking your junk, Carl? the girl's voice says in my head.

I rush out of my bedroom to the kitchen and fill a glass with water. I turn to the basement door, pause, and take a deep breath. I look at the glass in my hand. A peace offering?

Weren't you going to kill me, Carl? Why the peace offering?

Because I don't want dehydration to take away the joy of doing it myself, I'll say to her.

That would be a good comeback; I want to keep that one at the ready.

It puts the lotion in the basket, Buffalo Bill says in my mind.

I shake it off, taking another deep breath, and open the basement door, easing down the steps.

A small band of light falls through the basement window. The girl is an unmoving, and for once silent, pile of flesh secured to the chair. Her chin dips against her chest, her shirt's collar stretched a bit, revealing a liberal amount of cleavage. I fight the urge to get a peek.

Why? I can look if I want. Take a peek. It's my prerogative. If she didn't want to be gawked at, she shouldn't have gotten herself tied up in the basement.

Really? You're going with that excuse?

I push the voice aside and raise my eyebrows, scrunching my face—half in museum-goer appreciation, half in gawker-expecting retribution—taking in the plains and valleys of her bosom.

As if sensing my staring, her head snaps up, immediately alert.

I avert my eyes with a sudden surge of guilt.

She sizes me up, saying, "Used to think a man in uniform was sexy. But that's ruined."

"Think you can shut up long enough to drink this?" I place the glass against her lips.

She drinks.

"I'm going to work," I tell her.

She stops drinking and says, "Oh, okay, dear. Shall I pack you a lunch?"

As she drinks again, I say, "Need I remind you not to do anything stupid?"

She stops drinking and looks up. "Carl, I'm tied up, what the hell am I going to—" She stops short and inspects my uniform. "Wait a minute," she says, "you're not even a cop?"

"I am a member of the force," I say.

I've leaned on this response over the years. Mandy would tell me I'd be an embarrassment to Rudy if the other kids at school ever found out what his father did for a job. I told her they'd respect the truth: his father is on the police force. *Sure, that will help,* Mandy said. She was a worse bully than those kids could ever be.

I snap from the memory, the girl tied to the chair saying, "According to your uniform, you…are you a meter maid?"

"Parking Enforcement Officer."

The girl begins laughing and says, "You're a meter maid."

I ignore her taunting, saying, "As I said, just sit there and don't do anything stupid."

Continuing her laughing, she says, "I can't believe you're a meter maid."

"Enough of that," I say, and suddenly I note the hurt, whiny tone of my voice, and I quickly regain my calm and, with a little effort, work up the Caruso in my voice again, reminding her, "As I said, be good, or you will suffer dire consequences."

"Like what? A parking ticket?"

I literally bite my lip as I take three measured breaths, holding in the last one.

The girl says, "Tell me, is pressing your pen too hard against a parking ticket considered excessive force?"

I let out the breath and turn to leave, but she stops me, saying, "Wait, Carl, how about some breakfast?"

I turn toward her.

The girl says, "Some orange juice, maybe? Tropicana? Meter maid?" She bursts into maniacal laughter, saying, "Shit, that was way funnier than it should have been."

Her laughing continues as I climb the basement steps and shut the door. I envision burying the girl's corpse in the grave I've dug. If only I had the time. If only I didn't have to go to work. I'd show her. I'd teach her not to push me too far.

I pause at the house's front door, about to turn back.

Teach her now. Do it. Who cares about work? There is only righting the wrong. Balancing Karma's yang. Killing the thief. Burning the witch. A ritualistic cleansing of the universe. I need to commit to my convictions.

She finally stops laughing, seemingly with great effort, and I hear her call from the basement, "Hey, Parking Special Needs Enforcer, I need to pee."

I step out of my house, saying, "She's dead." But it will have to wait. I am already in my car and driving down the street.

4

I feel the sunlight on my skin, its hot caress almost overwhelming, but not quite. I welcome it, knowing that when I sit up, the boat's gunwales will no longer steal the breeze from me. I smell the sweat beading up on my skin—a summer-at-the-lake fragrance—and I hear the water kiss the boat's hull. I open my eyes, squint against the sunlight, raise my arm as if to hold that sun in my hand, and then, with the sideways lurch of the boat, there is a black form blocking out the sun.

I shake awake. Where am I?

In the basement, dummy.

"Oh, yeah," I say. I must have faded out at some point, and I'm not sure when I'd drifted into restless, ambiguous sleep.

Can sleep be described as ambiguous?

How the fuck should I know, and who's to argue with me? That's how I'm describing it.

I have no idea exactly how long I've been out. I'd probably faded out a little after Meter Maid Marian left. I begin laughing, a little more hysterically than I probably should at this joke, but whatever; gotta laugh at something, right?

I want nothing more than to doze off again—like sleeping in on a weekend, allowing this day to slip by without the fear and the worry and the rage. But I suppose my body has had all the rest it needs, and now I can't get comfortable enough, or mentally and emotionally settled enough, to drift back off to sleep, despite how broken and tortured that sleep has been.

After all, I've got things to do, places to be. Like anywhere not in this basement. I need to get the fuck out of here. It's as if I'm on *Survivor*, and I need to outwit and outplay the asshole that has me tied up.

What time is it? Even if I did wear a watch, it would be buried under layers of duct tape.

I'll just check my bladder clock…let's see, feels like it's about the year 2038. I have to fucking pee again so bad; I probably could have gotten him to take me to the bathroom again if I hadn't started off insulting him about being a meter maid.

No, he would have accused me of being up to something if I hadn't insulted him. And how am I supposed to resist with him dressed up as a fake cop? I fucking knew he was no cop.

Good for me. That and a quarter will buy me getting tied up in a basement.

I look at the basement window, trying to gauge the time again. I'm guessing it's about noon, but that assessment could be mistaken. Being tied up in a basement can really fuck with one's internal clock. Who'd have known? I suppose POWs and prisoners in solitary would have known? And slaves transported in the bowels of ships, and sex slaves kept in boxes, and children locked up in closets.... See? There have been a lot of people in my situation, and some of them survived.

Some?

Most probably died…horribly.

No, not most; I bet just as many made it, because there *is* a way out. And I'm going to find it.

I begin working my arms, trying to loosen the tape. But it bunches again, gaining strength and durability. I'm done with trying to bite through the stuff. I'd never be able to gnaw through the six zip ties. And I'm not quite to the point where I'll just gnaw off my hand like some fucking pathetic trapped animal…although…I am hungry…Jesus, will it get to that point?

Knock it off. That's desperate talk. And I ain't desperate…yet.

I inventory the basement for the millionth time, my attention continuously snapping back to the workbench and the shears. There has to be a way to use that shit. I drop my head back to think.

This is pretty comfortable, my head hanging back like this, the blood seeming to pool in my brain, and I begin to feel the ambiguous sleep creep back into my body.

5

I edge down a sidewalk, reading meters and issuing tickets. It is the same tedious routine that marks every day. Route is the same, the number of tickets is generally the same, even the cars become repeat offenders—lawyers and clerks who get shut out of the courthouse garage because they were late getting into work, or just too stupid and apathetic about getting ticketed. And now that we are heading into the busy season, spring and summer, it will be a free-for-all. At least it isn't October. Halloween always brings the worst elements.

I come to an expired meter and begin writing a ticket, but my ticket writing is interrupted when a woman's voice calls, "Excuse me."

I glance up from the ticket to see a woman with a large shopping bag step up to me. The woman is with a girl of about nine. This, also, is part of the monotony: disgruntled, mouthy assholes that have a hard time facing that they, too, are accountable to the rules.

I ignore the woman and return to writing the ticket.

"I said, excuse me," the woman repeats.

I continue writing, saying, "Yes, ma'am, what is it?"

"What do you mean, what is it?"

"What do you need, ma'am?" I say, keeping my tone authoritative.

The woman, not the least bit impressed with my authority, says, "What I need is for you to 'splain what you think you're doing."

"It's really quite simple, ma'am," I say. "If you really need me to *'splain* it, maybe you should go back to Driver's Ed."

The woman raises her eyebrows almost off her forehead and places her hands on her hips. "Look here, smartass, just because you're wearing a clown suit, it don't make you funny."

I try to maintain an even, authoritative voice. "Look, ma'am, you have received a ticket for an expired meter. I'm sorry, but it's the law, and you have broken it."

The woman gives a handful of quarters to the little girl. "Here, honey, put these in the meter, we're here in plenty-o-time."

I feel the veins tightening in my neck like angry cords. "No, ma'am you can't—"

The girl puts a quarter in the meter in front of their car.

I say, "Um, no, wait, you can't—"

The young girl then begins skipping down the sidewalk, putting quarters in all the meters like the Robin Hood of parking.

"Hey, wait, you can't do that. Come back here. You need to cease and desist immediately, or—"

With a shake of her head, the woman says, "Shit, you talk like a cop, but you ain't nothing but a meter bitch."

"That's Parking Enforcement Officer, ma'am, and— Hey...." I begin following the girl as the woman trails behind me.

The girl continues to pluck quarters from her hand and feed the meters.

I catch up to her, yelling, "Hey, I said stop." I turn to the woman, saying, "Ma'am, you need to stop your daughter here from—"

With another shake of her head and a raised finger, the woman says, "I don't *need* to do a thing. It's a free goddamn country."

"Ma'am, you need—"

The girl drops more quarters into meters.

"Hey, you need to stop that." I can hear that whiny quality in my voice. The one I hear while pleading with the girl in the basement.

The woman calls to the little girl, "You just keep on going, honey. You're doing a good deed, now. This Parking Enforcement-whatever ain't nothing."

"I said, *stop*." I trot after the girl, grabbing her by the arm, hollering, "I said, stop, you ni—need to stop."

I'd almost said it. And I don't know where it came from.

The girl bursts into tears. My hand is squeezing her arm.

The woman swings her bag at me, shouting, "You let go of her this instant, you let go, now. Help. Help. Police. Police."

I say, "Ma'am I am the po—"

"Real police. Real police."

The girl twists from my grip, and I look at my hand, feeling a surge of horror. It all happened so quickly, and I am once again racing to catch up with my instinct, only to realize how futile it is to even try reeling back my actions. It has always been this way for me, and I am reminded of being a kid, the beauty of an active bees' nest catching my eye, and before I even consider the function of the object, there it is in my hands. I look now at the girl, her shoulders hunched and shuddering, a bees' nest of the moment, and I pray I'd released her soon enough to avoid the coming stings.

The girl runs from me and continues crying as she sits on the curb between two parked cars. Her braids seem like rosary beads, and I fight the urge to bend and touch them.

The mid-spring sun is suddenly sweltering, as if the heat were cranked up a few notches in a matter of seconds. The skin on the back of my neck feels blistering, my face flushing.

The woman steps up to me and studies my nametag. "Carl…White is it?" she says. "Figures. Well, Carl *White*, we'll be going now to the real police to report this. You'll be hearing from our lawyer."

The woman storms to the curb, bending to comfort the girl, her child becoming an infant in her arms, and for a moment, I can imagine them rocking in a glider chair on a porch, looking out over a familiar neighborhood. And with that image implanted in my mind, I suddenly feel connected to them. *Connected* is the wrong word. I *envy* them.

The woman pulls the girl to her feet and they amble away like wounded soldiers retreating from battle. I call after them. "No. Wait. But she...."

I watch them go, the girl still sniveling.

I then close my eyes, trying to will myself gone.

6

Something wakes me. A sound upstairs. The front door. And footsteps (I'm getting good at recognizing these sounds now). What the fuck time is it? Glancing at the window, the light hasn't changed much. The basement door opens and I see the police uniform, and a moment of hope surges into my—

Correction: meter maid uniform. Carl comes down the steps.

He's here to kill me. This is it. He's holding a…

Bucket.

"Am I parked in a tow zone, sir?" I say.

"Please, not now with the bullshit. I'm having a really bad day."

I snort a loud, and frankly not very attractive, guffaw. "You're having a bad day?"

He pauses a moment, cogs turning, then says, "Do you want to piss or not?"

"Not in a bucket."

"It's your only shot. You think I'm going to take you back up to piss on my bathroom floor again? If you want to piss on floors, you can piss on this one. Or you can piss in the bucket."

"C'mon, Carl, don't be that—"

He interrupts, saying, "Don't be that way? Oh, I *am* going to be that way. Having no idea what exactly you pissed on, I had to wash everything in my bathroom last night. I didn't get to bed until almost midnight."

"Are you sure you got everything?" I ask him.

"Positive," he says. "Now hurry up; I'm on lunch break."

"Well, I assure you it won't happen again. Quick, untie me, we can head up to the bathroom, and you'll still have time for lunch."

He turns and walks away.

"C'mon, Carl, I can't fucking hold it for another twenty hours."

He turns back toward me and holds up the bucket.

Something tells me I'm pissing into a bucket from now on (now on; how long is that?) but I mount an argument anyway…"Carl, I told you, I'm not—"

His weak chin lowers and clenches and he gives me a look like he's looking at me over a pair of reading glasses—the look a fed-up mother gives a toddler or teenager.

I am definitely pissing in a bucket.

"Fine," I say, "Cut me loose and let's get this over with."

"No fucking way," he says. "I don't have time for your bullshit. You'll manage as is."

"Manage as is? I'm completely bound to a chair, how am I supposed to get my panties down?"

"I'll do it," he says.

"The hell you will," I say.

"I mean it; that's the only option. Otherwise, piss

yourself." He glances up the stairs, then back at me. "I'm running late, so hurry up and make your decision."

"Fine. Hurry up, then," I say, determined to stay in control, but as he approaches, the dread hits hard. I can feel my breathing quickening and my stomach clench—I don't know how my bladder doesn't let loose. And as he reaches up my skirt, I want to scream, *Fine, I'll just piss myself, leave me alone.* Or I want to literally beg, sobbing, for him to take me back up to the bathroom. But I can't let him see me break. I can't let him see me weak. And as I find myself shifting my hips up, so he can slip my panties down, I want to burst into tears, and I want to spit in his fucking face, and I look down at him and—

I see he has his head turned away and his eyes clenched shut, like a little kid afraid to look at a solar eclipse because someone told him it will burn out his eyes.

Somehow that surge of fear and dread I felt a moment ago is replaced with disdain—which isn't strange, given that is my default feeling toward him, but I have to admit it is mixed with a little pity toward this pathetic fuck. But it is mostly disdain. I almost relax to the point of letting my bladder go, and it occurs to me that if I do, I'll piss right in his face—which, his expression looks like he's preparing for. Now I want to fucking laugh, but I don't. Instead, I take the opportunity to snatch back control.

"You're going to need to get my panties down lower, Carl, I don't want to piss on them."

He obediently scoots them down my leg, looking like a blind man refusing to use his sense of touch to negotiate the world, careful not to touch the skin on my legs.

"Okay, grab the bucket," I tell him. "Get it between my legs."

He grabs the bucket and, with the slightest of brushes with his hand to determine where my legs are, he positions the bucket between my knees, still with his eyes pressed shut like someone thrust into a supernova.

"Don't want to see what you could have had, Carl?" I say.

"Shut up," he growls.

I shift my hips, thrusting my pelvis toward the edge of the chair, trying to aim for the bucket, my hooha now less than a foot from his face, right in line with his closed eyes. Wanting to somehow lower his comfort level even more, I say, "I need you to check, am I going to clear the edge of the chair?"

He opens his eyes and gets an eyeful of pussy, and his eyes snap wide and his jaw drops. I can't quite place his expression, but it goes beyond shock. There is legitimate fear in his eyes.

His eyes snap onto mine, and he says with panic in his voice, "How old are you?"

"What?" I say, and I want to laugh and ask what the fuck he's getting at, when it dawns on me. "Wait, have you never seen a shaved pussy before?"

"Shaved?" he says.

"Yes," I say, wanting to break into hysterical laughter and ask what kind of giant bushes he's had to endure all these years? But I don't, I reel it in; after all, I still need to pee, and it's pointless to enrage him now and get him to sulk off. "It's 2004, Carl, women shave their pussies now. You don't watch porn?"

"No," he says. "Just take your piss, will you? I'm late."

I begin to pee and he turns his head away, clenching his eyes again.

Can someone orgasm from peeing? Because I think I am. Jesus, thank God, this feels so fucking good.

As the bucket fills, drops of urine begin splashing up, and his head darts back.

"Don't want a golden shower, do you?"

"Shut up."

"Do you even know what one is, with no porn?"

"I said shut up." He shifts, balancing the bucket.

"What do you whack off to, Carl?"

"I don't," he says.

"No wonder," I say.

"What's that supposed to—" he begins to say, but he has to catch the bucket when it almost shifts from his grip.

My peeing begins to wane—Jesus, I would have thought there was a lot more in my bladder from how full it felt, but I guess, what would be in there? I've barely had anything to drink.

The final drips prompt him to say, "Finished?"

"Yes, Carl."

"Okay," he says, taking the bucket and turning to go.

"Um, you're just going to leave me here like this? It's a little breezy on my wet pussy."

"Will you stop using that word?"

"Why, Carl? You don't like pussy?"

"No. I…look, what do you want?"

"My panties back up, Carl. Think you can weather the scary pussy again?"

Without a word, he sets the bucket down and mopes back to me. Kneeling, and pressing his eyes shut again, he starts my panties back up my legs. "What about wiping, Carl?"

"What?"

"I need to wipe. You know, after peeing? You do understand how a pussy works, don't you?"

"What are you talking about?"

"You need to cut my hand free so I can at least wipe my pussy."

He takes a deep breath after cringing again at the word

pussy.

"Unless," I say in my seductive voice," You want to wipe for me."

He is frozen for a moment, glancing up the stairs again, the cogs in his head turning, and then he says, "You'll be fine," and finishes hiking up my undies. When the deed is done, he almost leaps away from me as if he's just hand-fed an alligator, and he returns to the bucket, taking it from the floor and turning to go. He wipes stray urine drops from his uniform. That stupid fucking wannabe cop uniform.

"Wait, Carl."

He turns back to me.

"I'm hungry," I say.

"I don't have time for this," he says.

"C'mon," I say, "I'm so hungry, and the Ritz crackers are right there. They've been parked there all night. You can't just leave them parked there, can you?"

He looks at the crackers, the cogs turning in his head, and then he looks back at me—and the shit-eating grin on my face.

"Shouldn't they have been towed by now?" I say.

I don't know why I'm saying it—I just can't fucking help myself—because I really am fucking hungry.

He picks up the box, turns toward me, and says, "Consider them towed." And he heads for the stairs.

"C'mon, Carl, don't be that way."

As he heads up the stairs, I call, "My meter is up, you gonna tow me, too? Hey, you better be careful, Carl, you might get your own ass impounded—or pounded—in prison, because…."

He shakes his head and shuts the basement door. I then hear the front door shutting as my laughter chases him from the house.

7

Again, I spot the pair of pruning shears hanging from the edge of the workbench to my left, like they're calling to me. My eyes narrow. I know I can't somehow mentally will them to me like Carrie White fucking everything up at the end of that movie; but even if I can't get them to me, I can theoretically get to them, right? I mean, sliding my chair to them is not out of the realm of possibility.

I struggle against the bindings on my wrists and ankles, attempting to coordinate my body to get the chair to move. But it isn't working.

Maybe sliding *isn't* in the realm of possibility—or technically it may be *possible*, but success is not *probable*. Maybe sliding is not the right idea, but…

Hopping is.

I try to launch my butt from the chair, but I don't get far; the bindings on my wrists and ankles yank me back down. I try again with more force. This time the chair bounces a bit. That's encouraging. I try again, the chair bouncing a bit more. The first thing I am reminded of, and yes, I know this is weird and random, but I'm reminded of one of those umbrella ornithopters—I'd researched ornithopters when a mark had told me he had Penaud's original model, but it turned out he'd been full of shit and I'd had to settle for his Hummel collection. And like the video I'd seen of one of the attempted umbrella contraptions, I'm only accomplishing bouncing up and down. I need to scoot my ass, not launch it straight up. Bunny hop it, like back when I was a kid hopping the BMX bikes with the boys in the neighborhood.

After a while, I get the motion down, starting with miniscule movements at first, and then moving on to actual chair-leg-skidding hops, shuffling slowly across the concrete. As I inchworm across the floor, I realize I might actually get to them. What I'm going to do when I get there, I've still yet to decide. At this point, I'm just glad my bladder is empty for this.

8

I walk into the police station's break room. I usually take lunch on the small strip of grass that serves as a pathetic attempt for a park across the street, eating peanut butter sandwiches while keeping an eye on pedestrians. The college up the block makes it a good spot to roost on a bench and scope out the parade of ass as it trots off to class. I've heard the place is a teacher factory, tailoring programs to education majors, and I often marvel that I'd never had teachers that looked half as good as some of those girls. I'd always been stuck with frumpy old biddies who'd looked the same, year after year, as if they'd been churned out of a different factory—one that served up weathered, defective models. But today, obviously I had other things to do. Had to go home and…walk the dog?

Woman, Carl; I'm a woman. Don't go trying to make your oh-so-clever puns about me being a bitch. It's woman to you. Or, if you want to really get technical: a prisoner.

I shake off the voice, along with the surge of panic the word *prisoner* brings.

But it gets worse. I need to pick up Rudy after work. And that will be…tricky? How about catastrophic? Even with having tomorrow off—I pray Walters won't make me work to atone for the day I'd missed—with Rudy in tow, how am I going to—

I suddenly realize I am standing at the vending machine

and I've already pumped the coins into the slot. I stare at the choices beyond the glass.

What do I want? Healthy? Junk? Is there healthy? There's trail mix. Should I get that? There is a nutrition bar. Is that healthier than trail mix? I doubt it. I squint through the glass, trying to take a gander at the ingredients. What I really want is Cheetos. Something comfortingly awful for me. But this is lunch, and I barely had a breakfast, only a stale donut left in the break room earlier. Trail mix is best, it has—

Jesus, Carl, you can't even make a decision about what to fucking eat?

The voice is in my head again, but at this point I can't even tell if it sounds more like Mandy or the girl in the basement.

I answer the voice with a hardy *fuck you* and press the button for Cheetos.

The metal rings holding the Cheetos begin turning and then stop, the bag dangling without dropping.

"What the…you…you fucking—"

I suddenly notice a moving reflection in the vending machine's glass. Steve Riley—a slick looking cop—stands behind me. I turn and see, on the far end of the room, two other police officers, Tommy Adams and Chet Harris, are sitting at a table.

Steve motions toward the hanging Cheetos, saying, "Hate when that happens."

"Yeah," I say, turning back to the machine, biting the inside of my lip, wishing I could climb in there behind the glass and get away from the *real cops*. Steve Riley isn't that bad, but Tommy and Chet are the same bullying jocks found in any middle school.

I back away from the vending machine and sit in a chair, watching the Cheetos dangling defiantly on the other side of the glass. I try making the maneuver seem natural, as if I'd planned the vending request to remain unfulfilled, and I suddenly feel as if I'm back in eighth grade. Feeling their attention on my back the same way I'd felt everyone's eyes the day of my impromptu erection in gym class. That day, I'd employed a similar tactic, sitting and pretending I had a cramp, while silently begging my Johnson to stand down. Now I silently begged the dangling Cheetos to do the same.

Steve joins the other two officers seated at the table.

I watch the real cops in the reflection of the vending machine's glass. The reflected-Tommy motions toward me, whispering something to the other two. Then Chet raises his voice, loud enough for me to hear. "That EMT chick, little Venezuelan honey. What is her name?"

I know what he's trying to do. Her name is Anna. I'm sure he's talking about Anna, just to get a rise out of me.

Steve says, "Anna?"

"Anna, that's right," Chet continues. "She's something. I saw her in the parking garage with—what's that big goofy guy's name? Other EMT driver. Big Bird-looking fella."

"Monroe," Steve says, "Sean Monroe."

"Yeah, Sean Monroe. I never can remember that big doofus's name."

Tommy calls out. "Hey, Carl, weren't you trying to hit that for a while? I seem to remember that time you played poker with us—"

"Would you really call that playing?" Chet says. "More like giving out free money. Goddamn ATM machine, this one."

Chet and Tommy laugh.

Not looking at the three men, I say, "That's redundant."

"What's redundant?" Chet says.

"It's when something is repea—" Tommy begins to say.

"I know what the word means, dickhead," Chet says.

"ATM machine," I say to the glass. "The M stands for machine. So adding the word *machine* is redundant."

Chet says, "What's redundant was you handing over your poker chips to me." He glances at Tommy. "That was fucking redundant."

Tommy smirks, and then says, "Anyway, I remember you saying you wanted to hit that."

Still staring at the reflection of the men in the glass of the vending machine, I say, "Hit what, Tommy?"

Chet says, "Rescue Annie."

"I thought her name was Anna?" Tommy says.

"Rescue Annie is the name of the CPR mannequin," Steve says.

"Oh, shit. Really?" Tommy says and then bursts out laughing.

The other two men chuckle.

Tommy stifles his laughter and calls over to Carl, "No, not your girl Rescue Annie. We already know you hit that—" He stifles another chuckle. "I meant little Anna smoke-a-the-banana," he says this in a voice mocking a Spanish accent. "Weren't you trying to work that for awhile?"

I turn my head and draw a deep breath. I can imagine Mandy sitting over there with them, smirking. Mandy daring me to do something stupid. Like take the bait from this piece of shit and hit him in front of his goony friends who outrank me both on the job and in life's meritless social hierarchy.

"Smoke-a-the-banana," I say as if to myself. My fingers curl into fists. I stand and turn. "Yeah, Tommy, I was trying to hit that," I say, my nostrils flaring. "You got something to say about it?" I stride over to the three men. "Not the best of luck with women, I suppose, that what you want me to say?" I'm shouting. The other men are standing now, their hands out in that calm-down-manner cops are taught to use. I say, "Maybe you'd like to join my latest failed relationship, I've already got the fucking hole dug, you want to spend eternity side by side with my latest sweetie? Maybe I'll-a smoke-a you, you fucking sniveling asshole." I grasp the handle of the coffee pot on the side counter, watching as Tommy's hand moves to the grip of his sidearm. "How fast can you draw that thing?" I say, swinging the coffee pot and smashing it into Tommy's face. Tommy drops, screaming, covering his face. "Whoops, not fast enough, I'm afraid," I scream as I rain blows down on the *real* cop.

I shake from the fantasy, still sitting in the chair, and I return my attention to the hanging Cheetos.

Steve says, "C'mon, Tommy, don't be a dick."

Tommy responds in a high, who-me? tone, "What? Just making conversation with the Meter-Peter, here. Look, he's smiling about it."

The ghost of a smile, remnants of my imagined smashing of Tommy with a coffee pot, falls from my face.

Tommy stands from the table and walks up behind me. I see his reflection in the vending machine's glass. He says, "So, how about it, Meter-Peter, were you able to give her your shaft before she shafted you?"

Chet calls from the table, "Technically a girl needs to be dating you before she can shaft you."

Tommy snaps his fingers, as if a light bulb appears over his head—it is the sound I imagine his neck would make as I pressed it to the floor with my shoe and tugged his head upward. "That's right," Tommy says. "I was confused, because the amount of time and effort he spent on Little Anna-smokes-the-banana made me think he *was* dating her."

Chet says, "Maybe if she were made of plastic like his girl Annie...." He shrugs, letting the statement hang in the air. Tommy and Chet both laugh. Steve does not this time.

"Or, if only he were still an EMT technician," Tommy says, stepping to the vending machine and dropping coins into the slot. "Oh, I suppose EMT technician is redundant, too, right?" He presses the required buttons, making his choice on the machine's keypad: Cheetos. Both his choice, as well as my bag, drop into the dispenser.

Chet and Steve are now heading for the break room's door, Tommy tossing one of the bags of Cheetos to Chet. Tommy says, "Look, extra bag. Lucky me."

Chet catches the bag, laughing, as he and Steve exit the room.

Tommy turns back toward Carl and says, "Don't sweat it. Anna-smoke-a-the-banana is a tough one to crack. We've all tried. Got my own banana smoked once or twice. But I guess it wasn't to be."

Tommy leaves the break room.

I stare at my own reflection in the vending machine's glass. I then stand and flick the coin return. Then kick the machine. "You stupid piece of...you...piece of..." I howl, pounding on the machine. "You fucking bitch...you fucking bitch. Fucking bitch."

9

I'm close. The apparent distance between me and those shears has shrunk from an ocean to a pond to a stream, and now the shears loom large in front of me. Maybe about five more feet. I take a moment to rest again. A little out of breath. My heart pounding. I don't remember bunny-hopping those bikes as being quite this exerting. I take a moment to inspect the shears. They are the big ones requiring two hands to work. The kind used to trim larger shrubs.

How am I supposed to work these things? Never mind two hands, I don't even have one hand available.

I suppose I can get them in my lap maybe, somehow without an unintended and horrifically unpleasant penetration to my nether regions? And then open them? And maneuver them to cut the binds? Is that even possible? I wish I hadn't skipped all those physics classes in high school. Who'd have thought when I'd argued *I'll never use this in real life* that, in order to escape some psycho's basement, I would need to understand compound levers and fulcrums and rates of descent (hey, maybe I remember more than I thought)?

Fuck physics. I don't need physics to know this ain't gonna work. It's common sense. It just isn't going to happen. There is no way. Do I abort the mission, scoot back to my spot in the middle of the room and avoid sending Carl into another blind rage—or more likely a whiny bitch session about how bad a day *he's* having— when he comes home and finds my impromptu journey?

No. Fuck common sense and that negativity shit. I really think I can do this. I just need to get the shears open. Position one handle against the inside of the chair and pull with my fingers. Open sesame. Then cut the ties. All I need is a slight tear in the tape, and rip. Voila. Hand free. And hand free equals *hands* free. Then legs free. Then I can kick through that door and use the shears as a weapon—I envision me dueling Carl, shears versus bayonet—or as a way to cut through the thick woods out back maybe?

I chuckle out loud at this last thought, imagining the woods thick enough to need to be cut through like a rain forest, and imagining the stupidity of choosing to cut through the forest instead of strolling out the front door and down the fucking street.

The shears are close.

Few more feet.

I can do it.

I start shuffling again.

10

The vocal gyrations of NSYNC fill the car, and I sing along with a few lines, procrastinating the game face I know I should be putting on. It is a bad habit of mine: approaching unpleasant situations with my emotions threading the distant hope that everything will fall into place on its own. I even did it as a kid—walking home from school with a sub-mediocre report card weighing down my book bag, my mind preoccupied with Jackson 5 performances instead of crafting an explanation for when my mom would ask why I'd spent another term subpar. Time after time, I'd accept the loss before even trying to change it. Now, I have to tell Mandy that I can't take Rudy.

I turn the car into the cul-de-sac and take the gentle curve slowly, even though I know I should be stepping on it, time has gotten away from me, and I am late. Mandy will be pissed. The last thing I need, however, is to squeal my tires and invite some unpleasant confrontation with an asshole neighborhood-speed-vigilante (which, ironically, I'd been when I lived here). If I'm a few minutes late, then I'm a few minutes late. The bitch can wait.

You sure about that? The voice says in my mind.

And I answer, "Yup. I am. Bitch can wait." I take a deep breath and feel my face nearly relax, my fingers loosening on the steering wheel, but then a car backs out into the street. The dipshit not even bothering to look. I slam on the brakes and flip off the driver, shouting, "Pluck yew."

For me, road rage is like dandruff, no matter how much I vow to get rid of it, I always end up wearing it on my sleeve.

The driver is a young woman—probably hurrying off to make some poor bastard's life even more miserable—and she pulls up beside me, looking me up and down with a sneer. "Fuck you, too, sweetie," She says. She eyes my car and adds, "Nice shitbox."

Any comeback I may have had is lodged at the base of my throat in a pocket of stale air, and I bite the inside of my lip in frustration—another neat trick I learned during childhood. Belittling remarks from a teacher, humiliating rebukes from the jocks, or a girl, whatever; I would bite the inside of the lower lip, and the pain somehow made everything a bit more palatable.

"Fucking bitch," I say under my breath as the girl drives off. I imagine for a moment tying this girl up in my basement beside the other one, and as I allow the fantasy to take hold, I barely notice I'd unconsciously continued down the street and parked in front of my former home. I snap from my thoughts and regard the lawn and the bed of perennials. At least one benefit of divorce is not having to weed that pain in the ass garden anymore. I do wonder, however, whom she is banging to get it done.

I walk up the front path toward the door, noticing a corner of gutter dangling away from the soffit beneath the roof (apparently she's not banging someone enough to fix that) and I hope it falls off, even though I'll end up paying for it eventually.

At the screen door, I draw a deep breath, raising my hand to knock, but before my knuckles land, Mandy appears on the other side of the screen, bitching already. "Took you long enough."

"Look, Mandy, I can't—"

"I don't want to hear that you can't take Rudy. Do I need to call the lawyer? Are you admitting you don't want to be a part of his life?"

I pause a moment, looking away from her and watch my former neighbor walking his dog (neither of us bother to wave). Countless scenarios are flashing through my mind, and I try to calculate them all, but it is just too much, keeping all the factors straight in my mind, and I find myself saying, as if my voice is independent of my brain, "Is he ready?"

"That's better. I'll get him."

The scenarios are flashing through my mind again, and I just want to sit down for a moment. I pull at the screen door to let myself in, but it is locked. "Mind if I come in?"

"Yeah, I do." She then disappears, calling into the house, "Rudy, it's time to go."

I sigh and look around the porch. The mailbox beside the door reads: AND MANDY WHITE. What had been my name is now only scratches in the metal.

11

I make it to the workbench, the shears hanging there from a nail in the bench's edge.

I need the shears to get the shears. It's a situation worthy of Joseph Heller—I'd once swiped a signed first edition of *Catch 22*, but because it was signed to the full name of the guy I'd swiped it from, I couldn't sell the thing; go figure.

There has to be some kind of maneuver I can attempt to configure my body and chair in a manner to get them. But do I still have enough in me for another maneuver, or should I rest?

There's no time to rest. I need to make my move now.

This time, instead of bunny hops, I go with rocking. After all, it's the best tactic when a car is stuck in the muck—and I'm certainly stuck in the muck. Put it in drive. Put it in reverse. Drive. Reverse. Forward. Back. Get the chair rocking toward the shears, then away, then toward them again until I can hit the table hard enough to knock them off the hook. I just need to be sure that, when righting the chair from hitting the table's edge, I'm able to catch the shears in my lap.

Simple, right?

The danger—besides the very real possibility of the pruning-shears impaling rather sensitive areas—is in rocking too far, falling away from the shears, onto the floor, and then spending the rest of the day trying to right myself like an overturned beetle.

I make my move, swaying against the binds to get that chair a-rocking. And rock it does. Tipping forward, and tipping back.

Forward.

Back.

Forward.

Then back—a little more than expected, my heart dropping for a moment like someone almost slipping on ice.

Then forward again, and I strike the bench.

The shears swinging ever so slightly on their hook.

Back.
Forward.
Hit.
Swing.
Repeat.
I rock the chair forward again, this time too much, striking the bench harder than intended, and the chair's legs begin to scoot out from under me. I try desperately to counterbalance my weight, leaning back, hoping to plant the chair's rear legs firmly on the floor to stabilize it, and then hopefully gently lean it forward onto all four legs again—which would be the proper maneuver on one of those BMX bikes when a jump goes wrong. But it's too late for that; gravity already has its eager grip on me, and I've already overcompensated.

With a last ditch, hopping maneuver—hoping to shift the center of gravity in the air and avoid the skidding momentum—I scoot forward, but the back legs of the chair fall out from under me, and I land on my back with a loud, breath-stealing, "Ooomph."

I've ended up like that overturned beetle after all, now looking up at the basement's ceiling and at the edge of the table and at the shears. The shears dangling precariously above my face.

A handful of objects topple off of the bench. A few screws, a black magic marker, a roll of electrical tape. I close my eyes as they bounce off my face. When I open my eyes again, I see the shears still swinging above me. Back and forth, the blades walk their way to the edge of the hook in a macabre march. I shut my eyes again, waiting for the blades to plunge through the muscle and sinew and bones of my face, hoping that they will at least hit something vital and kill me quickly.

One final swing should just about bring my demise,

and, with my eyes still shut tight, I can sense the blades falling.

Bracing, cringing, and letting out a mouse-like squeak, I hear a loud clang on the concrete floor beside my right ear.

PART 4

1

When I get home, I open the basement door and walk down the steps with a glass of water. My breath catches in an audible intake of air, my fingers loosening almost to the point of dropping the glass.

The girl is gone.

I dart my eyes around frantically, until I hear a scratching sound. I look over to see the overturned chair with the girl still tied to it. She'd somehow made it to the side of the room. The scratching of the chair against the concrete floor intensifies as she worms toward the pruning shears now on the floor. She teases the rubber handle with the fingers of her still-bound hand.

"Holy shit," I say, walking over to her, my eyes bugging in disbelief.

The girl looks up with a disgusted smile. "Welcome home, limp-dick."

"Did I not explicitly state that you weren't to do anything stupid?"

"Obviously those instructions weren't explicit enough, Carl," she says, worming with a little more vigor.

I grunt as I right her in the chair, saying, "Looks like you almost took off your head with those shears." I drag her toward the center of the basement.

"Almost saved you the trouble of killing me," she says.

I stop dragging her for a moment, but then continue dragging her to the center of the room. I return to the workbench, cleaning up the objects off the floor and placing the shears further back on the bench.

I turn for the stairs.

"Do I actually get any of that water you brought down?" she says.

I stop short, looking around the room. I retrieve the water from where I'd set it down on the floor. Allowing her to drain the glass, I say, "Not too fast, who knows when you'll actually get to pee again."

She stops drinking and says, "At least that indicates there will be another chance?"

I look at her for a moment, not saying anything.

"I could really go now," she says.

"Can't now," I say and then turn back for the steps, saying over my shoulder, "I'm going to mow the lawn."

"You're going to mow the lawn? You're telling the girl you have tied in your basement that you're going to mow the lawn as if we've been married for years? Jesus, Carl, does the obsessive compulsion in you ever end?"

"I have to mow it…I have…my…." I stop, choosing to ignore her attempt to goad me, and I certainly don't have time to explain myself now. And why should I? After all, I am in charge. "What is it to you? I have to mow my lawn."

See? *I* am in charge.

I am in *charge*.

I am in charge.

I say, "I know this is probably too much to ask, but do

you think you can try and behave?"

"I can surely try, Carl."

"Let's see if I can be more explicit this time. Do *not* do anything stupid, got it?"

"Sure, Carl, whatever you say."

I turn to exit, but she stops me, saying, "So how long do you expect I'll be staying here needing to pee, Carl?"

I stand, with my back to her, take three deep breaths, then climb the stairs, closing the basement door behind me.

2

He wasn't kidding. He really did go out to mow the lawn.

I mutter, "Guy has a girl tied up in his basement, and he decides to go out and do yard work?"

The sound of the mower's engine approaches, becoming louder as it sweeps past the window, and then fades again into the distance.

"What a fucking lunatic." I take a deep breath and let it out before saying, "I'm not going to be one of those people that keeps talking to themselves, am I?" I pause as if waiting for an answer and then say, "I guess I already am one."

I twitch my head, thinking maybe I just heard something. Something more than the distant approach and recede of the mower outside. A bang from upstairs. The slam of a screen door snapping shut. And then there are footsteps on the floor above me. But the Doppler runs of the mower's engine continue to sweep past the basement window, and I can only assume that it is Carl out there propelling that mower.

Then who is upstairs?

My heart, like a kite—catching the air of some emotion, I'm not sure which—rises to my throat, but then it nosedives to my bowels. I'm not quite sure how to feel. It could be a rescuer. But, with the way things have been going, I'm guessing it's more likely an executioner.

Maybe Carl can't bring himself to kill me, and he found someone else to do the deed.

Dirty deeds, done dirt-cheap?

Maybe that's why he's decided to choose this very moment to do yard work. Something to keep him occupied, something to drown out my screams as the girl in his basement is being dispatched.

"Fucking coward," I say.

The basement door opens. And then two sneaker-clad feet appear on the steps.

The mower sweeps by the window.

The sneaker-clad feet begin to cautiously edge down the steps, bringing the sneakers' owner into view. A boy of about eleven. I immediately recognize him as the boy in the pictures up in the living room.

The kid, edging down the steps, suddenly spots me. He stops his descent of the steps and stares at me as expressionless as he stares from the pictures upstairs.

I have my first true pangs of hope, although I'm not quite sure what to make of this development—I still have the lingering thoughts of a possible execution crawling in my mind, but is Carl the type to outsource my death to his preteen son?

Definitely not—if I weren't tied up, with a glimmer of hope for escape, I'd take the time to laugh at the notion. The prominent display of the photographs in his bookcase proves Carl clearly cares for the boy. Which means Carl won't want the boy to know about my presence here. He'd probably told the kid to stay out of the basement, and the kid came down anyway. After all, disobeying Carl is just so damn easy. Which makes me think this kid is somehow going to be the catalyst for my escape. Either I will be able to get this kid to free me, or his father will now *have* to let me go. Carl is deranged, angry, hateful, impotent, and feckless, but he isn't the type to allow his son to think him a killer. And he certainly isn't going to eliminate *this* witness.

I watch the kid watch me, and just to be sure he realizes this isn't a case of his dad being involved in some demented sex-game with a consenting adult, I mouth the word, "Help."

The kid tentatively descends the final steps, but freezes as the mower sweeps by the window again. All the while, there is no change in his demeanor or expression, the kid apparently having all the charisma of his father. When the mower is heading away from the window, the boy continues to edge toward me.

I whisper, "Oh, god, thank you, thank you," and it feels good not to be whispering it to myself. "Quick, you've got to free me."

The boy doesn't say a word. He has an expression on his face I can't quite read. An intensity in his eyes, as if he is shocked his father has a girl tied in the basement, but not entirely phased by it.

I whisper to the boy, "It's okay. Hurry. You've got to get me out of here. Find help."

The kid walks up close, a foot or so from me, and bends over to peer into my face. He stares at me with that expressionless gaze, as if studying me for a time that stretches on for several seconds.

I move my head back, raising my eyebrows, saying, "Um—"

The kid jumps up and down, flapping his hands in the

air and hooting, looking like an epileptic owl trying to take flight.

"You've got to be shitting me," I say.

Upstairs, there is the bang of the screen door slamming shut, then footsteps crossing the floor. The warden is back, and my only savior is a kid who I can only assume is autistic, or brain damaged, or mentally retarded, or I don't know what.

In the friendly, soothing voice one might use with a toddler or a puppy—someone one doesn't want to spook—I say, "Hey. Hi. Hi."

The kid keeps staring at the wall, hooting and groaning and flapping his hands. I try to bob my head into the line of the boy's vision. Trying to get his attention. "Hey," I say in my soothing way, trying to remember if Carl told me the kid's name, but no name comes to me. "Hey, can you undo this tape? Hey. Tape? Can you undo it? Do you know how?"

The kid's father calls from upstairs, "Rudy?"

I say to the boy, "Rudy? Rudy, is it? Can you get this tape undone, Rudy?"

Carl calls, "Rudy? Rudy, where are—oh, shit."

"C'mon, Rudy," I say. "The tape."

But Rudy keeps flapping and hooting.

I whistle sharply as if hailing a cab, saying, "Yo, Rudy, over here, buddy."

Rudy's father comes barreling down the stairs, striding over to his son. Carl, like his son, doesn't even look at me. He places his hand comfortingly on the boy's shoulder, leading him toward the stairs, the guy telling his son, like he is Ward-fucking-Cleaver, "It's mowing time, buddy. We always mow the lawn when you visit. Come back outside and leave Daddy's friend alone."

I call, "C'mon, Rudy, undo the tape, won't you? You

can do it."

Never looking back toward me, the two go back up the stairs.

I call after them, "Rudy? Rudy? Oh, no, please don't go, Rudy. Hey, Rudy, do me a favor and smack your dad in the nuts for me. Can you do that? Yo, Rudy—"

But they disappear into the kitchen, the basement door shutting behind them.

3

I slam the microwave door shut harder than I intended, startling myself.

I've been a little on edge lately.

A *little* on edge? I have become a rabbit in the gaze of a perpetual predator. Why wouldn't I be on edge?

You have a fucking girl tied up in your basement, a voice yells inside my head. This time it is my own voice. Not Mandy's. Not the girl's. Mine.

Even I'm yelling at me now.

The hot dogs I've been heating up are too hot, but Rudy is reaching for them, making me have to dance them above his head.

"No, Rudy. Hot."

Rudy jumps for them.

"They're hot, Rudy."

He continues to jump and begins to hoot.

"Rudy, not yet, they're hot."

He continues his jumping and hooting.

"No, Rudy, they…ah, whatever."

I give Rudy the plate.

Sighing and leaning against the kitchen counter, I see faces leap across my mind's eye like a broken strip of film stuttering past the projection bulb. I see Mandy's glare, her goddamn lawyer's smirk, the girls at the magazine rack laying their disapproving scowls on me, the leers of those pricks in the station break room, even the bitch who'd backed into my path earlier in the afternoon. And to top it all off, the girl downstairs and her expression of shock when I'd caught her stealing *my* things.

Part of me wants to run away from it all. Just pack my shit up into a box and hit the road. Simply drive off into a new life.

Until, of course, they find the girl in the basement and put out an APB for me.

Rudy bites into the hot dog and immediately begins yelping and then groaning in his hooting way. I hustle the plate to the sink, running cold water over the dogs. While the water rushes over them, I look over my shoulder at the boy. He has a tube of lipstick in his hands, watching the way the tip climbs in and out of its plastic base.

"What the hell?" I say in a breathy groan. I shut off the water and, before I can ask where he'd gotten the lipstick, I spot the purse in the corner of the room. The girl's personal contents are spilled out on the floor.

I eye the objects—wondering why I hadn't seen any of these things when going through the purse earlier; they must have been in an inside pocket I hadn't bothered to open—then look up at Rudy. A smear of lipstick rings his lips in a scarlet goatee.

If only Mandy could see us now.

Despite my desire to clean up the items from the purse, and the nagging to do so in my own head, I ignore it for now. *Fuck it. Leave it*, I tell myself.

"Come on, buddy, let's eat." I place the plate of hot dogs in front of Rudy.

As Rudy eats and plays with the tube of lipstick—the

boy exchanging one phallic object for the other, part of me wondering if he'll accidently bite the wrong one—I dart my eyes to the bag and its spilled contents. *I'm not cleaning that up*, I think.

I say to Rudy, "C'mon, buddy, clean that up—I mean, eat that up."

Rudy stares at me a moment and then continues his eating.

"Screw it," I say, striding to the bag. It isn't only my desire to clean up the mess that spurs me to it. There is the curiosity.

Among the items, I find a miniature pencil sharpener, half a dozen sticks of eyeliner. A pack of gum. A strip of condoms. "Guess she does put out for someone, at least," I say.

Rudy stops eating and looks at me, as if to respond, but then he returns to his lipstick inspection and eats his hotdog.

As if on cue, the girl begins calling from the basement. "Carl. Oh, Carl."

I scoop the items back into the purse and shove it into the cabinet beneath the sink. I let out a loud sigh.

I grab the lipstick from Rudy, shoving it into my pocket and, pointing at the hot dogs, I tell the boy, "C'mon, eat up."

Rudy looks at me as if to say, *I have been eating up, dumbass*, but he doesn't actually say anything.

The girl continues calling, "Carl. Oh, Carl."

I open the basement door and call down the steps, "What?"

"Carl? Oh, Carl?"

"What do you want?"

"Carl, I'm thirsty. I'm really, really thirsty."

"I already gave you some water earlier. That was

plenty.”

"It wasn't enough, Carl. I'm still really thirsty."

"Yeah? So what? I told you, the less liquid the better. Maybe you won't pee all over my stuff again."

"C'mon, Carl, don't be that way. My throat is so—" She adds a hacking cough and then continues, "—dry. I can barely…swallow." She punctuates this with another hacking cough.

"Good. Maybe you'll actually shut up."

"Carl, you're not being much of a host. Are you going to give me a fucking drink, or what?"

I cringe when she drops the F-bomb. That's all I need is for Rudy to return to Mandy with a fresh vocabulary. It's not like he says much as it is, but when he develops an affinity for a new word, he is like a pubescent boy who's just discovered his pecker.

"If you're going to be that way about it, then no," I tell her, shutting the basement door, feeling rather pleased with myself.

The girl employs her teakettle scream again. "Caaaaarrrrrrl."

Sitting at the kitchen table, Rudy covers his ears and begins moaning.

I open the door, the scream becoming louder, and call down the steps, "All right, all right. Hey. Shut up. Hold on."

The screaming stops.

"I'll get you a drink."

"Thank you, Carl," she calls sweetly.

I shut the door to temporarily divide my worlds. I don't want her getting her talons into Rudy. Exposure to her verbal bullshit can't be good for anyone, even the nonverbal. I start toward the kitchen sink and stop short when I see my son. It is too late to avoid the exposure entirely, and I can see Rudy's mind cranking behind the blue lenses of his eyes. Does the boy wonder if she is his father's girlfriend? A playmate? Live-in maid? A cattle rustler and I'm the posse waiting for the sheriff? Does he wonder anything at all?

We regard one another for a moment, and then Rudy hoots and bounces in his chair. I suddenly realize I've been glaring at the boy. I often catch myself glaring at him with jaw locked in an awkward position, molars grinding together, tongue pressed against the roof of my mouth. I know, of course, that the kid can't help the way he is, but my tolerance can only go so far, and it tends to reach its limit more quickly each time we are together. But I suppose it would be that way with any kid, or any person, for that matter.

You hit your limit with that girl almost immediately.
She fucking robbed me.
Still, pretty extreme knocking her out. Kidnapping her.
Kidnapping. It is the first time the word is brought to mind. I've kidnapped someone.

I didn't kidnap her. She robbed me. *I'm* the fucking victim. I need to teach her a lesson.
She ain't getting that lesson.
She will. Or else—
Or else what?
Rudy is jumping and hooting.
"Don't you start, too," I say to the boy.
You going to tie him up, too. Maybe dig a hole for him?
"I would never hurt Rudy," I snap. I only realize I said it out loud when Rudy stops his hooting.

Rudy looks at me, his eyes full of understanding, but unable to voice that awareness. It is the look of someone observing the world from beyond a pane of glass. One summer, when Rudy was about six, I took him to the

Franklin Park Zoo. Rudy and one of the gorillas had engaged in a stare down. At the time, the surrounding zoo-goers had thought it cute, a few obnoxious tourist-types even snapping pictures of him. They'd gushed, "oooh" and "aaah," sounding like the fucking monkeys down the hall, fawning all over this cute kid and a 300-pound ape locked in a staring contest. But their smiles melted away after a few minutes when it was apparent Rudy was incapable of breaking from the trance-like state on his own. When I finally intervened, the tourists began shuffling away uncomfortably. Even the gorilla began to look confused and uncomfortable. I remember wishing at the time that I could release that gorilla from its captivity.

Turns out the thing did break free from its cage a year or so ago, leading authorities on a two-hour hard-target search. It was splashed all over the news, the thing sitting at a bus stop at one point, casually waiting for his ride. I wonder if Rudy will ever break free from his own captivity, if only for a fleeting two-hour respite.

I dig the lipstick from my pocket and give it back to him, saying, "Here, stare aimlessly at this for a few hours."

Rudy snatches the lipstick from me, raising and lowering the tip a few times. I take it as a sign of forgiveness, and I head to the sink to fill a glass with water, being fairly certain the water is not enough for the girl's forgiveness.

What did she have to forgive *me* for? She is the whole reason for this mess. The 300-pound gorilla in the room. Only, she broke *into* captivity. Why am I even placating her with this water in the first place?

As water gushes into the glass, my mind is gushing full of all sorts of scenarios. I consider filling the glass with scalding water and throwing it in the bitch's face. Or pissing in the glass as payback for her treatment of my bathroom. Maybe I should lace the water with bleach or some sort of poison to eradicate the problem once and for all.

But I won't do any of that. Instead, I will wait. There has to be a logical way out of this…endeavor. Even though all the logical ways seem to be diminishing rapidly.

After making sure Rudy is pacified with the lipstick, I head down the basement steps with the water held out before me.

The girl says, "Oh, you're a doll, Carl."

Holding the glass before her face, I say, "You want this, or not?"

"Actually, a beer would be nice, Carl. When I was growing up in Minnesota, my mom and aunt would sit on the porch enjoying a nice, cold—"

I shake the glass, spilling a little of the water over its lip. "Hurry up and drink."

"Okay, Carl, thank you." She drinks from the glass.

As she drinks, I say, "By the way, you're from Pittsburgh, remember?"

Choking on the water, she tries to mount an argument.

I take away the glass as she coughs.

She smiles and says seductively, "Carl, let's not argue. Forget the water or the beer; why don't you go get the whiskey, and we can—"

Upstairs, the doorbell rings.

We stare at one another, unsure which one of us is the deer and which is the headlights.

She reacts first, screaming, "Help. Help. I'm in the basement. Help—"

I dart behind her, trying to clasp my hand over her mouth. It's like wrestling an alligator, and she sinks her teeth into my palm.

Grunting, I drop the glass of water and it shatters

against the floor. I lean into the bite for leverage and grab her hair, proposing a wordless deal: if she lets go with her teeth, I'll let go of her hair.

There is a trickle of blood creeping from her teeth, tiny rivulets running onto my wrist. *I should have poisoned the bitch while I had the chance*, I think, releasing her hair and taking the bayonet from my back pocket and placing it against her throat.

The doorbell rings again.

I whisper in her ear, "Not a word. Got me?"

She nods, and her teeth go slack.

The blade stays where it is.

The doorbell rings again.

I return the blade to my back pocket, and, without removing my hand from her mouth, I slip off my work shirt to the wrist. I then gag her with it before she can scream again, securing the gag and stepping away to test its effectiveness. In the ensuing silence, I think, *why didn't I gag her to begin with?*

I don't really have an answer for that. I just never thought to do it. Or did part of me not want to do it?

From the workbench along the far wall, I grab a rag and wrap my hand. The doorbell rings again.

Go the fuck away. Ever hear of someone not being home?

What if Rudy answers the door? What if it is the police? Or one of the girl's friends coming to look for her. Some muscle-bound douchebag boyfriend about to smash through the door? Would he hurt Rudy? Would the police accidentally shoot Rudy?

If whoever is knocking heard her scream, and no one answers the door, it will raise suspicion. I *have* to answer it.

I can handle this. And for some reason, my eighth

grade English class springs to mind. Remembering the time we'd read the story "The Tell-Tale Heart." The guy in that story invites the police into his house after burying a body under the floor. I could invite them in if I want. After all, I am in control.

The guy in "The Tell-Tale Heart" gets caught.

Only because he loses control. He loses focus.

This is how I can take back control. Show this bitch *I* am the one calling the shots. I can come back down and say, *Cops were here. Too bad they won't be back.* I *took care of them.*

With a renewed sense of confidence, I say to her, "Remember, not a sound."

After checking my hand and smoothing the tee shirt I've been wearing under my work shirt, I start up the basement stairs. The bayonet slips from my pocket and bounces down the steps and slides toward the girl, its tip pointing at her like the spinner of a child's game. I start back down the steps, but another ring of the doorbell brings groans from Rudy.

Fuck it. Her last attempts at cutting her binds proved so catastrophically futile, bitch can have a chainsaw for all I care.

And I run up the steps.

4

At the top of the stairs, I spot Rudy staring accusingly at me, the lipstick held before him with its tip peeking from the cylinder.

"Sit tight, buddy," I say to him and trot to the front door. By the time I whip open the door, my heart is creating a visible pulsing imprint against my thin cotton tee shirt. I mop away the sweat trails on my forehead with the back of my hand.

A girl of about nineteen or twenty is starting back down the stoop. When the door opens, she whirls around, clasping her hand over her heart, saying, "Oh, you scared me."

I catch my breath. "Yeah, sorry. I was out back. Didn't hear you at first. My son called to me and said you were ringing the doorbell."

This statement gives me pause. For a moment, I am living in a reality where my son is normal. Where I lead a normal life. Where I am a father and a responsible homeowner, and not a kidnapper and potential murderer.

The girl is small, athletic, her blond hair in a runner's ponytail. She wears soccer shorts and a Salem State sweatshirt. I size her up almost immediately, and I want to say to her, *I heard the bell each of the dozen times you rang it, you stupid little girl. No matter what your overly zealous teacher or leftie college professor might have told you, persistence is really not something to be admired in every context.*

The girl says, "I was a little nervous. I thought I heard screaming."

I stand quiet a moment, assessing the situation. Wondering, *Well, why didn't you run then? Professor didn't teach you that one in How Not To Be a Dumbass 101?*

I say, "Probably neighborhood kids. They sometimes play in the woods out back. What can I do for you?" The lie came so easily off the tongue, there was a surge of dopamine just from uttering it. A thrill to the concept of having a foot in two different realities.

The girl starts back up the stoop.

I cock my head, almost saying, *What are you doing? Didn't you just say you thought you heard screaming? Are you insane?* But I don't say a word.

She brandishes pamphlets and has already launched into a rehearsed pitch. "Well, sir, this is your lucky day. I have come to offer you the opportunity to save, not only energy and money, but also the very future of the human race. May I take a moment of your time to tell you about it?"

I regard the girl for a moment and say, "You mean, you want to come *in* my *house* right now?"

I didn't intend to emphasize the words *in* and *house*, but still, I had.

"If you don't mind, sir. Could be the most important decision of your life."

Again I consider the situation, Poe's story popping into my head, and I smile and for some reason say, "Okay. Why not? Come on in."

I hold the door open and the girl walks past me and into the living room. As she passes, I catch a whiff of the same cheap floral perfume the girls in the bookstore had been wearing. I shake my head unbelievingly and say, "Have a seat." My voice tinged with baffled amusement.

The girl sits on the couch, and I shut the door. The click of the door's catch seems loud in the quiet room. As I stand, looking at the girl, a strange smile creeps onto my face. I fight it back. I feel giddy and not sure why. Probably because here is this girl sitting casually in my living room, while *another* girl is tied up in my basement.

More dopamine floods my system. Is this the rush criminals and adrenaline junkies get?

I am suddenly gripped by a vision: this chick and the one in the basement dressed in red Dr. Seuss jumpers with the words *Stupid Girl 1* and *Stupid Girl 2* emblazoned across their chests.

Now *this* is a story to tell at the Dutch Horse Pub. I imagine myself sitting at the bar, surrounded by the bartender, and the fishermen, and the old guy that always sits in the corner. I tell them, *As soon as* Idol *is over, I'll tell you a* real *fucking story.*

Or maybe it could be a funny story to tell a girl on a first date…?

No, probably not.

I almost burst out laughing, but I stifle it, saying, "So, go ahead. What is this"—I wave my hands—"big emergency?"

The girl flicks her eyes around the living room a moment and then launches into her rehearsed speech, saying, "Well, sir, every year an exorbitant amount of greenhouse gases are released into the air by—"

I interrupt her in my almost giddy tone, "So, wait, before you start. I have a question, if you don't mind."

"Yes, sir?"

"Does anyone know you're here?"

All expression falls from the girl's face. I catch the sudden trepidation in her eyes, and my giddiness fades, my brain scrambling back to eighth grade, trying to remember how the guy in Poe's story had screwed up.

Poe's guy heard the tell-tale heartbeat, dumbass, the girl in the basement—Stupid Girl 1's—voice says in my mind.

Well this young girl here ain't gonna hear dick, because I got you gagged, my inner voice retorts.

The giddiness returns.

Not giddiness, Stupid Girl 1's voice says. *Smugness. And that's how Poe's character got nabbed.*

Well I'm not Poe's character.

I say to Stupid Girl 2, "I'm just asking if it's wise for a young, attractive girl to be so eager to waltz into some stranger's house. I mean, what if I were some kind of deranged murderer?"

The girl's foot starts tapping on the carpet like she's

fucking Thumper, her wide eyes even look like the eyes of the Disney character. She is clearly nervous now, but she seems unsure of what to do.

She is unsure what to do? What the hell am *I* doing? I've gone too far. I just told this girl I'm a deranged murderer.

Now, when they find Stupid Girl 1 buried in a shallow grave, this girl says, *Hey, I met this guy that told me he was a murderer. He lives right* here, *officers.*

All traces of giddiness are gone now.

Am I really going to kill the girl downstairs?

I'm going to have this argument of conscience now?

And do I now have to kill *this* girl, too?

"Shit," I say under my breath. I look at the young, college girl. She is sitting ramrod straight on the couch, eyes wide, and I can't even tell if she is breathing or not. She's fucking scared. I need to fix this.

I smile, trying to look harmless, but her expression still suggests a different version of the face I am trying to project.

"Don't be nervous. I'm no murder…" my voice trails off, my eyes wandering in the direction of the basement door. I then look at her, forcing my slack expression into a painfully faux smile, the moment in a job interview where one tries to shrug off an awkward moment with feigned, unprompted confidence. But this will be a tough fix. The girl's face is a broadcast of terror.

<h1 style="text-align:center">5</h1>

I can hear footsteps upstairs. More than one person. More than just Carl. Carl and Rudy? Or is someone else in the house? The possibility of a hired executioner again surfaces in my mind.

But Carl was genuinely shocked when the doorbell rang.

Can it be cops? Carl's wife? Anyone with the conscience and capability to help me?

I need to get this gag out. I try to bite it and move my head to maneuver it off my mouth, but it's on there pretty good. Removing it in that manner will most likely be as tedious and pointless as chewing through duct tape.

The bayonet is not far from me. But with my hands and ankles bound as they are, and after my failed attempt with the pruning shears, it might as well be miles from my grasp.

The bayonet, however, will not require any mechanical manipulation like the shears. I just need to stabilize the blade enough to cut the zip ties and the tape. I think I can do it with one hand. Get the gag out of my mouth. And call for help.

I can do it, I think as I reemploy my bunny hopping skills.

6

I continue to force my smile, trying to ease the fear from the girl's face.

It isn't working. She looks like that chipmunk watching as tires bear down.

Why did I allow the situation to snowball like this? Why did I invite her into this house? What was I even trying to prove? That I'm not someone for women to fear? Or that I am?

I think you're merely proving you're a dick. And a pretty foolish one at that. It was the voice of Stupid Girl 1, sounding so very much like Mandy.

I should tell Stupid Girl 2 she'd have better luck peddling her tree-hugger paraphernalia someplace where the apathy doesn't run so deep and the hopelessness isn't leashed with such permanence. Or maybe that is too harsh.

Just tell her you're not interested, dipshit. Send her on her way.

But it is too late. I *can't* do that now. She thinks I'm a murderer.

You are a murderer, aren't you?

I suddenly find myself saying out loud, "I mean…do I look like a murderer?"

The girl squeaks, "No."

"Okay," I say, taking the moment to contemplate the girl's response. I shake my head, as if to clear it and say, "So, you came here to talk about global warming. Is that right?"

The girl nods.

7

Each scraping bunny hop seems incredibly loud, though I know it probably only registers as white noise to anyone upstairs. But I'm almost there. And when I get the gag out of my mouth, I'll scream so loud that there will definitely be no mistaking it as white noise.

I am now close enough to see the scars of battle gleaming on the blade's polished steel.

Almost there. Almost free.

8

I suddenly want this young college girl gone. Not just from my house, but from existence.

That sounds an awful lot like something a murderer would say, Carl.

No. Not her, specifically. Those like her.

That's exactly what you said about me. How many girls do you want to kill, here? Is mass murder your thing now, Carl? You gonna be a serial killer?

No. I mean I want to kill her naiveté, her stupid compulsion to fix what can not be fixed.

I say to the young girl in my living room, "So let me guess, you're going to tell me how the polar caps are crackling like ice in scotch, Manhattan will be underwater within the next forty years, and the polar bears are dying off because their weenies are shrinking. Is that about right?" I don't even pause, never mind give her time to respond. I continue, saying, "I feel like I'm smothered by this bullshit every time I turn around. From companies who promise sin-no-more with wasteful packaging to the celebrity and political-hack profiteers like Al Gore trying to sell it like a religion." I scrutinize the brochures in my hand. "My question is, do you have anything to really offer me? Anything more than brochures telling me to turn off lights when I'm not in a room, or buy a hybrid car? Because it's actual answers I need. Do you have any real answers for me?"

9

The blade is beside me now—well, beside the chair at least. I can just about touch it with my toe, making it about a mere 27 inches from my hand—give or take. My *bound* hand. I need to somehow either get my hand to the bayonet or the bayonet to my hand. And seeing as I've already established a lack of telekinesis, I need to rely on the former.

I again begin rocking my chair as I'd done the day before.

Only, this time, toppling over *is* the intent.

10

The girl is visibly trembling now, but I can't stop talking. It is just pouring from me as if I am a medium channeling some asshole.

Just channeling your inner self, Carl.

I don't even take the time to register Stupid Girl 1's voice in my head; I just keep spewing out the ugly vitriol within me.

It's called verbal diarrhea, Carl. And it is one of your most persistent character traits.

"Anything in that brochure about the fact that nothing will ever change? Anything in it about how there's just too much money tied up in big business for anyone to do a damn thing? I mean, we're in the middle of an energy crisis, and what do the car companies do? Do you know?"

She opens her mouth as if to answer, but shuts it quickly when nothing comes out. It doesn't matter because I wasn't going to let her answer anyway.

"They bring back the fucking muscle car. Does the world really need a new Mustang? Not to mention the SUVs and Hummers, and who knows what else. Car companies have somehow convinced the common shmuck that a six-hundred horsepower gas-guzzler is a good idea even though gas prices are higher than ever and the air is shit. And we're supposed to pin our hopes on a young, peppy girl, without the fucking brains to not walk into a stranger's house, even after claiming to hear someone screaming?"

The girl's gaze has wandered down to the fresh blood trickling along the edge of my hand.

She makes an audible, high-pitched groan.

11

Whoever came knocking, this chair is a-rocking.

Forward.

Backward.

Forward.

Backward.

Biting against the gag, I scream an inaudible, muffled, "C'mon…."

Forward.

Backward…backward…and backward; I'm falling.

"C'mon, you son of a—"

12

I say, "I mean, for all you know I could have someone tied up in the basement right now. Did you even think of that before you came in here?"

A loud crash erupts from the basement.

My attention snaps toward the basement door, and I freeze, looking like a hunting dog on point.

The sound was so shockingly loud that it sounded like the whole house was falling down, but I quickly realize it's my guest in the basement having probably decided to make another attempt at chair-locomotion, and she'd toppled to the floor.

Good, I think, imagining her lying there with her shattered cheek pressed to the concrete, maybe her arm is splintered beneath the twisted wreckage of the chair, a spoke of bone poking out through the skin beneath her blackening elbow. Or maybe she'd impaled herself with the bayonet she'd been most likely trying to retrieve. This fantasy elates me, but then the panic rushes through me.

If she is hurt, I'll have to take her to the hospital.

Why would I bring someone I intend to kill to the hospital?

Because you have no intention of killing me, that's why.

Yes I do. I'll make you pay, you thieving bitch.

Even if she is hurt, it doesn't matter, I can avoid the hospital. I have plenty of first aid skills and supplies. There was a time I intended to be a paramedic, back when I still seemed to have a future, still had aspirations. I'd gone through most of the EMT training, but then…well, then shit went sour.

I hear a ticking rise up in the room. A muffled sound *like a watch enveloped in cotton.*

It isn't so much that I hear it. I *feel* it. My own heartbeat. There is seemingly nothing else in the room, just the ticking of my heart, and the heavy gulping breaths of the young girl standing beside the couch. She now looks more than ever like the chipmunk in the middle of the road. Her eyes staring dumbly at me.

Rudy runs into the living room, hooting and waving his hands. The lipstick smeared all over his face looks like a cheap blood effect in a B vampire movie.

The girl's response is no longer a high-pitched groan. It is the heavy, deep moan of a pipe organ. She looks as if she is about to vomit her vegan lunch all over my coffee table. I follow her glassy gaze to my son.

The situation that has been spinning so profoundly out of control has somehow become grounded.

I say, "Sorry. That's my son Rudy. He's autistic."

The girl says, "That's nice." Not seeming to realize what she is saying. "Is that...paint on his face?"

My shoulders, which had been tensed up around my jawline, now relax. My voice does the same. "Lipstick," I say. "He must have gotten into his mother's lipstick." This time, the fantasy of a normal family life brings no rush of dopamine. "Look, you hit a nerve with this global warming thing. Maybe I'll help you out after all. Just leave the brochure, if you don't mind."

I lead Rudy into the kitchen, never turning to see the girl race from the house, she not bothering to shut the door behind her.

13

In the kitchen, I hand Rudy an empty glass. The boy stares at the light refracting from it as I clean lipstick from his face. Even though I can't tell if my son is upset or not, I say, "It's okay, buddy."

Maybe it isn't the boy I am trying to comfort. *It's okay* has become the lie of my life.

It's okay that my marriage is a failed experiment.

It's okay that I've sacrificed my dignity for so many years.

It's okay that my legacy can't communicate a complete sentence to the world.

When I finish cleaning my son's face, leaving Rudy at the table to watch the light refractions, I head toward the basement. For a moment, I am struck with the thought of having two girls tied up down there. Stupid Girl 1 *and* Stupid Girl 2. They could tag-team nag me. *Carl, I need this. Carl, I need that. I need the bathroom. I need a glass of water. I need clean oceans.*

I shake away the thought and open the door, descending the steps by twos.

Stupid Girl 1 is toppled over in the chair, somehow on her side—I'm not sure how she managed that without breaking something—still struggling to get the bayonet. I hunch down and pick it up—the blade catching a glint of light as I swivel it back and forth for a few seconds like a kid who'd found a new toy. I press my finger against its tip and, for the first time since coming into possession of the thing, wondered just how much pressure would be needed to make it hurt, to draw blood, to kill.

I stand up, saying, "Shitty time to ask for water. If I hadn't been down here when that girl rang the doorbell, I never would've been able to shut you up in time."

I look at the broken glass on the floor, needing to clean it up.

Fuck it, I don't need to clean it up.

I turn and walk up the basement steps, leaving her on the floor, still tied to the chair and still with the shirt gagging her mouth. She screams against the gag, but I leave it, not bothering to clean up that mess either. I close the door to muffle her cries.

14

I'm standing on the *American Idol* stage, singing "Measure of a Man." The veins in my neck are bulging as my voice captures the true emotional essence of the song. The bright flares of the stage lights hide the faces of countless girls screaming and swooning in the crowd. Near the end of the song, the house lights brighten enough to notice a few homemade signs bobbing on the surf of screaming fans. *Cali for Carl!* reads one. Another proclaiming, *Carl White is my Knight!*

I feel the surge of a hard-on fighting against the crotch of my leather pants, and I hope the television cameras don't pick it up, or that the audience notices it. Or maybe I hope they do. When I finish the climactic note, I drop my raised hand with a dramatic flourish. The crowd is spastic. I take an exaggerated bow before Ryan Seacrest joins me on stage. I hold the microphone down to conceal the hard-on. Together, Ryan and I look down at Randy Jackson, who tries to quiet the crowd.

"Okay, okay," Randy says, bobbing his head. "All right, dog. Well that was fantastic, dog. You nailed it, dog."

The crowd goes wild.

Randy says, "It was better than Clay, yo. If that is even possible. But I guess we found it possible, huh? Bravo, dog."

The crowd goes wild again.

Seacrest then turns to Paula. "And what did you think, Ms. Abdul?"

"Well, I gotta tell you, Carl," Paula says. "I can't disagree more with Randy."

The smile drops from my face.

Paula continues, "I can't decide if your stage presence is like a man impotent, or that of an outright dickless eunuch. Tell you what, go grow some balls, and then come back and give that song a shot."

The crowd's cheers are now louder than before as my pecker shrivels, and I wonder if any of the girls in the audience will still want to screw now that Paula has gelded me.

Seacrest says, "Holy shit. I can't wait to see what Simon has to say."

Simon Cowell looks me dead in the eyes, as if about to say something profound, and when he opens his mouth, he issues a droning hooting.

I sit upright in my bed. Rudy is standing beside me, droning and brandishing the bayonet.

"What the fuck?" I howl, startling both my son and myself.

I snatch the bayonet from Rudy's hand, unable to focus my thoughts for a moment. Rudy continues to make his noises. Then panic sets in. Like a fast-acting fever. And I run to the basement door, throwing it open and scrambling down the steps.

In the basement, the girl is still tied to, and toppled over in, the chair in the middle of the room. Still gagged, as well. I can smell the acidic tang of urine and can see a drying puddle around her hip. She looks up at me in her usual disgusted manner.

I right the chair and remove her gag.

"Back to kill me, Carl? Still can't do it, I bet? Why don't you grow a nutsack and—"

I gag her, turn, and walk up the steps, shutting the basement door behind me.

15

"Rudy, sit still," Carl's voice says to me.

I am sitting in a booth. The smells of cooking grease and meat, the starchy stench of French fries, and the sounds of people are overwhelming. But I love the grease and the starch and the explosions of taste.

Explosions of taste. Explosions of taste. Explosions of taste.

Grease melting in my mouth and pooling and going down into my belly. And the taste of the sugary soda.

Sugary soda. Sugary soda. Sugary soda.

The food is then before me. The burger out of its wrapper. Fries pouring out on the open wrapper. Soda with a straw piercing the plastic cover.

Piercing the plastic. Piercing the plastic. Piercing the plastic.

My hands are under the table, nestled between my knees, and I pat my hands together in the ASL sign for hamburger. No one sees me doing this, and even if they did, they probably wouldn't understand it anyway. My new teachers would just call it a *stim*. My old teacher, Ms. Parker, taught me several signs a while ago. But no one has taught me a sign for some time. After signing hamburger three times, I bring my hands from under the table to begin my meal.

I take the straw from the soda's pierced plastic lid.

Pierced plastic. Pierced plastic. Pierced plastic.

And I sip the soda that spills from a hole in the plastic. The hole shaped like an X.

An X-hole.

X-hole. X-hole. X-hole.

The cup is taken from me, and Carl's voice says, "No, buddy, you need the straw to drink."

The straw pierces the plastic with a loud squeal.

Pierced plastic. Pierced plastic. Pierced plastic.

Through the X-hole. X-hole. X-hole.

I try to say X-hole, but it comes out like a braying burrow.

Braying burrow. Braying burrow. Braying burrow.

The cup is before me again. I remove the straw from the lid and suck at the soda spilling from the hole.

Soda spilling. Soda spilling. Soda spilling from the X-hole.

Carl says, "No, Rudy. Not like that. You need the straw."

The cup goes away. It squeals and returns with the straw in the X-hole again.

I remove the straw.

The cup is taken. Squeal. The cup returns with the straw.

I remove the straw.

The cup is taken. Squeal. The cup returns with the straw.

I remove the straw.

The cup is taken. Squeal. The cup returns with the straw. Carl saying, "Jesus Christ, no, Rudy, use the straw."

I try to tell him that I want to drink the soda through the X-hole. But my words come out braying again.

Braying. Bray-ing. Br-rrr-ay-ing.

Carl says, "Fine, do it the hard way," dropping the straw on the table.

Carl is being an X-hole.

I begin laughing hysterically, droplets of soda spraying from my mouth.

Soda spraying. Soda spraying. Soda spraying.

After a moment, Carl's voice is saying, "He's autistic."

To the right of us is a table with two young children sitting at it. And an old woman. They stare at me as if I were on television. I often feel as if I'm looking out from inside a television set.

The woman says, "Oh, isn't that nice."

Carl says, "No, not artistic—" He stops, even though it seems like he is going to say more.

Other people at other tables stare at us as if we both are on the television now.

Artistic. Autistic. Artistic. Autistic. Artistic. Autistic.

I sip from the X-hole and laugh again.

Carl says, "C'mon, Rudy, eat your burger. Starving children in China, and all that."

Chinese children. Chinese children. Chinese children.

Carl nudges the burger toward me. Carl saying, "C'mon, eat up."

I stop slurping the X-hole and take a bite of the burger. *A burger bite. Burger bite. Burger bite with its explosion of taste.*

Carl says, "Do you know how they make hamburgers?"

I take a burger bite with another explosion of taste.

Carl says, "They feed cows all kinds of crazy stuff to fatten them up. Then when they're real fat, they put them on a big conveyer belt. And when the cows come to the end of the conveyer belt, they drop off the edge, breaking their legs because they didn't even see the drop coming. And even if they did see it…well, they're just overweight cows, what are they going to be able to do about it?"

The picture is suddenly in my mind. A picture of an overweight cow.

Overweight cow. Over, weight cow. It's over, wait, cow.

I say, "Wait. Cow." The words coming out very loudly from my mouth.

Carl says, "Not like the cows can put on the brakes and jump off the conveyer belt and make a run for it."

I like this picture in my head even more. An overweight cow jumping for it. An overweight cow jumping over the moon. I say, "Cow. Moooon." Again, my voice louder than I intended.

Carl says, "Yeah, cow, moo."

Moo is not what I said, so I correct him, saying, "Mooooon."

Correct Carl. Correct Carl. Correct Carl.

"Moo, right," Carl says.

"Mooooon."

"Okay, enough with the mooing. Anyway, in some

cases, cattle farmers feed the parts of dead cows to the live cows to cut down on the cost of feed. Recycling in action, you might say."

Cows eating parts of dead cows causes me to no longer want my burger, and I push it away from me. I sip at the X-hole.

Carl says, "After a while of going all cannibalistic, the cows begin acting crazy."

Crazy cannibalistic cows. Crazy cannibalistic cows. Crazy cannibalistic cows.

"Turns out, an enzyme that's produced through cannibalism is eating away at their brains. This enzyme can't be destroyed, but still, we eat the beef, even though we can get infected. They call it Mad Cow Disease."

I stare at the soda spilling up through the X-hole. I like the picture in my head of a mad cow.

Mad cow. Mad cow. Mad cow.

I laugh, saying, "Mad cows."

Carl says, "Yeah, mad cows. I guess if they're being fed their relatives, they have a right to be mad. I'd be pissed."

Pissed. Piiiisssed. Piiiisssssssed.

I say, "Pisssssssed."

Carl says, "People are kind of the same way. Cannibalistic. Only they don't feed on flesh. They feed on souls."

Flesh-feeding. Flesh-feeding. Flesh-feeding.

Carl says, "And this cannibalistic soul-feeding can make people a little mad, too."

Soul-feeding. Soul-feeding. Soul-feeding.

I say, "Soul-feeding." But I say it loudly and as if one word, sounding like, *So-fee.*

"Well, the soul-feeding of my life is not something I want you to stay and see."

Stay and see. Stay and see. Stay and see.

"Stay and see," I say, sounding like one word: Stay-see.

Carl cocks his head and stares at me. Carl saying, "What did you say?"

I say, "Stay and see." Coming out sounding like *Stain-in-sea*. Then I say, "Mad too." Liking the way it sounds coming off my lips. Sounding like Maddoo.

Carl chuckles, and says, "Ah, Stay-see, right. Stay and see. Stacey. Sounds about right. Imagine, the only people I can talk to in my life are you, who can't talk back, and Stacey, the soul-feeding leach of a girl tied up in my basement."

I suddenly see a picture I don't like in my mind. The girl tied up in the basement.

Girl in basement. Girl in basement. Girl in basement. Girl in basement. Girl in basement. The picture fills me up. The image of the girl in the basement. And I say, "Girl in basement." Saying it very loudly. And very clearly. I say it again, "Girl in basement." And again, "Girl in basement."

Carl pushes the burger in front of me. Carl saying, "Okay, pal, why don't you finish up your burger, here."

Girl in basement. Girl in basement. Girl in basement. Girl in basement. Girl in basement.

Very loudly, "Girl in basement."

The burger and the fries and the soda cup are all scooped up into a pile in the middle of the table. Carl saying, "Okay, Rudy, I think it's time to go home."

"Girl in basement. Girl in basement. Girl in basement."

Carl pulls me from the booth. Carl saying, "Let's go, buddy." Carl's hand on my arm pokes me sharply.

"Girl in basement," I shout. My voice very clear.

The people at the other table, the little girl and little boy, the old woman, are watching me and Carl from outside the television set. In fact, everyone is watching us.

Carl leaves the trash on the table and turns to the old woman at the table beside us. Carl chuckling, saying, "Never should have let him watch *Silence of the Lambs* last night."

The woman nods. She is looking at him as if he were speaking another language.

"Girl in basement. Girl in basement. Girl in basement," I shout.

Carl's fingers wrap around my arm and squeeze. It hurts. Carl pulls me from the restaurant as I keep shouting, "The girl is in the basement."

16

I pull the car out of the McDonalds' parking lot. Rudy is sitting in the passenger seat, rocking and moaning.

"Rudy. Quiet."

He continues moaning.

"Rudy, I said quiet."

He keeps moaning.

I turn on the radio. LMC's "Take Me to the Clouds Above" fills the car and I feel much more at ease.

Rudy looks at me.

The two of us staring at each other.

Rudy changes the radio station, a Led Zeppelin song blasting into the car.

I switch the radio back to the pop station.

Rudy presses the button again, bringing forth "Kashmir."

I switch it back to LMC.

Rudy presses another button, this time landing on NPR.

"For Christ's sake, Rudy, can't we listen to something

worthwhile?" I say, switching back to the pop station, catching the beginning of Maroon 5's "This Love." I begin singing along with it, returning my attention to the road, but the little bugger reaches for the button again. I shoo his hand away. "No, Rudy, this is my radio."

Rudy begins hooting as my cell phone rings.

I dig for the phone in my pocket, telling Rudy to, "knock it off," then, managing to flip open the phone with one hand, I say into it, "Yeah?"

"Carl. It's Walters."

Even on my day off this asshole has to find a way to worsen an already bad situation.

"Yes, sir?"

"Want to tell me about the girl?"

I swerve the car, nearly dropping the phone. A guy in the oncoming lane wails his horn. I wait a moment, breathing heavy, as the inevitable finger emerges from the guy's window.

Rudy hoots and waves back at the guy.

I straighten the car and put the phone to my ear. On numb lips, I choke the words, "What girl?"

"Goddamn it, Carl, what girl do you think?"

Rudy rocks in the passenger seat, murmuring, "Girl in basement. Girl in basement…" as I try to focus on the conversation with Walters. A conversation about *the* girl.

How does he know? Are there cops waiting for me at home now?

"Um…sir?"

Walters barks on the other end of the phone, "The girl with the quarters that you accosted yesterday. Ring any bells?"

My heart is an untying knot, unraveling, flaccid in my stomach. "Oh, yeah, her."

Beside me, Rudy rocks like a metronome and

continues to murmur about the girl in the basement.

"Rudy, quiet."

Rudy's voice grows louder. "Girl in basement. Girl in basement."

Walters says, "What is that?"

I turn to Rudy, saying, "Shut up. Please."

"What did you just say to me?" Walters growls through the phone.

"No, not you. Sorry, sir. It's my son."

Rudy continues his low droning about the girl in the basement. His eyes bulging, fists curling up and down as if using invisible dumbbells.

I stop the car at a red light and hold the phone away from my ear. I want to lower the window and throw the thing, shatter it against the asphalt, erase Walters and his questions. Erase this situation altogether. I can drop Rudy off on Mandy's front lawn and run away to Florida or someplace. I could find work at some Miami beachside resort, doling out bocce sets and inflatable tubes to wealthy assholes from the North. Until someone catches up with me—Child Services, or some such thing— looking for answers as to why I'd left my autistic kid on the curb. Maybe a bounty hunter will net me as a deadbeat for non-payment of child support. Then, eventually, someone will come looking for an explanation for the pile of bones tied to a chair in my basement. I've now entered a phase of my life where the only person who'd ever miss me is someone I've tied up in my basement. And the only reason she'd care is because I am the only one, besides Rudy, who knows she is there. At the moment, she is the only person in the world that actually *needs* me.

But I realize running to Florida is a dumb fantasy. Because there *is* no escape.

I put the phone to my ear while clasping my hand over

a struggling Rudy's mouth.

"Sir?" I say into the phone.

Walters is saying, "You need to get in here and square this away. The girl and her mother are here now."

Rudy continues struggling.

To Rudy, I say, "Stop." Into the phone, I say, "Can't, sir."

Walters says, "What?"

"Can't, sir. I have my son here."

"That's too bad, find a way to get in here."

Rudy squirms free of my grip. He leans over and punches me in the crotch, dead center in my balls.

My eyes cross momentarily, and I choke on an, "Oomph," then, grimacing and grunting, I say into the phone, "Can't come in, sir."

"Well, you're just going to have to find a way."

"And you're just gonna have to find a way to go fuck yourself, sir."

I hang up the phone, dropping it to the car's floor, and I cock my hand as if to strike Rudy.

Rudy cowers.

I spot my face in the rearview mirror, a stranger's eyes catching the mask of anger reflecting back. Those stranger's eyes then soften back to my own, as if I am waking from a dream.

The traffic light turns green, other cars beeping, and the world is closing in around me.

I look at Rudy, who is still cowering, and I say, "I need to get that girl out of my basement."

Rudy looks back at me, and I can only imagine his response, if he could formulate it, would be, "No shit."

"Let's go," I say to him. But I know the damage is done.

17

I'd dozed off again.

My new sleep pattern.

Flashes that last for who knows how long.

Five hours? Five minutes? Five seconds?

Could be any one of them.

I'll fall into bizarre, intense dreams, only to realize, mid-dream, that I'm not flying over New York City, or on a hike with forgotten high school classmates, but that I am, in fact, still tied up in a basement, waking in the chair with duct tape binding my wrists and ankles.

This time, it is the front door's slamming that wakes me. Then I hear the dickhead's heavy footsteps trudging about upstairs. The basement door whips open and the shithead comes down the stairs with a folding, metal TV Dinner table—the kind only owned by grandmothers. He places the table before me, and without a word, turns and goes back up the steps. More trudging about upstairs, and then he comes back down, this time with a small washcloth, a sandwich, and a glass of water balanced on the chess set from his coffee table. He places the chess set, the washcloth, the sandwich, and the glass of water on the TV Dinner table, then steps behind me and removes the gag.

"I'm going to untie one of your hands so you can clean yourself and eat," he says. "I'm only telling you this once, don't do anything stupid, got it?"

"Nice to see you, too, Carl."

"Are we clear?" he says. "Nothing stupid."

"Loud and clear, Carl. But what makes you think I want to play chess right now?"

"What else are you going to do? You have to be bored out of your tits right now. Not to mention hungry."

He produces the bayonet and cuts free my right hand, then moves the TV Dinner table closer to me so the sandwich and water are within reach. The sight of the food makes my stomach grumble audibly, and my thirst is unbearable, but he wants something here, and I can't quite see the angle. My impromptu diagnosis of the situation is that he is lonely and in need of a companion, whether it is a puppy on a leash or a girl bound to a chair, it doesn't matter. But there is more. He's been riding the teetering seesaw of his needs and wants vs. the harsh reality of…well, reality. His need for control against his utter abandonment of all hope for life in general. This is a dangerous moment. He is in the grip of some deep darkness, which could push him either into remorseful shame—leading potentially to my release—or into a spiraling self-loathing rage—in which he'll kill me.

Or, there is still the possibility that I can bark this omega dog into submission and convince him to release me. But any misstep, and I will most likely end up dead.

I take a small sip of water and a dainty, lady-like bite of the sandwich, as if Carl and I were sitting down for tea and finger sandwiches. It is a bologna sandwich with orange Kraft slices, but at the moment, to me, it is prime rib. I want to chug the water as if it is the last beer in a frat party boat race, and I want to stuff the sandwich whole into my mouth a la Belushi in *Animal House*, but I need to stay in control. He can't realize I rely on him so profoundly for survival. He cannot be the master of my fate so entirely.

I take the washcloth, which has been dampened, and I wipe away the dried urine from my hip and leg. I do this with a flair of royalty, refusing to yield an iota of dignity. I then nibble on the sandwich, the stench of the bologna overwhelming.

He places the plate and the glass of water on the floor, out of my reach. I eye the water, wanting more, but I will not let him know this.

The asshole pulls the other chair in the basement's corner over to the TV Dinner table and he sets up the chess pieces on the board. When he's finished setting it up, he says, "White moves first."

"White as in the pieces, or the surname?"

"Don't be difficult. Just move."

"I'm not sure a bologna sandwich is worth a chess game, Carl."

He sighs and says, "Can you take time off from insulting me long enough to make a move?"

There is real sadness in his voice.

I need to be smart about this; there is more than the chess game being played here.

I make my opening move—king's pawn, two spaces forward—saying, "So where's Rudy?"

Carl counters with his own king's pawn, saying, "Brought him home to his mother."

White bishop three spaces. "Visiting time's over?"

His own bishop comes out, nestling in front of his king. He says, "Not exactly. But I couldn't have him around here while I have company."

"Company, huh?" I say, leaning over, stretching to reach the glass of water on the floor. I can't reach it, but Carl hops out of his seat and places the glass in my hand.

An encouraging sign.

"Thanks," I say and sip the water. "So what did the ex—what's her name?"

"Mandy."

"What did Mandy have to say about that?"

"I don't care."

"Sure you do." I take another sip of water and place

the glass on the floor, this time within reach.

"What makes you think I care?"

"I can just tell."

"So you're the expert on Carl White now, huh?"

I don't like the sudden turn in tone this exchange is taking. The conversation has had the potential of being civil, but now a shift. Should I try to shift it back to civility, or bitch-slap him back into his omega position where he belongs? I err on civility, saying, "I like to think that I'm getting to know you pretty well."

That sounded weak on my part, and I knew it as soon as I'd said it—it gives him a seeming upper hand—and he is suddenly emboldened.

"Well you don't know shit about me, or how I feel."

Civility didn't work. I'd struck a nerve. And now he is trying to back me down. Looks like I might need the bitch-slap approach after all.

"Carl, you're easier to read than a parking meter."

"Very funny."

"Seriously. I hope you don't play poker."

"I'm good at poker," he snaps.

"See? Right there. Your tone. The way you emphasized your poker prowess tells me it's a lie." I bring the queen out, saying to him, "I'd say you've been cleaned out more than a few times in poker games. Maybe with your meter maid biddies?"

He shoots me a glare.

"No," I say. "The cops. You've played with the actual cops."

Another nerve. C'mon Omega Dog, bow-wow down to your master. I've found my angle, and I jump on it.

"You play with them often?" I ask. "No wonder your car sucks. You lose your other one in a high stakes game?"

"Did you ever think that maybe I don't have a nice car

because I don't have any money because I have a blood-sucking wife and a son with special needs?"

Oh, some honesty, and vulnerability. What to do? Therapeutic or domineering?

Let's shift back to therapeutic; see where it goes. Maybe I can get him weeping and reexamining the mistakes he's made in life. You know, like marrying the wrong woman, sticking with the wrong job, tying up a girl in his fucking basement.

Carl is regarding the chessboard again, contemplating his next move. He says, "Doesn't matter. Poker's a game of luck. Anything can happen. Cards just don't fall my way all the time."

Realizing he isn't talking about poker, I say, "Life's not a card game, Carl."

He shoots me a look, as if I'd read his mind.

I say, "You can't rely on the cards falling your way. Life is more of a chess match than a card game. You've got to make the right moves." I motion toward my queen, wondering if he'll get his head out of his ass and see it, so we can move this game along, laying the foundation for a conversation about life and choices—me being the therapist working him through his life's problems, he being so grateful he will unbind me from a fucking chair.

But the dipshit moves his queen's knight forward on the board, saying, "Making right moves?" He chuckles, saying, "Making right moves, huh? This from the girl tied up in my basement? Unbelievable," he says, shaking his head. "You can be such a cunt."

And so much for the therapy session.

I'm trying to breathe and stay calm. Trying desperately to remember everything I'd learned about breathing from yoga, the Ujjayi Pranayama and all that other shit, but it's too late. Something within me is surging. It grips me from the inside out.

This asshole and his smug, entitled, woe-is-me attitude. He has a young woman tied in a fucking chair, and he is going to lecture *me* on choices? And did he really just call me a *cunt?*

A rush of adrenalin, a feeling of total empowerment rushes through my appendages, like fiery, liquid metal filling my core. I no longer care about anything. No therapeutic approach, no careful contemplation, nothing other than the phoenix rising within me. I can feel its flames rush through my every being. And it's not the first time. I've had these moments ever since I was a kid, when something deep down within me gives way, some dam of submission, and I'll suddenly stand up to the bully, or in high school when, with the whole cafeteria as witness, I'd told my "mean girl" friends to fuck off, I'd had enough of them, or my domineering douchebag boyfriends I'd dumped in some dramatic fashion—knees to balls, keyed cars, shit-smeared interiors…the phoenix is coming; it is surging through every part of me and about to spill from my mouth. Carl is about to have a reckoning despite a clear, but futile, voice in the back of my head begging me to reconsider.

I need to think this through. Do nothing brash. Be a good girl.

I flex my hands.

Nope. This fucker is mine.

Hands flexing again. Another Ujjayi Pranayama gulp of air.

Relax. Calculate the next move. Plan an endgame. Prepare a cold dish of whoop ass.

Why am I sitting here arguing this shit in my mind? I need to get out of this chair. Am I going to spend the next fucking week in therapy sessions with this asshole?

Yes, if need be. Deep breath, in through the—

I can't tame it, and maybe I will just be able to burn these bindings off my limbs with my rage. And if not, who gives a fuck. Knock the motherfucker down a few pegs and get him to let me go. See the way he jumped-to-it when he handed me the glass?

Forget being a good girl. You've got him.

"Checkmate." I say with a growling edge to my voice as I move my queen forward to take f7.

He stares at the board for what seems a long moment, a cryptologist deciphering a code. Then he looks up at me. Child-like hurt in his eyes.

Which only infuriates me more.

Despite my mind not really agreeing to the words now flowing from me, I say, "My being tied up here was your fucking bonehead move, you pathetic splash of diarrhea juice. You see, shit stain, all the bad things in your pathetic life have nothing to do with luck or fate or falling cards. They have only to do with you being a dumb flaccid piece of limp man meat."

What the hell am I doing? that Ujjayi Pranayama part inside me is saying, but the phoenix is doing the talking now.

I say, "You lose because you're a loser."

He sits staring at the board with that slow, gear-turning coming to understanding, but then he stands and launches the table across the basement.

The phoenix has obviously taken hold of him, too.

He screams, "You're just so sure of yourself. Just so fucking smart. Well, you weren't so smart when you betrayed *me*, were you? Not so fucking smart as to not take *my* things. Or smart enough to not get knocked the fuck out. Or smart enough to not get tied up down here, were you? It's laughable for the fly to tell the spider how stupid *he* is being, while she's in the spider's web."

"Again, with the spider and fly shit," I say. "If anyone is the fly here, it's you, you clueless asshole. But your analogy is wrong on several levels. Even if I were your so-called fly, there was nothing haphazard about my taking your shit. You actually still think I saw your stupid bubblegum cards and just suddenly decided I needed them? A moment of compulsion on my part? Oh, my, look, my dream history memorabilia is finally within reach. I just can't help myself, I have to have it."

"Given that's what happened? Yes, I believe it."

"You think I'm really a history buff?" I say. "You seriously still think that I went out on a date with a guy I have so much history-love in common with, only to see his historical treasures and, oh no, I can't help myself, I have to have those cards? You still think that's it? A hot, young history buff that came back to *your* house? You still think it was a pleasant evening that I ruined because the devil made me take your shit? That makes sense to you?"

"Um. Well—"

"You were a rube, you dumb fuck. A mark. Don't you get it yet?"

"What are you talking about?"

"I had you set up from the start, fucktard. Think about it. You really think a girl like me would suggest a dweeb like you take her home? And to see history memorabilia? That didn't seem a little odd to you? Jesus, that type of thing only happens in pornos and John Hughes movies. Losers like you don't actually get the girl, asshole."

"But, wait...." That infuriating, slow, trying to grasp the situation expression again. I want so badly to reach him with my free hand and smack that look off his fucking dumb face.

"I advertise on Craigslist looking for marks. And this

time, you were it."

"What are you—?"

"What am I talking about? Are you really this fucking slow and dimwitted? Jesus, you're more freaking retarded than your kid. Let me spell it out for you: you were set up in a con. It wasn't that I found you so interesting during our phone conversation that I just needed to meet you, my history-buff soulmate. The only thing I discovered during that phone call was that you were enough of a clueless moron to hand over your collectables to me. But if it makes you feel any better, you're not the first jackass to fall for this."

"I don't believe it."

"Really, Carl? You don't believe it? Because the alternative makes so much more sense? A beautiful girl happens to be in town and wants to meet up for drinks, sight unseen. And you—*you*—woo her into meeting up for a date. And then *you* woo her to your *house*? That makes sense to you? I get an average of two hundred responses a city. The only real work in this whole endeavor is figuring out which shithead will yield the most. Must be a slow week in Boston, because that shithead was you."

"But—"

"Couple of martinis and suddenly I've got some rare comic book or Babe Ruth's jockstrap. A few shots of tequila and a first edition Hemingway is mine. Or, in your case, a little whiskey, and I get the elusive Infamy Cards and all those old Nazi medals your lame-ass uncle swiped off dead Germans. In fact, my name's not even Stacey. It's Sophie, nice to fucking meet you."

"You're lying."

"Oh, no, Carl, I'm far from lying. I've been using Craigslist to scam schmucks like you for a while. I call it 'nocking the list.' You know, like nocking an arrow onto a bow? I gather a quiver of rubes, city to city, string them up and let them go, seeing what kind of a bull's-eye I can hit. So, you know, Carl, you can stop talking about me like I'm the unfortunate, small-town girl that took a wrong turn in her decision making, only to fall in with the Big Bad Wolf." I lean forward and take a sip of water—just for a dramatic pause, let it all sink in for him; not to mention I have a feeling it might be the last sip of water I have for a while. I return the glass to the floor and say, "You know what, Carl? I'd like to thank you for freeing my hand here." I hold up my hand and flex my fingers. "There's something I've been really wanting to do for a while." I jam my hand in the air, extending the middle finger. It feels so good, that little action, as if all my hatred is surging out of that one fingertip. "I've been so wanting to give you this nice proper ole fuck you for some time now." I shake the finger for emphasis. "Fuck you, Carl."

He stares at the finger for what seems like several minutes, but it is really only a few seconds; the time it takes for it to all sink into his clueless comprehension. Finally, he appears to come back to himself, shaking his head and standing from his chair, saying, "Give me your hand."

I hold the hand and finger steady in the air, and with a deadpan expression, say, "Fuck you, Carl."

He is upon me in a blur, the speed of it shocking me. The cold steel of the bayonet is beneath my chin, and for a moment, I actually think he's gone through with slashing my throat. I'm waiting for the shock to subside and the nerves of my neck to register the burning severing of the metal through my flesh, and the pouring of blood pulling the life from my body. But he hasn't slit it. Not yet. No rush of blood. Nothing but the feeling of steel and his growling voice in my ear, "I said, give me your fucking hand or I *will* kill you."

This time, I actually believe him, and I focus on keeping my trembling imperceptible to him, being sure that, as far as he is concerned, I am as steely as ever. But I'm fucking scared. And I pray he can't smell it on me. Or sense it like some kind of animal. I take a deep breath, summoning the phoenix, and glance casually up at him, saying, "Again with the idle threats. We both know that you're not going to kill me, you dickless-wonder. But fine, you spineless schmuck, here's my hand, duct tape away."

He takes the bayonet away from my throat, and my fear dissipates some. But not fully. I have no idea where this is going.

He binds my arm back to the chair and then turns and walks up the basement steps, disappearing into the kitchen.

"Later, Carl," I casually call after him.

Maybe *that's* where it is going. Nowhere. As usual. Again, we've fallen into the predictable pattern of a married couple. Him trying to get control. Me berating him to partial-submission. He threatens me. I call his bluff until he goes off and sulks. At least he forgot to put the zip ties on this time. Looks like I'll be trying to chew through the tape again.

But he comes back after a couple of minutes, and there is something about the calm control in his face I don't like. Anyone who's ever seen a sleepwalker would recognize the expression. There is a difference between someone who has lost control, and someone who has been taken over by something deep within. This is the latter, and that is bad. Really bad. Someone who has lost control will generally tire themselves out like a tantruming child, but someone taken over, they won't stop until they've completed whatever task deemed necessary by whatever has taken the reins. I also don't like that he is carrying something wrapped in a towel.

He's been all pomp and circumstance with his threats to this point, brandishing his bayonet like a conductor's baton, but now, with this calm, determined look on his face, and the hidden something wrapped in the towel, I'm realizing that whatever threat he has planned may not be so idle.

I keep my steely expression and say, "What you got wrapped up there, Hitler's mustache comb?"

He doesn't answer. Instead, he sits in the chair across from me and places the towel on the basement floor. He takes a moment to gather his thoughts, crosses his legs and folds his hands in his lap. He's going to give another speech, but this time he's actually achieving a little David Caruso vibe as he says, "As you may have gathered, I enjoy history, and I have studied it rather extensively."

"You may have mentioned it once or twice."

"Well, I don't think I mentioned this piece of history," he says. "Do you know where the concept of the good ole *fuck you* came from? When and where people started to"— he holds up his hand, middle finger extended—"give the finger?"

"No. But I have a feeling you're about to tell me."

He grins serenely, folding his hands in his lap again, and he says, "During the Hundred Years War—you know, England verses France, Joan of Arc, Henry the Fifth, and all that shit—the most effective weapon of the war was the English longbow."

"For Christ's sake, is your mode of murder to bore your victims to death?" I say—I want to glance at the something in the towel on the floor, but I keep my eyes locked on him.

He ignores me and continues his stupid fucking history lecture. "So dangerous was an English archer with a longbow, that when the French captured a bowman, they would sever his middle finger so that he could no longer draw back a bowstring, which was known as plucking the yew, because the bows were made of yew wood."

"Fascinating."

"I think so. Anyway, during the Battle of Agincourt in 1415, the English were vastly outnumbered. But, the English rallied and won. And what do they do to taunt the French?"

"Tie them up in a basement?"

"Nope," he says, thrusting his middle finger into the air. "They flip off the French and they scream, we can still pluck yew."

"I get it. Pluck yew. That's funny. And this has all been real interesting, but what does any of this have to do with us?" I sound cool and collected. And part of me, after my verbal beat-down of Carl a few moments ago, actually *feels* cool and collected. Zen-like. Like nothing can harm me.

The phoenix won't allow it.

But there is a growing pit in my stomach, because I also know the *anything* the history lesson has to do with is wrapped up in that towel beside his seat.

He stands up, smoothing the thighs of his pants in an obvious attempt for dramatic effect. Then he bends down to retrieve the towel. My heart picks up cadence as he unravels it to reveal its contents.

A spool of dental floss.

My initial thought is a logical one; he is going to strangle me with it. My second thought is he is going to use it in place of the duct tape to tie me to the chair. My third thought is that he is going to floss my teeth.

But none of these prospects makes much sense. Floss doesn't have the strength to strangle or tie. And flossing my teeth...? I suppose he is weird enough to do it. But it is more likely the floss has to do with this Agincourt story somehow. Carl is never random when it comes to his history lessons.

I say, "Was your story about how the British discovered dental care or something? Because I hate to break it to you, it didn't help. I've met a lot of Brits and their teeth still su—"

He doesn't interrupt me; I just stop talking. The phoenix has flown off to hide for the moment. Because something isn't right. Something in his eyes. It's not the dog fighting rage, or the usual confusion. I don't know what it is; I can only describe it as spinning wheels, like a car stuck in drive racing toward a cliff…or more accurately a wall. And I am the wall. There is a scent coming off of him. I no longer detect that underlying sweaty scent of confusion. He smells like something else. Like hot steel.

He steps to my right hand, and while I'm hoping he's changing the mode of bondage to the chair, he instead loops the dental floss beneath my middle finger, binding my other fingers to the chair's arm. He then ties more dental floss, tightly—like tourniquet tight—around my middle finger.

I definitely don't like where this is going as I make the connection between the story and the floss.

He turns and walks toward the workbench.

I say, "String's tied a little tight here, Carl." My voice is quivering.

When he turns back toward me, he is holding the pruning shears that had almost impaled my face.

He walks toward me, holding them ceremoniously in front of him.

"What do you think you're going to do with those, Carl?" My voice is outright quaking now.

He grins, but there is absolutely no humor in his eyes. Instead, there is steadfast determination. A determination to hate and to harm.

He says, "You've plucked your last yew."

PART 5

1

Blackness.

Floating.

Enveloped in warmth.

Shaking violently. Spasms.

Distant chimes of dripping, swirling water.

I am filled with some sense of being. Dread. Like waking from a panic dream. Something not remembered. Or not wanting to remember.

My thoughts, blurring, smearing, are traveling off over the horizon of violent spasms and floating blackness.

Then the hellish sun of pain rises over that horizon.

Pain never quite pinpointed.

Seemingly allover.

Encompassing me along with the shaking.

I feel the need to open my eyes, but I don't want to. Wanting only to slip back into the painless unconsciousness.

Was I shaking in my unconsciousness, too? Was my unconsciousness painless?

Eyelids fluttering. Fighting against blinding starbursts. Trying to recall where I am. How I got here. Why the pain? Why the shaking?

There is a form above me. And the sound of deep sobbing.

But not my sobbing.

A man's sobbing.

Am I dead?

Travelling the obligatory tunnel to the light.

But there is no light. Just swirling colors.

And who is this weeping man greeting me at heaven's door?

There are memories. There have to be memories of where I am, or why I am here, but they are grease-soaked eels slithering, sliding from my grip.

I open my eyes. And there is the tunnel. Spreading as my eyes adjust painfully against the light. My eyes focusing on…Heaven?

I am floating in a sea of red water, and I begin pinpointing the pain and the edges of the sea as white porcelain walls.

Is it Heaven?

Or Hell?

The fire running up inside my right hand through my arm and into my shoulder is more like Hell.

But there is no Heaven or Hell, I think—or at least I try to think it. The pain is gripping my mind, and I begin imagining a bank of light switches, and, like a stagehand, I snap them off one by one until all the world's stage is again in darkness, and the hellish red sun drops back below the horizon, banishing the pain and the shaking to happen somewhere else.

2

No longer in water, but still floating.

This time it is different.

Different.

I can see that word in my mind's eye.

Different.

The word changing font and color and size.

My thoughts are morphing, and the warm water from before is no longer encompassing my body, now it is inside my body, tingling and fluttering. My sternum is attached to a cord and being lifted, weightless, or so it felt, feels…

Feels….

But this could not be. Because I feel a mattress beneath me—a contradiction, feeling gravity's fight for me upon the mattress, and gravity's loss of me to the floating.

There is a brushing of a hand against my hair, and I hear the sobbing man again.

Is it my father sobbing. I see him clear as day.

But that fucker never cried a day in his life, and how can I see him if my eyes are closed? And I realize again that I must be dead. And again, I have no idea if it is Heaven or Hell in which I now reside—my father's presence certainly no indication.

I laugh inside my head at the notion. The laughter tangible and echoing and visible, flying off into space. My thoughts are fluid, holding no more permanence than shifting clouds in a child's eye. I want to laugh again, want to say those words out loud: *shifting clouds* and *child's eyes*, and *holy shit, I'm stoned*, but my thoughts are struggling again to remember where and why and who.

Or is it whom?

I like that word.

No I don't. I always get it wrong.

I want to say it. *Whom.*

It's a word I can see floating before me like each letter is a balloon.

What the fuck does that even mean?

Am I supposed to be in pain? I don't feel it. But it is there. Hidden as a mad dog shut away in a room where it cannot bite.

Bite looks like a word made of slashes.

Who the fuck is crying?

Whom?

I want to laugh at the word, rising from the cord in my sternum and still feeling my body on the mattress in that contradiction of opposing sensations.

Fuck it.

I'll sleep. Laughing inside and floating away.

3

My eyes are open. I'm on my side. The world tilting slightly as if I'm tied to a clock's second hand. My world is now a bedroom. My country a mattress. Turning on the clock's second hand, I hear tinny laughter echoing in rhythmic waves, then banter, then rhythmic laughter again. The people sounding like they are talking inside a metal box. I catch movement from the corner of my eye.

Carl is sitting in a chair.

The fucker, seeing I'm awake now, shifts in his seat, halfway between standing and sitting, as if spooked and unsure what to make of my consciousness. I'm dizzy from my ride around the second hand and the rhythmic laughter from the people in the metal box, all of it making me feel sick, and I want out of here, and my voice comes, sounding like a returning echo, "Carl…Carl…."

He stands fully from the chair and scurries to my bedside. He strokes my hair like a comforting parent.

"Please, Carl…just let me go…I'll sleep with you if you want. Don't you want to fuck me?"

"Don't say that," he says. He sounds sad.

I'm still spinning, and I close my eyes. The tin box's voice and laughter seeming to spin inside my head on that slow second hand crawl, and I fall back to sleep.

Waking again, feeling my head being lifted and a cup coming to my lips, water rushing into my throat, and I gag and cough and gasp, and I hear Carl's voice saying, "Careful.…"

Did he just tell me to be careful?

The memories flood back. I can feel the ghost of the dental floss tight on my finger. That is the horror of the memory. Of the reality. Not the searing severing of my finger…the feeling that most haunts my memory is that suffocating dental floss turning my finger a bright purple. Then the red. And now he tells me to be careful? After cutting my fucking finger off—the pain of the finger now beginning to radiate up my arm like the mad dog scratching at the closed door—the asshole tells me to be careful?

"Carl—" I begin to say, but the cup is again at my mouth, and I drink the water. The water with a chalky bitter taste. I swallow it all. "Carl…" I begin saying again, but my voice and thoughts swim and fade.

He leans closer to hear me.

"Carl, you…" My voice sounds distant to me, coming out as a low groan. And the floating, turning feeling returns, the planet seeming to rotate the wrong direction, the mad dog stopping its scratching. "Carl, you—"

"Shh," he says. "You need to rest."

"No, I need my…need my.…" My thoughts are getting harder to follow. "No, Carl, I need my finger, you…asshole."

"Shh."

"Carl, what did you do to me?"

"Shh. Rest."

"Carl…Carl…you're an asshole—"

"Shh. Quiet."

"No…really…a real cocksucker—"

"Stop. Go to sleep."

"Carl…you…pussy—"

His voice rises, saying, "I told you to be quiet. Any more shit from you, and I'll cut something else off. Jesus Christ, you never stop."

Then the sound of a slamming door, and some little girl inside me is laughing and laughing until I fall asleep.

4

I'm sitting in my living room, my head in my hands, when a car door slams outside. I rush to the window and look out. A lone police car is parked silently at the end of the driveway. A police officer, wearing mirrored aviator sunglasses, looks up at the house.

"Oh, god…" I whisper, unsure if the statement is exasperation or the fumbled start of a prayer. I look toward the bedroom, options racing through my head: do I run out the back door and into the woods, or face the cop at the door?

Why is a cop here?

You know why.

For me?

No. Probably just a lost kitty or something, dumbass.

Should I answer the door with fingers rubbing eyes, feigning I've been suddenly pulled from a deep slumber? Or I could always not answer it at all.

Is that really an option?

Here is where Rudy could have been helpful. I could tell the cop: *Sorry, I need to take care of my boy here. I need to take him to the doctor?*

Why is that statement a question? See? You can't even pull this off in your imagination.

I spot the bayonet on the coffee table. Another option?

Again, why is that a question? It is an option.

The police officer heads up the walkway. "No. No. No," I whisper, looking at the bayonet again, my eyes then dart around the room for any remaining options.

If it were because of the girl, would they send only one officer?

Is it only one? Maybe the rest of them are hiding outside, ready to raid the house. Maybe a whole SWAT team.

Isn't that redundant, Carl? SWAT team?

No, the T stands for *tactics*, which—fuck, stop pestering me, this is serious.

Peaking out the window again, I realize it's not a Mystic Island police cruiser. The car is from Salem, and the cop is Steve Riley.

I spring to the table, shoving the bayonet into my back pocket. The blade pokes through the fabric and drops down through the bottom of the pocket, its hilt stopping it from falling further. Its point tickles the back of my knee. I race to the door in a penguin-like shuffle, the blade swinging against my skin.

Before Steve can ring the bell, I whip open the door. Steve's head darts back, the police officer's hand going instinctively to his sidearm.

In a low, casual tone, as if not surprised at all to see him standing on my front step, I say, "Hey, Steve, what can I do for you?"

Steve's eyebrows lower, the skin creasing between them. "You really have to ask?" he says.

"Um…yes?" I say.

Steve's eyebrows crease the skin further. "The girl."

"Girl?"

5

I begin to stir out of sleep again. The drugs still have their grip on me, creating a funhouse of moving shapes and color blobs. I think maybe I hear voices. Distant. Not the tinny voices of the television.

These voices seem real.

For some reason I envision Carl is speaking with a priest. The priest asking for his confession. Offering forgiveness. I can't quite make out the words. But that seems the gist of it from their tones.

The tones and the colorful blobs pull apart and then coalesce into a wave pulling me back down toward sleep.

6

Steve says, "Little girl. Quarters? You telling Walters to basically fuck off?"

"Oh, yeah, Walters," I say in a hushed tone. "Tell him I'm sorry, would you?"

"You want me to tell him…no, Carl, that's not the half of it…"

We stand on opposite sides of the opened door, the

threshold separating more trouble than Steve can ever imagine. Steve is doing the talking while I do my best to look attentive, wondering if my face is glazed with sweat or turning an odd shade of red. My wandering mind reduces the police officer's words to unglued phrases that I've stopped following, and I am unsure if I will be able to adhere their meanings together again.

Steve looks dumbfounded, like a guy who's just lost a sure bet, as he speaks about "the little girl you grabbed" and my "not showing up for the past few days." He is in search of an explanation for my "not answering phone calls" and my "insubordination."

7

Swimming again to the surface of consciousness, I search for the owners of the voices, unable to quite gauge their distance from me, but they are not in the bedroom; I can gauge that much at least. I open my eyes, the blur of light and seesawing of reality causing a brief, vicious bout of vertigo, but then I'm able to make out the surrounding landscape.

Bed. I'm on that.

Bureau.

Television. It is not on. The voices *are* real. They are out in the living room.

I try to clear the blur from my vision, rubbing my eyes with my fingertips—all nine of them. I shut my eyes again. Sleep pulling me back to its depths. I begin floating back out into space with the funhouse colors, back to the priest and Carl discussing his sins. The ghost of my fingers' tips still on my eyelids.

My fingertips.

Fingertips. The word in sharp colors, floating off into space.

Fingertips attached to the hands attached to my wrists attached to my arms attached to…

Nothing.

My arms aren't bound to anything. I am free.

8

I still don't invite Steve in. I do, for some reason, have the awareness, despite my pounding heart and spinning mind, to note the situation's similarity to "The Tell-Tale Heart" again. But this time, instead of a tree-hugger-clueless-hipster-chick, it is an actual cop.

And the cop is asking, "Did you really tell Walters to go fuck himself?"

"I'm afraid so. Look, Steve, I've been real sick. And I've had my autistic son to look after—"

"Why are you whispering?"

"Am I? Oh."

9

I lift my head, but then drop it back on the pillow. I am free of the bindings, but not free of the drugs. I want to stand, but I feel very heavy.

Like several hundreds of pounds heavy. Like several thousands of pounds heavy.

I should call out. But my voice is heavy, too. And I note the dream-like quality of my inability to move or speak.

Is this a dream?

In my mind's eye, I can see Carl and the priest clearly. But it isn't a priest.

I try to follow the snatches of conversation coming in through the door.

I try to speak, my voice squelched by the dryness of the words in my mouth, like cotton wadding. I try again, only able to get one word out like a nightmare scream that fizzles at the vocal cords. "Carl…?"

10

Steve says, "You all right, Carl? You've been acting really off lately."

"Me? All right? Yeah. Fine." Why is my voice so high?

"Look, I know the guys have been tough on you lately," Steve says. "But they just like to ride you a little."

"It's fine. Tell them it's fine."

"Well, yeah. But I know it's not fine. I know it's tough, the rumors about you fucking the CPR dummy during EMT training and all."

"I never fucked that thing."

"Well, forcing it to blow you, or whatever."

"That never happened."

Steve shrugs. "Look, they were going to send Tommy to check in on you, but I said I'd do it. Figuring Tommy'd just make it worse. Look, Carl, if you need to talk—"

"Talk? Um, no. Nope. I'm good."

11

In my mind's eye, I can see Carl clear as day. Talking to…

It's not a priest.

The men's voices are coming from the distance, but seemingly so close in my mind. I can see the imagined form of the priest morphing into someone else. He is…

A concerned neighbor?

A teacher?

Rudy's teacher?

A cop?

It's a cop.

I raise my head again, calling, "Help?" But softly, too softly.

12

I hear the voice from the bedroom. The low muffled call of a wounded animal. I cock my head slightly, just to be sure. Yup, there it is again.

Steve is still talking, not seeming to notice, but the moment the conversation takes its inevitable awkward pause, I might be in some real trouble. Steve only needs to hear one yelp and I'm cooked.

The point of the bayonet is scratching the back of my knee. My palms are sweating, and I curl them in and out of slippery fists. Reaching back to rub my thigh, I feel the blade, and I run my fingers up to the hilt. How quickly could I whip it out of the pocket?

Nausea grips me, and I rub my stomach.

"You all right, White? Can I come in? Like I said, if you want to talk—"

"I'm Good. Talk? No. Look, Steve—Officer Riley, I'm good. Really. Just been sick, stomach bug, I think. And my son…you know."

Steve narrows his eyes, saying, "All right, if you say so. I need to tell you, though, Walters wants you in tomorrow for a review. You're probably going to lose your job, man."

The voice from the bedroom again, this time a little louder. "Help?"

I can detect my voice quickening and rising in pitch and volume as I say, "Yeah. I know. Look, Steve, I think my son's calling for me. I need to get going. But thanks for your concern. And tell Walters I'll be in tomorrow."

Steve pauses, searching for something to say. "All right, White. Well…good luck with the review."

"Right. You bet. Bye, now." I shut the door, releasing a whale-like exhale of air.

13

Carl is again in the room, cupping the back of my head, lifting my lips to a glass of water. I sip from it.

"Thought I heard people talking," I murmur.

"Television," Carl said.

"Thought you were talking to a priest."

"Just the television. A show about a mobster, confessing to a priest, saying…." He stops. "Just rest," he says.

He is gone. The door clicking behind him.

I rub my eyes again. My hands still free.

14

I hear singing. A lilting tenor singing "Bridge Over Troubled Water" a cappella. It is more than pleasant. It is actually lovely. I lift off to sleep on the notes.

When I'm carried back into consciousness, the mad

dog of pain is still locked away behind the door, but the room is not spinning quite so much.

Either Carl backed off the drug dosage, or my body is getting used to it.

Sports announcers are speaking on the television. The calm demeanor of the announcers and the almost passive cheering of the fans make it most likely a baseball game.

I open my eyes.

Carl sits, looking like something slowly deflating in a chair beside the bed, his eyes staring off as if the television screen is beyond the walls of the house. He is holding the swastika doorknob, turning it over in his hands.

I close my eyes again, feeling the slight shift of the room; its spinning has slowed more but is still there. I focus on the announcers' conversation. Two bobble heads discussing the legitimacy of baseball records during the steroid era. They cite the records of Babe Ruth for comparison. All these years later. All these broken records. Babe Ruth. Still the standard. Still the prized ball in John Thompson's collection.

In my mind, the word *immortality* floats in kaleidoscopic funhouse colors. I want to say it out loud.

"Immortality."

Wait, did I just say it out loud?

Carl flinches and drops the swastika doorknob. The asshole saying, "Damn."

"Damn, damned, damned immortality," I say out loud, again, not sure why I've said it, the pictures of words in my mind twisting slightly, dreamily. The words *damned* and *immortality* marry into a knotted concept that I suddenly feel is very real for me. The words floating off like balloons and then popping.

There is a sudden bolt of panic, and I'm gripped by the thought that what I've done with my life *is* damnable.

Maybe I *am* in Hell, spending that eternal damnation with this fuckhead, Carl. But this bolt of panic passes quickly, blowing off with the clouds on which I've been floating.

I'm feeling a little more alert.

"What are you talking about?" he says, and I think for a moment that perhaps I've spoken my contemplations on Hell aloud, but then remember I'd been talking about immortality and…what else?

Oh, yeah… "The Babe," I say, liking the way the word feels in my mouth. Saying, "The guy will never die."

This concept feels vital at the moment, but then that, too, blows off with the clouds.

Carl picks the door knocker up off the floor and places it on the nightstand beside the bed. "I hate to break this to you, but Babe Ruth's been dead for a while."

"But they still talk about him as the one end-all ballplayer." I feel for the moment that I am actually standing in John Thompson's living room and holding that stupid signed baseball, looking at the signature and thinking about the fact that an immortal being had touched that very ball. Or, at least his bat had touched it. And his pen, I suppose. "He's more famous than any guy still playing the game, even though there's barely anyone old enough to remember seeing the guy play."

"You're a baseball fan?"

"I did grow up in Oakland," I say. Not knowing why I said it.

"I thought you grew up in Pittsburgh. No, wait, it was Ohio, wasn't it? Nope, it was Minnesota, remember?"

When did I tell him I grew up in Ohio?

I say, "I had a Ricky Henderson rookie card when I was a kid." For some reason I keep going on about Oakland, even though I know he knows I am lying my ass off. It's like I just can't stop the lies spilling from my lips.

"My brother told me to hang onto that card, because someday it would be worth a lot of money."

I can almost see John Thompson standing in his living room, a big goofy smile on his face as he places Ricky Henderson's rookie card on his bookcase.

By the way, I did have that Ricky Henderson card—it was one of my first scores, convincing Jimmy Robbins to trade it to me for a promised kiss that never came.

But I never had the brother.

Wait, did I say that out loud?

"What happened to you being an only child?"

I ignore him, saying, "I don't know what even happened to that card." Sold it, dipshit. "Or to Ricky Henderson, for that matter."

Carl says, "Henderson ended his career here in Boston."

"L.A., actually," I say.

Carl looks over as if to point out more of my contradictions, but instead he deflates further in his seat and says, "L.A. Right again you are."

I begin laughing and say in a Yoda-type voice, "Mmm, right again you are." Then, realizing it didn't sound anything like Yoda, I laugh again, feeling the room turn ever so slightly.

Carl regards me for a moment, then says, "Henderson didn't know when to quit. Guy practically needed a walker in the end just to steal a base. Then he just kind of faded away like that General MacArthur saying." He watches the television for a moment and says, "I had baseball cards, too. A shitload of them, actually. I lost them a long time ago, so you won't be able to steal them."

I glance over at him, but don't say anything. I almost laugh. Thinking it funny. But then I didn't.

He says, "I spent hours on end building card houses

with them. Got pretty good at them, too. I'd build these giant cathedrals made totally from balanced cards. I'd be so proud and go find my mom to show her. Thought it made me seem more grownup somehow, you know, that I could build things that were so intricate."

The floating sensation in my body is returning. But not drug-induced so much. More pure exhaustion. My finger hurts. Throbbing. But I am tilting off to sleep. Thoughts liquefying and filling the crevasses of my mind and running away like water. I see Rudy building card houses and bringing his father to see them with a big smile on the kid's face. "Was she impressed?" I say, my voice seeming to run off like water, too.

Carl says, "Well, I had a brother…a real one." I can sense Carl glancing my way. "And he'd get to my card cathedrals before I ever had the chance to show anyone. He'd crush whatever it was I'd built."

"Isn't that what brothers do?"

"I guess."

"Where is he now? Your brother?"

"Gone the way of Ricky Henderson."

"Your folks?" I say as my thoughts are running off and pooling into growing distortions.

"Dad died when I was young. Mom died about ten years ago."

I am falling, but then slam back onto the mattress, my whole body twitching me awake again. The throbbing rising in my finger like a drumbeat.

Carl sits in the chair, watching the baseball game. He is not so much deflating, but shrinking in the seat like some kind of *Alice in Wonderland* character, melting away into his own world, the loneliness washing him away.

"Guess we're just a couple of loners, Carl."

Wait, did I say that out loud? I must have, because he

answers.

"Guess so. Only your loneliness is by choice." He looks like an abandoned child sitting in that chair. More sad than pathetic. Like he just now watches as his brother crushes his cathedral of cards.

"My loneliness is more a necessity," I say, shifting a little on the bed to see the baseball game. The mad dog begins barking for a moment, bringing me back some from sleep, but the real pain still stays locked away.

Red Sox were up on the Yankees, 3-0.

"What does that mean, loneliness as a necessity?" he says.

"Being alone helps me survive. Always having to cover my tracks. Although, I suppose now it's finally caught up with me. Turns out, I've covered my tracks so well that no one even knows I'm gone."

"So why do you choose this—profession, is it?"

"It's a lifestyle."

He chuckles—it is a humorless sound—and says, "Lifestyle? No. Hiking is a lifestyle. Surfing is a lifestyle. What you do is…what is it? Grifter? Con-artist? Prostitute?"

"I'd say I'm a collector."

He scoffs. "Collector. That's a good one."

"I just negotiate a real good price for the stuff I collect."

Scoffing again. "Yeah, a real steal for you."

"Steal? No, Carl, I pay a very fair price for my things. I give men the feeling they want to feel. For a short time, they are the men they want to be, doted on by a girl of their dreams."

"Like I said: prostitute."

"Oh no, it's more than prostitution. I give much more than sex." I suddenly stop talking, not entirely sure what has spilled from my mouth. I retrace the words as if pulling on an anchor line.

Carl says nothing. He stares at the baseball game, and for once, I can't read him. Not sure if it is the drugs, or if I am just slipping. Or if it is some new thought process slithering into his demeanor.

I retrace the conversation to Carl's question.

Why I chose this profession, by Sophie Monroe. I can see myself standing in front of a classroom of grade-schoolers, only I am an adult, presenting a report I've never completed.

"Truth is," I say, "Being this type of professional—as you call it—is all I've ever been good at."

"Given your current predicament, you may want to reconsider that."

I ignore this, having no quip in volley. For one thing, I am too damn tired to get into it at the moment, feeling the room spinning its slow, counter planetary rotation, and hearing the drone of the baseball announcers and the crowd noise on the television. I am drifting again. Not to mention, this is the first time since I'd tried snatching Carl's memorabilia that we seemingly don't want to kill each other. Or, at least I don't want to kill him as much.

I close my eyes, feeling that pulling, floating sensation lift me off the bed, and I say, "When I was a little girl, I'd stay at my grandmother's house in the summer."

"Are you really going to bullshit me with some when-I-was-a-little-girl story?"

In my mind I am standing in front of that classroom again, but I know I am saying the words in real life. "This one's true," I say to little Susie Hamilton in the front row. Susie was always a little bitch.

Susie says, with Carl's voice, "Yeah, right. Well, save it. I don't want to hear it." I open my eyes briefly, seeing him watching the television in silence. After a moment, he says, "So what happened at your grandmother's house?"

I close my eyes again and say to the class, "She had this pond behind the place. A little murky thing with lily pads and shit like that. I can't believe we ever swam in it. There was this big old rowboat down there. I'd drag the thing out into the pond and just lie in it, getting lost in the day."

The classroom disappears, and for a moment, I am in that rowboat, lying there, floating and looking up as the clouds morph and change from shape to shape. I say, still looking up at the clouds, "Anyway, sometimes my uncles and cousins would come over."

"But I thought you said—" Carl starts to say, but stops. "Never mind."

"Anyway, no one else wants anything to do with that pond. Which is fine because it is my special place. This one day, I'm in the boat, and I must've fallen asleep. Next thing I know, the boat takes this deep dipping rocking motion, and then my uncle is in the boat with me. He holds his finger to his lips, but I think he's joking, so I squeal with laughter. He clasps his hand over my mouth and jams his hand inside my bathing suit bottom, shushing me and telling me it will be over soon. And, believe me, it *was* over quick." In my mind, in that boat, I chuckle and say right into my uncle's face, "Guy didn't even get it out of his shorts in time." Then my uncle is gone, and I am musing up at the cloud-strewn sky again, I can hear the water kiss the boat's hull.

Carl's voice brings me back again. "Why didn't you scream or knee him in the balls or something?"

"At first, because I was scared and shocked, but then I took back control of the situation. If I'd screamed, everyone would have come running to see what the commotion was."

"And he'd have been caught red-handed."

"No. He would've denied it." I now feel as if I'm talking down at Carl from the ceiling. When did I begin floating upward again? "He'd have said he was just joking and he'd never touched me, saying he was only trying to scare me or whatever and I had turned it into something else. You see, I had a bit of a reputation already then, because I was pretty and sarcastic, and many people found it flirty and sexualized, although I never understood why. So no one would believe me. And then I'd have to live with a kind of shame, forever feeling that fucker's eyes on me and remembering his finger in my crotch. And I'd have to face him at family gatherings as everyone wondered which one of us was the liar. It would've become nothing more than the family's dirty little secret."

"So how'd you keep control?" Carl says, seemingly from below me, his tone that of an eager housewife getting her fortune told.

"I'm no dummy, Carl. I was thirteen. He was forty. By letting him get his rocks off for about ten seconds, I was able to prey on his guilt and fears for years. He didn't know why I hadn't turned him in immediately. So I had that fucker sending me checks every month for eight years."

"Why would he send you the checks? The more time that passed, the less leverage you'd have."

"Not true. If I'd spoken up immediately, it looks reactionary, and he could label me a drama queen. But, as time goes by, and if I were to keep waking my parents with nightmares, and if they were to take me to the doctor, and if I were to tell the doctor what had happened…suddenly my uncle has a real situation on his hands."

"You relied on your uncle coming to that conclusion on his own?"

"I may have outlined the situation for him when I first requested the checks. Most expensive pussy he'd ever had."

I'm about to break through the ceiling now, and I hear Carl's voice from what seems a great distance.

"You still bleeding him."

"He hung himself two years ago. He neglected to mention me in his will."

I break through the ceiling and I am floating now above the house.

"You have a good singing voice, Carl," I murmur.

"You really think so? You really—hey, Sophie, you really…?"

But I no longer hear him. I am now high above, and I can see the roof of the house and the forest stretch off to a distant sea.

15

I'm sitting on the toilet, head in my hands, praying to evacuate what feels like a shot put in my stomach. How many freaking days has it been since I've had a movement? First, I had to hold my piss like a dog whose owner had forgotten it over vacation, and now…? Now, whatever drugs Carl is giving me are stopping me up. I can hear the commercial in my mind: *Do you have captivity constipation?*

Speaking of which, the pills are kicking in again. The pit of nausea is opening up into a thing with wings, fluttering in my stomach. Perched as I am on the toilet, I feel high up, like I might fall off, or fly off, a gargoyle over a cityscape.

I put my face in my hands and feel a bandage on my right cheek…

No, dummy, the bandage is on my right hand. "Right finger," I murmur, pulling my hand away from my face and looking at the bandage on my middle finger, a red dot beginning to bleed through the white gauze.

Hey, bleed through, I think. *It's bleeding and it's bleeding through*. This is funny to me for some reason. And then it is not.

The winged thing in my stomach tucks its wings and drops into a falcon's dive.

I need to get out of here. The bathroom is getting too bright. The porcelain too slick.

"I need to get out of more than just the bathroom," I murmur, as the thing in my stomach spreads its wings and rises again.

I lean over from the toilet and raise a single window blind with the middle finger of my left hand, not sure why I use that finger to do the job—maybe out of some strange defiance.

Behind the house, the black mass of the forest is tinged silver in moonlit brushstrokes. How long have I fucking been here? Full moon? What was the moon when last I'd seen it?

Must have been waning.

No, waxing.

Waning or waxing? Which is getting bigger? Waxing. They should get rid of the word waning and say the moon is waxing-on or waxing-off.

"The moon is waxing-on, Sophie-san," I mutter.

The thing flying in my stomach tickles my inside with its feathers, and I laugh.

I stand from the toilet and hike up my undies, no longer worried about constipation, or my finger. No longer worried about much, actually. My limbs feel as if filled with liquid metal, like the robot in the *Terminator* movie, and I feel like I can just melt out under the door and maybe extend my now-missing finger into a pointed spike through Carl's eye, watching him twitch and convulse until he goes still with his stupid expression frozen on his face.

I giggle again, as the overwhelming pine stench of the forest calls to me.

I can't smell the forest, dingbat, it's outside.

"I can smell it," I murmur. "Smells like a fucking Christmas tree."

I look up and see a green Yankee Candle on top of the medicine cabinet.

Stinky-shit-camouflage for when company is afoot.

Meaning the candle will need to be lit at a moment's notice.

Meaning there is an emergency lighter in here.

Meaning I can have a light source for the darkened woods.

Lighter's not gonna light your way through those woods.

"I'll make a fucking torch," I murmur. I see myself running through the woods as if I'm part of the freaking Olympic torch relay, humming *Chariots of Fire* as I go. I have to stifle a laugh.

I could always just burn the house down.

Is it smart to burn down the building I'm trapped in? Do I even fucking care anymore?

I could distract him while he's trying to put out the fire and make a break for it.

No. Again, why give him a reason to kill me in a panic? Or, what if he grabs me in a final act of desperation and lets us both burn to death? Suddenly, somehow the bayonet seems a better fate than burning alive.

The torch-as-light-source idea again seems viable. I

could run into the woods and hide, and then sneak back out of the woods using the lighter to light my way. I begin quietly opening drawers and cabinets. He wouldn't leave it where Rudy can get at it. I stand on tiptoes, reaching up to the top of the medicine cabinet, and sure enough, it is behind the candle.

It is one of those grill lighters with the trigger guard. I light the thing and hold it inches from my face, engrossed in the flame's salsa dance, feeling the flame's heat flush my skin. When the first drops of sweat begin to gather along my hairline, I let the flame flicker out, blowing on the barrel like a gunslinger before stashing it in the waistband of my skirt.

I take a deep breath and burst through the bathroom door.

Carl is seated at the kitchen table, and he stands as soon as I come through the door. "Are you all right?" he says, his voice rising in panic.

No, fuckhead. I'm stoned and sans a finger.

I want to laugh at this, but instead I look as desperate as I can, crumpling to my knees on the floor. "Carl," I say in a whispered plea. "Carl, I'm in so much pain. I need more pills. Please."

"But I just gave you some."

"They aren't working. Please, Carl, I need more."

"But…no, I can't give—"

"Carl…Carl, the pain…it's too much. Just one more. Hurry, please." I begin sobbing, collapsing fully to the floor and curling up on the linoleum. "Hurry, please." I say these last words in a breathy squeak.

Carl turns and heads for his office.

I pop up, almost leaving my feet like a gymnast sticking a dismount, and I dart to the back door, unlock it, and burst into the night.

16

I sprint for the trees, knowing I am weaving, my legs the uncooperative tangle of a drunk's. But I concentrate on keeping my balance—even managing to sidestep a fire pit in the middle of the yard—and pull the lighter from my waistband like a warrior preparing for battle.

This isn't going to work.

Yes it will.

I burst into the trees, and it is as if some black membrane has enveloped me; Carl's sudden calls of my name—as he realizes what has happened and he, too, bursts from the house in pursuit—sound strangely muted and further off than they should. Streamers of moonlight cast down, lighting my path, the fallen branches and stones and roots seeming to get out of my way, as if the forest is welcoming me into it.

I still hear Carl calling, but it is becoming more muted, more distant. There is movement in the woods, and now the trees seem to be gathering around me, their forms more person-like, their leaves rustling like eager rubbing hands, the wind through their branches groaning. The moonlight is fading, winking away under the thickening canopy, that black membrane seeming to become thick oozing goo.

I flick the trigger of the lighter, but it blinks out as I run. I stop, flick the lighter again. It lights, and I get my bearings, gingerly picking my way through the branches. The trees are closer. More person-like. Not only person-like in form, but also, the patterns of bark are beginning to resemble faces.

I hear my name called on the wind. But it doesn't sound like Carl. It sounds like…literally my name called by the wind.

I stop and let the lighter wink out.

How close is he?

I wait, silent, listening for snapping branches—which seems to be coming from all over the woods—and searching for the wink of his flashlight's beam through the trees.

I crouch between two trees. My heart seeming to fill my entire chest cavity. I can feel every blood cell surge through my arteries, feel the life-giving burn of every oxygen molecule processed in my lungs.

A sudden gust of wind creaks the limbs around me with groans and growls that slip off into the night—even hearing what sounds like the distant roar of a lion—all going quiet again as the gust passes.

I hear my name again…

closer…

whispering along the leaves. Something is winding along my shoulders, like the coils of a giant snake. I stand and shake it off, but there is nothing there. Turning and flicking the lighter, I find the tree's bark has become the face of a child screaming a silent cry into the night.

I shriek, dropping the lighter, turning and running, tripping over a root. My limbs feel heavier, as if hardening. My hands, planted on the ground, seem to be burrowing into the soil. The trees are grabbing me. There is a flash of light, and the wind now sounds just like Carl, no longer muted. "Jesus, Sophie, Jesus Christ. I need to get you out of here."

17

My toes are lengthening and burrowing like roots through the soil. I hold my hands before my face and watch my lengthening fingers stretch and twist as tiny offshoot fingerlings branch from my growing digits. I see their many tiny fingernails glowing in the fragmented moonlight. Leaves spring from the fingers' tips.

I scream, shaking awake.

I am on a bed. Carl's bed. My wrists bound to the headrest with the zip ties. I begin to inspect them, trying to formulate a plan, but I am just too fucking tired for plans.

I look around the bedroom. The door is shut. Television turned off. The rocking chair, where he's spent his bedside vigil after my "surgery," is now empty. The nightstand beside me has three framed pictures on it. Pictures of Carl with Rudy.

I squint, and upon closer inspection, I notice that the photographs have been cropped. People, or more likely a single person, appear to have been cut from them.

A chill runs through my body, and I am quite sure this time it is not from the drugs.

Carl is not the type to plan and then calmly cut someone—most likely his ex-wife—out of a photograph. He is more the cut-someone-from-a-picture in a blind rage type of guy. The sudden reaction of someone at the end of his line. Maybe he'd contemplated cutting her out of the pictures several times, but in the end, he'd been *pushed* into grabbing those scissors and sheering her out of the landscapes. And then he most likely had no recollection of doing it. He may have had the rationality, during one of those prior contemplations, to think, *why would I ruin these one-of-a-kind pictures by altering them?* But in the end, he'd reacted, and was most likely filled with regret in the aftermath. Now he lives with these altered abominations on his nightstand—the first things he sees upon waking, the last thing seen before falling off to sleep.

Maybe he'd even framed them as a reminder of what his rage had wrought.

He can't frame a mutilated girl he's kidnapped and tortured and keep her on his bedstand. Even if he doesn't have it in him, so to speak, to murder me, in the end, he has no other choice. The fact that the binds are around my wrists again is the final proverbial nail in the coffin. He expects to keep me here, but of course, he can't keep me here. He has no choice but to kill me.

Beside the pictures is the swastika door knocker.

The Avon Fräulein has most likely made her last call.

18

I lean on the shovel, staring off into the night. My eyes adjust to the dark, making out the tall grass and low dunes playing hide-and-seek just beyond the flashlight's beam. I then look down at the now half-filled grave I'd dug a few days earlier. I've already filled it in and dug it out again, and now filling it back in. *I* am the chipmunk in the road, frozen with indecision while the tires bear down.

"Fuck," I shout into the night, my voice lost in the area's solitude.

I jam the shovel's head into the earth, leaving it standing upright, and walk off toward the car. Getting in the car and starting it, I sit still a moment, engine idling, radio turned down to a small din. With my forehead pressed against the steering wheel, I feel like an inflatable person low on air.

Mandy would have enjoyed seeing me this way. She beat me down for so many years, berating me in public and private, and she never gets to see the payoff of my Sisyphus-like slope of defeat. Because that is where I am now. Rock bottom defeat.

"I don't know what to do," I say out loud. My voice sounds foreign to my own ears.

"You're no killer, Carl." It is Sophie's voice I hear in response.

I look to my right, and she is sitting there, her bare feet tucked up onto the seat, her back leaning against the passenger side door, her arms folded, tightly hugging her body. It is how I'd imagine she'd look if we'd taken a drive out to the beach one night to watch the rollers breaking in the moonlight.

"Go ahead, give me your shit," I say. "Tell me how you told me so."

She says, "Nah. There's no need for that, Carl. I get it. You were confused. Confused and hurting. You weren't thinking straight. But now you are."

"I just wanted you to pay for what you'd done. I just wanted you to admit you were wrong and ask for forgiveness." I begin sobbing. "I hurt you so badly."

In her soothing way, she says, "*You* didn't do that, Carl. It was the anger. The hurt and the rage that did it. It had control of you. But now it's over. Now it's time to heal and move on."

I take a series of deep breaths to stave off tears. My cheeks are wet with them and I push my hands across my face. "You mean, you can forgive me?"

"Of course."

"But, how?" I say through my tears.

"Things happen for a reason. People find each other for a reason, often in strange ways. We found each other because we're the only ones that understand one another. We were both lost, but now we're found. I saved you from your self-destruction, you saved me from the life I was leading. It was meant to be. In a way, you could say we're soul mates."

"That's just the Stockholm Syndrome talking."

"No, Carl, we're connected. Like that Christmas Eve during World War I when the Allies and the Germans climbed from their trenches, enemies that suddenly understood one another, comrades fighting against the hell that is life."

I force a grin. "Maybe in some alternate universe, meeting under different circumstances, we're happy together, huh?"

"Maybe," she says with a grin of her own.

I chuckle and put the car into gear, not bothering to retrieve my shovel. I drive along the secluded dirt road, watching the rhythmic glow of the lighthouse's light flaring occasionally over the dunes.

I say, "As soon as I get home, I'm letting you go. That's it."

"Thank you, Carl," she says.

Another voice suddenly speaks up, this time from the backseat. "And as soon as she walks out that door, we won't be far behind to put your dumb ass in prison."

I look into the rearview mirror to see Tommy Adams sitting behind me. "Know what the sentence is for kidnapping, White? Life in prison."

"Life? But I'm letting her go," I tell him.

"How much sympathy you expect from a jury that hears how you tortured a young girl by denying her food, water, the bathroom, and, oh yeah, that little cutting off of the finger bit?"

"But they'll understand that I was lost, that I was confused, that it wasn't me. And in the end, I did let her go. I did redeem the sin."

Tommy says, "Redeeming a sin? You can't kidnap someone, torture her, and then say, oops, my bad, guess

I'll just redeem my sin by letting her go."

Chet's voice joins in. "That's called being a pussy."

I glance into the backseat and see Chet sitting beside Tommy. Chet saying, "That's called not being able to go through with what you started. Getting spooked and cutting the problem loose."

Sophie, turning and looking at the two men in the backseat, says, "Don't listen to them, Carl." She looks at me again, saying, "You'll redeem yourself with me. They don't understand."

"*We* don't understand?" Chet says. "You've been telling him he's dickless since the beginning."

"I didn't say he was dickless. I said he wasn't a killer," she says.

Chet says, "No, I think you used the term dickless quite a few times. But you're right, he's not a killer. Yet. Just a kidnapper. And a torturer. But it doesn't matter what you call him, because where he's going, he won't be needing a dick. Believe me, Carl, where you're going, you won't be pitching; you'll definitely be the catcher."

"You're about to lose the rest of your life, White," Tommy says with a matter-of-fact tone.

Chet chuckles. "Not to mention your cherry."

Mandy's voice pipes in, "I always knew you were a loser."

I glance again into the mirror, seeing her sitting there between Chet and Tommy in the backseat. Mandy saying, "Just proving what I've said all along. But, of course, you've always known it anyway."

Chet says, "He's got to look in a mirror at least once a day."

"And you can say goodbye to Rudy, too," Mandy says. "Think I'm going to allow my child anywhere around your warped mind? Not for visiting day, not for nothing. You'll never see him again."

Rudy's hooting fills the car.

I look in the mirror to see my son.

Mandy says, "I always knew it was your fucked up genes that did this to him."

"Shut up," I shout.

Tommy cautions, "Watch that temper, White."

Chet saying, "Why don't you just cut off her finger?"

Tommy and Chet break into laughter, and an old cackle joins them from the backseat. In the mirror, I can see the old woman from McDonalds. Beside her, the stupid tree-hugging girl that came by the house peddling her save the planet bullshit.

"He was talking about a woman in his basement," the old woman says.

"He told me he was a murderer," the tree-hugger says.

All of them begin talking at once, their voices becoming louder and more frantic, like a crowd spilling into a street in anticipation of a riot. Rudy is hooting, everyone else shouting and laughing and arguing.

Simon Cowell appears among them, saying, "Your life is truly dreadful, Carl. The worst I've ever heard."

Sophie, who has been regarding the crowded backseat, turns to me and says, "Is it me or is it getting crowded in here?"

I slam on the brakes. The car coming to a skidding halt. I turn and bat hands around the empty space in the backseat, as if shooing mosquitos, and I can only imagine how I'd look to anyone stumbling upon this scene. A man in the midst of a bad acid trip.

Or just going crazy.

I turn forward and grip the steering wheel, staring ahead through the windshield where the headlights slash into the darkness. I say, "They are right."

Sophie's voice again. "Yes. They are. It's okay, Carl. You have to do what you have to do."

I turn my head to see her sitting beside me again. I say, "I have no choice."

"It's time," she says. "I'll forgive you."

19

Carl bursts through the bedroom door, bayonet in hand. He rushes toward me.

I don't even brace for the impact of the blade; I just close my eyes, take a deep breath and imagine, almost welcoming, the abrupt burn across my skin, prepared to accept my fate as my life bleeds out onto the floor. But instead, he cuts the zip ties binding my wrists.

I am visibly trembling with fear. I have no snappy comeback. No cool, unflinching eyes.

"You're free," he tells me. "Go on."

I rub my wrists and look at him, unsure.

He steps back and tosses the bayonet out of the room. "Go ahead. Get out of here."

I stand. Almost falling, I brace myself on the bedpost.

Carl takes a step toward me to help, but I hold up my four-fingered hand, saying, "I've got it." Taking a moment to regain my composure from the swoon, I then say, "What's going to happen to you?"

He looks at the floor, taking a deep breath, and then raises his eyes to mine. "I don't know. Whatever it is, I'm going to have to face the consequences."

I swallow with some difficulty. Saying on dry lips, "I need water."

Carl nods, a child sent on a mission, rushing out of the room.

20

In the kitchen, I fill a glass with water. I look up from the rushing faucet to the window above the sink. My body is seized by a rush of adrenaline as I find a stranger looking in at me. Eyes wide and frantic and pleading and…tired. Once I realize it is my own reflection, I quickly look away, closing my eyes and taking another deep breath.

"It'll be okay," I whisper, turning off the faucet and taking the glass to the bedroom, striding past the bayonet discarded on the linoleum floor.

Entering the room, I find Sophie steadying herself with one hand on the bedpost and the other on the nightstand. I rush toward her with the water.

I stop and look down at the hand that is resting on the nightstand. It holds the swastika door knocker. I look up into her eyes as she brings the hunk of metal up with a swift, smooth swing, catching me in the face.

I drop to the floor, trying to rise up on my hands and knees. But she is hitting me, raining blows down upon me. The last things I see are two of my teeth swimming in splatters of blood on the floor, and then my own feeble hand rising in defense.

21

I dope-slap the motherfucker, smacking him upside his lowered head.

"Psst. Hey, Carl. Hey, asshole, wake up."

I smack him again.

Still nothing.

I must have smashed him with that door knocker harder than I'd thought. I entwine the fingers of my left hand into his hair and raise his head, lifting his chin off of his chest.

"Hey, fuckhead," I say, adding, "Avon Fräulein calling."

He groans.

"Hey, fuck-nut, wake up."

Groaning again, he tries to roll his head, his hair still in my grip.

I say, "C'mon, asswipe, time to wake up."

He opens his eyes, his pupils trying to focus. Coming to full consciousness, he stupidly regards my face looming over him.

I smile and let go of his hair, dropping his chin back onto his chest.

The fucker groans again and then flinches fully awake. The asshole now realizing *he* is in the basement, bound to a chair with duct tape. He raises his chin again, looking up at me with groggy eyes.

He says, "Wait…what…? Wait…." His groggy eyes clear. "But, you can't do this."

Fucker actually looking indignant, like how could *I* so inconvenience *him* at this moment?

He licks his swollen, bloody lip and says, "Sophie, what are you doing? What is this?"

I produce his bayonet, and his pupils snap to the steel as if they are magnets.

I say, "So you really thought you were just going to let me go?"

His eyes don't leave the bayonet as I hold it to my finger, casually checking its sharpness.

I say, "You kidnap me, cut off my finger, and when you finally decide to free me, you think I'm just going to say thank you, and be on my way?"

His eyes finally leave the bayonet, and he looks at me

with an earnest, hurt-puppy look, and in a whining voice, he says, "But, Sophie, please, just listen to me. I was fucked up. You've got to understand that. I needed help, and you helped me. Don't you understand? You're my salvation."

I lunge with the bayonet, placing the blade against his throat.

The crotch of his pants darkens with urine, and he begins sobbing uncontrollably, "Oh God, Sophie, please don't. Please don't kill me."

I break into a giggling fit and back away from him. Through hitches of laughter, I say, "I'm not going to kill you, Carl. And I'm not going to the cops, either. I'm in enough trouble. You have any idea how many states I'm wanted in? I'd probably get more jail time for all the things I've stolen than you would for kidnapping me."

I grin and kick at a box at my feet. It's filled with his war memorabilia, nicely packed and ready to go.

I say, "But I am taking this shit. All of it. Swastika door knocker and all. We can call it partial payment for the whole kidnapping-torture-cutting-off-my-finger thing. The rest of the payment is that you don't say a fucking word about me to anyone. But, of course, keeping quiet about this whole ordeal will probably benefit you as much as me."

He begins sobbing again. "Please, Sophie. Please forgive me. Don't leave me like this."

I bend down so that I am face to face with him, like a parent explaining something to her bratty kid. "No, Carl, I will never forgive you." I nod at the duct tape around his wrists, saying, "Better start gnawing at that. It takes longer than you think."

He looks down at his wrists and sobs, saying, "Oh, please don't do this."

"I am doing it, Carl. And you know what else?" I thrust my hand inches from his face, raising what is left of my middle finger. "I can still pluck yew, cunt."

22

I troll through the Craigslist personals, absentmindedly working my tongue into the gap of my two missing teeth: a new habit. I'd never gotten the teeth fixed, telling people I'd tripped going down my basement stairs. The cuts on my face are only now healed.

Trolling the Craigslist ads is my new daily routine.

Looking for someone, but never finding her.

There's been plenty of time to perform this ritual, having lost my job. I'm being sued by the woman with the quarter-toting daughter. I'm also being sued by Mandy for custody of Rudy. That doesn't matter though. Rudy wants nothing to do with me—the boy running away and cowering at my approach. I am also being evicted, just to top it all off. But still, with all this piling on, all I seem to care about lately is trolling these Craigslist personals for a single girl. Not single as in relationship status. Single as in, she is one of a kind.

Looking out the back window at the darkness, I shut down my computer. I grab a pile of papers from my desk and walk out of the room. Then out of the house and into the overgrown backyard. The last time I'd come out this far into the yard was to chase Sophie into the woods.

Chase her? At that point it was a rescue mission.

I chuckle at this thought. She'd have been fine. She always is. She'd have figured out how to get back out of those woods. Or talk her way out, convincing the trees to part their branches into easily navigated paths.

No, she wouldn't have come back out. No one comes out of those woods.

I stop in the middle of my yard and drop the pile of papers into one of those round metal fire pits. A subpoena to appear in court, a notice from the sheriff's office to remove my person from the property by the end of the month, construction paper birthday cards penned by the erratic hand of my son. The last thing I drop in is the ballooning bill for the credit card she apparently took from me—I never bothered contacting the credit card company, hoping the expenditures would give some kind of indication to her whereabouts, but the purchases are so random that I can't even imagine her making them. I squat and tent the papers amid the scattered coals of long ago late-night fire pit sessions. Remembering times sitting alone and staring at the stars while the tinny sounds of Backstreet Boys soothed from the boombox by my side. Nick, Brian, Howie, Kevin and AJ. My unwavering companions. It has been a while since I've sat out here, and I somehow miss the simplicity of the ritual while at the same time loathe those moments for a reason I can't quite finger.

Finger. Interesting use of words, a voice says in my mind. I don't recognize it as anyone's voice I know, and I wonder where it comes from. I've been hearing it more and more lately.

I reach into the tented papers—the structure looking like a deformed version of one of my card cathedrals from childhood—and flick the lighter I'd grabbed from the bathroom. The edges of the papers begin to curl gently, consumed by flame, and I watch the blackening of my last unpaid credit card statement before the whole tent expands like a phoenix.

As I turn away from the fire, I realize I am singing

Backstreet's "I Want it That Way" to the empty audience of my backyard. A line about fire and desire, and it being too late.

And that brings the closest thing to a smile I've felt in a long time.

I walk toward the woods and pause on the apron of grass at the back perimeter of my yard. Who am I kidding, *my* yard? It's never been mine. I stop at the spot where it roughens into thorny brush and the uncertainty of old growth trees. I bend down and pull a clump of turf, the blades of grass feeling sharp to the touch. I caress the soil in my hand as particles of dirt escape through my fingers and sprinkle back to the ground.

I look back at the house, no longer a home, and I reflect on my time spent there. It had been a new beginning filled with possibilities after my disastrous marriage. A clean slate for me, and I'd envisioned transitioning Rudy into an agreeable, conflict-free environment during the time I had custody. And as for the time when I wasn't with Rudy, I'd anticipated getting out to meet people. Maybe even find a woman who was normal. Someone with potential who could help me move on from Mandy. Someone like Sophie had seemed to be during the brief spell of our…friendship? Those few hours before she'd robbed me.

Of everything.

I stare out into the trees, eyes wending through the shadows of oddly shaped limbs. It has always been a place I'd warned Rudy about. Telling him stories of troll-like creatures and long-fanged monsters living out there in order to keep him from venturing into the woods. I told myself that the stories were only meant to deter the boy, so that I didn't have to go in there to retrieve him. But they were more a deterrent to my having to explain to

Mandy the thorn scrapes and other possible injuries the boy might have obtained under my watch.

I'd always make up stories about the unknown in order to avoid anything unplanned from happening. And I actively labored to pass on those fears to my unsuspecting son. Would I have still done this if the boy were "normal?" Would I still have instilled in the boy a take-no-chances attitude? Convincing the boy to live in the safety of boredom and subservient existence? That's how it has always been for me, anyway.

That's how it has always been for me.... That statement became the signature of my being. My entire life has been nothing more than a car with tires racing in mud. Stuck, with no way of breaking free. No way of moving forward. I've always accepted the ways things have been. Until Sophie came along. Those brief hours in the beginning, she'd challenged those conventions. She was dynamic and fun and beautiful, and she was interested in me and the things I loved. And, after all was said and done, like some bizarre Schrodinger's Cat, that girl existed and didn't exist at the same time. Throughout it all, isn't it the authenticity of that perfect companion that she'd really robbed me of?

I wipe the remaining soil from my hands onto my pants. Maybe it isn't that I told my son to avoid going into those woods because of the inconvenience of having to retrieve him or having to make poor excuses to Mandy. Maybe it's because those woods *are* dangerous. With a substantial body count to its credit.

Can you have a body count when no bodies are recovered? that unknown voice says in my head.

I ignore it.

Thunder rumbles from the gray clouds sailing overhead, and rain spits on me while I remain at the woods' edge. Under normal circumstances, I would raise my hand to shield my eyes or else run back to the house for cover from the pending storm. But those instincts are foreign to me now. They are pieces to a somewhat familiar jigsaw puzzle that belongs to somebody else. Instead, I hold my ground, face tilted toward the clouds, and allow my mind to unfold the possibilities that lay ahead.

Maybe the woods *are* actually inhabited by trolls, their eyes spotted among the trees, watching me, hands ready to clutch me by the arm and lead me into the dark recesses. Perhaps they will lead me to a clearing amid a fairy ring, a place to lie in wait for the next move toward the future of Carl White. Or, as I've heard local legend tell, would it be a small house-like structure built of rough-hewn stones waiting for me in there? A refuge away from the prying eyes of society and the accusatory fingers of my own past? It is the kind of scenario that would naturally draw a line in the sand, and I'd be forced to make a choice—fight or flight. I imagine Rudy's face, chiseled with wonder, trying to figure out how his father could go and live in the very recesses of danger he had warned against with such passion. Rudy would be another piece of that fading puzzle, partially completed and cast aside, waiting for someone else to finish.

The rain comes harder now, and I turn my head and regard the fire, now spewing white steam. The phoenix drowned in its own bed.

I take a few steps into the low brush of the woods, twigs snapping beneath my shoes and thorns barbing onto my pant legs, holding me back, or more likely pulling me forward, with gentle resistance. I push on toward comforting darkness, the tangle of limbs welcoming me into their embrace.

Maybe here I'll find what I'm looking for.

23

She is breathtakingly beautiful.

And she is with me.

If only my friends could see me now. Or maybe they'll meet her soon enough.

If all goes well, that is.

She has dark, chestnut hair drawn up atop her head, her light, gray eyes focusing on me.

Focused solely on *me*.

Her full lips slide easily off her bright teeth, so naturally. Her shoulders, exposed by her strapless, black dress, look smooth, like gold. I marvel at the way that dress so perfectly teases her breasts, and the delicate shape of her arms running down to her exquisite, folded hands, and her…finger. Or rather, lack of a finger.

Her hands shift and she unconsciously rubs at the nub of her missing middle finger.

What the heck happened to her finger?

With a sharp intake of air, I shoot my gaze back to her eyes.

She is staring at me, her eyebrow arching slightly.

Shit, she's caught me staring at the finger again.

"You can just ask me about it," she says. Her voice is confident and steady, but with the tiniest hint of child-like charm.

"Shoot, sorry, that was rude," I say, feeling the flush come to my cheeks.

"No, it isn't, it's only natural to peek at a deformity and wonder what happened."

"Yeah, guess so," I say. "Guess it's just jarring to see imperfection in someone so perfect." I twist my face into a sourball expression. "I can't believe I just said that."

She laughs a refined, elegant giggle. "It was cute, and

thank you," she says. Her eyes flash from confident steadiness to one of knowing mischief. "I don't mind telling you how it happened."

"No," I say, as if she's accused me of voyeurism. "It's none of my business."

"It's quite a story. And not one you'd tell in a Match.com profile." She leans forward, regarding me with her perfect gray eyes, and she says "Tell you what, let's get the check, and we can go back to your place. I'll tell you all about it."

"Yeah?" Did my voice just crack? I still can't believe this. I glance around the restaurant for the waiter, waving my hand for the check.

The girl says, "Besides, you need to show me this priceless comic book collection you've been raving about."

Read More from **STONE Pulp Press** at:
stonepulp.com

Mystic Island Stories

The Book of Ira

The Nocker

White Cover Series

Sas-squash

No Ire

Sloanebug Books

*Quest for Dreaming Mountain:
A Fairy's Tale*

Find More **Mystic Island** Content at:
mysticislandstories.com